THE NEW RELIGION

Paperback = ISBN	978-1-7771454-0-8
Hardback = ISBN	978-1-7771454-1-5
E-book = ISBN	978-1-7771454-2-2

THE NEW RELIGION

A novel

by

Geo Kirakos

Prologue

Humanity was on the brink of extinction. From rural China a respiratory virus had arisen more lethal than any in history, and it had been advancing across the globe for a year. Scientists had given it the unwieldy name of NH3N25, but social media had quickly dubbed it the "apocalypse virus" or simply AV.

Transmission took place like a run-of-the-mill influenza virus, through saliva, mucous, and other bodily fluids. Sneezing and coughing spread it in the tiny droplets. Even touching a door handle with bare skin was enough for infection to occur. It was detectable two to seven days after infection and remained detectable for as long as the person survived—typically six to seven months in an otherwise healthy individual, less in the very young, the very old, and those already compromised by other health conditions.

Initially, the symptoms were relatively benign: low-grade fever, coughing, lack of energy, and overall achiness. Within a month, however, the patient would begin to deteriorate rapidly, eventually succumbing to oxygen deprivation, secondary infections, or a combination. The mortality rate was 100%, and in the year since its first appearance, absolutely nothing had been found to stop or even slow the virus's progress.

It was as though the universe was trying to eliminate the human race so Earth could recover from the devastation of the Anthropocene epoch. Our species had wrought mind-boggling destruction. Environmental degradation compounded by increasing inequality in the distribution of essential resources had displaced record numbers of people fleeing natural disasters, wars, famine, and persecution. And this was but one of a multitude of ills arising from these core failures. After the apparent progress of the late twentieth and early twenty-first centuries, millions of children around the world continued to be homeless and hungry, violence against women was on the rise, and sectarian persecution ensured that disadvantaged minorities became even less able to defend themselves.

The only minority not suffering was the top one percent—those who had amassed the vast majority of the world's wealth and resources. Not only were they indifferent to others' misery; they ensured that through misinformation via the elite-controlled mass media, those suffering the most would blame and turn against each other.

Until the arrival of the apocalypse virus.

Then, no amount of money, land, or military might could protect them. The one percent were dying almost as rapidly as everyone else—and there were far, far fewer of the obscenely rich to die.

In retrospect, it seemed like the universe had delivered the ultimate in "tough love" to humanity, to give us a second chance. After bringing us to our knees, it gave to one individual the ability and enlightenment to halt the virus—not to save us outright but to tell us how to save ourselves.

My name is Tom Newman, I'm a journalist who had the extraordinary privilege of meeting and befriending this enlightened human, known as the Divine Blood, God's Messenger, and the Light Worker. At his request, I will tell you the story of how I met and followed this man who gave true power to the people, fundamentally changing the world and saving both humanity and planet Earth.

Chapter 1

"Reports continue to pour in from Columbia Hospital, Vancouver General Hospital, and other emergency departments throughout the Greater Vancouver Area and beyond, as the number of new cases of the NH3N25 virus skyrockets."

Sipping a beer, I listened to the radio announcer's measured cadences. Like any media professional, he was trying to keep a lid on his own emotions, but I wondered how long it would be before radio and TV coverage became patchier, as employees either succumbed to the virus or refused to come to work, fearing infection. I was struggling with the decision myself, but had opted for precautionary measures so I could continue my work. Still, my "work attire" was looking more like a hazmat suit each day.

As I looked out from my garage, where I'd been doing some tidying and reorganizing, it seemed hard to grasp that on such a gorgeous Saturday in early May, the human race could at last be facing a problem beyond its capacity to solve or even survive.

Next door, a large moving truck had just pulled up. Despite the escalating fear of a global epidemic, people still wanted to move, I thought. But then, this cozy cul-de-sac with just ten other houses, nestled against dense forest, was a better place than many in which to face the possible impending social chaos. Most of the neighbours had already met a few times to talk about options, although none of us was quite ready to take things to the next level of planning.

Being curious by nature, I strolled over to welcome the new arrivals. As I approached, I saw two of the movers taking a break and having a smoke. There was a nice-looking SUV in the driveway and a minivan already inside the garage. I'd heard these arrive earlier but hadn't wanted to rush over and appear nosey, rather than simply friendly. The sound of conversation was coming from the front door, muffled slightly by a thick, sculpted juniper bush that just about reached the eaves.

A deep voice boomed: "Honey, the truck is here. Let the fun begin!" The accented voice contained a dose of good-humoured sarcasm.

"Hello!" I said from the path between the sidewalk and their front steps, catching a first glimpse of the voice's owner.

"Hi there!" he said cheerfully, turning from the house interior and beaming a broad smile.

I'm by no means a small guy, but this man was a lot larger. About six-foot-three and 200 pounds, he sported a mop of golden-brown, curly hair trimmed short on the sides. Laughing eyes gazed out over full lips, set in a smooth, olive complexion. His age was difficult to gauge, but I guessed somewhere in his late thirties.

My extended hand was quickly gripped in what resembled a baseball mitt, engulfing part of my wrist as well. Beneath an emerald-green t-shirt sporting an airplane turbine graphic, muscles moved prominently, but his was more the build of a sportsman than a weightlifter.

"I know the moving guys, and you're not one of them. How can I help you?" He continued smiling.

"I'm Tom—Tom Newman, your next-door neighbour." I gestured over my left shoulder. "I just came by to welcome you to the cul-de-sac and ask whether you need any help with moving in. I'd be happy to lend a hand." I raised my hand with a smile, still feeling the pressure of his grip against my right palm.

"My name is Tasos Perasmas, and I'm very pleased to meet you. I must say, if all the other neighbours are as friendly as you, we certainly made the right choice in coming here. Some help would be great, thanks. But first, let me introduce you to my family. Please come in, Tom."

Walking down a wide hallway, we reached a huge open-plan space where living room, dining area, and kitchen merged. At a kidney-shaped island in the kitchen area stood a woman in her early thirties, about five-foot-eight, with wavy brown hair worn a little past her shoulders. As she looked up over a jumble of half-unpacked cloth shopping bags, green eyes met mine with the same kind of candid welcome as I'd seen in her husband's. The weather was unusually warm for May, and when she came out from around the island, hand extended, I saw she was wearing a pair of orange jean shorts with a white tank top that accentuated her light brown skin. A gangly boy who looked to be about eleven or twelve smiled tentatively from a tall chair.

"This is my wife Christine and my son Themis," Tasos said. "This is Tom Newman, our next-door neighbour. He's offered to help us move in."

"Pleased to meet you, Tom," Christine said warmly, giving my hand a quick squeeze.

Themis, who had stood up at his name, likewise shook hands. "It's a pleasure to meet you, Tom," he said, with more maturity than I was used to hearing in a kid of that age.

"It's great to meet you, Christine, Themis," I smiled. "Welcome to the neighbourhood! May I ask how old you are, Themis?"

"I'm ten," he said, then quickly added, "but turning eleven in two months." With the emphasis kids that age placed on the importance of becoming older.

"Well that's a bonus, because I have a son, Jake, who's also ten. And I have an eight-year-old daughter named Brit. My wife's name is Claire. Would you folks like to have dinner at our place once you've moved in? There's nothing worse than having to cook after moving. And you can meet my family and relax."

Christine laughed. "It's like you read my mind, Tom," she said. "I was thinking the only thing I'd have energy for later would be to phone for pizza. Tasos?" She looked inquiringly at him.

"We'd love to come for dinner!" he boomed, arms wide. "But you'll let us bring some beverages, will you? I have some nice wines, and unlike most of the other things in boxes, I know exactly where they are."

It took us and the movers about two hours to unload the truck and get the various boxes into their assigned rooms. Everything went pretty smoothly except for a minor incident with a large statue of Aphrodite that one of the movers nearly dropped.

"You'd better handle that piece of art more carefully; my wife will be very unhappy if you damage it," Tasos said, momentarily frowning.

The mover apologized profusely, and Tasos's face cleared. "It's OK. You guys are doing an excellent job, for the most part."

Shortly after that, I went home to help Claire with dinner preparations. I'd already phoned her when the plans were made, so she had checked that we had enough food on hand. About six months into the AV outbreak, we had adjusted our routine so that we did just one large shopping trip to the city every four weeks, to reduce our risk of exposure. We'd had our own greenhouses and hydroponics garden for years, to grow fresh vegetables year round. And our daughter had taught herself how to make bread and other baked goods, so she was now our resident baker. Hence, to some extent, we were less dependent on the food-supply chain than others. In this case, it was easy to expand our dinner menu to accommodate a few guests.

Claire was talking on the phone when I entered the kitchen. She waved, blew me a kiss, and signaled that she'd be just another minute or two. The May heat had prompted her to bring out her summer dresses early, and she was wearing one that subtly emphasized her effortless femininity. She was a natural beauty and rarely had the patience to fuss with makeup or fashion. With her dark-blonde hair pulled back in a loose ponytail, she still took my breath away after a dozen years of marriage.

"How are the new neighbours?" Claire asked when she ended the call, turning her beautiful blue-grey eyes to me.

"They're great," I said. "Easy going, smart. And they love the outdoors, good food, and nice wine. Tasos is a foreman in a steel shop, and Christine is a hair stylist. Their son Themis is the same age as Jake and seems like a really nice kid. I have a feeling we'll all become good friends."

"That's a pretty strong set of first impressions!" Claire laughed. "Anything in particular that makes you think so?"

"I don't know the exact reason, no. It's more of an instinct, I guess. There's something different about them in a very good way, especially Tasos. Well, you'll see when they get here." I glanced at my watch. "They'll be over in about an hour and a half, so I'm going to wrap up what I was doing in the garage, have a quick shower, then come and help you with dinner prep."

"OK, honey," she replied. "Just don't get sidetracked in the garage; you know what you're like."

I laughed, knowing full well she was right.

When the doorbell rang at 6:30 p.m. on the dot, our kids were watching TV in the living room, and Claire and I had just put the finishing touches on some appetizer trays.

I answered the front door and ushered them into the kitchen. After the introductions and handshakes, the three kids went back to the living room, Jake carrying a tray of appies and Brit three plates with some napkins. We adults settled at the L-shaped island in the kitchen for drinks and nibbles while the barbecue on the back deck finished heating up.

In the usual so-how-did-you-two-meet conversation of couples, we learned that Tasos had been working on a cruise ship as an engine room officer when he met Christine. He had been on deck, leaning against the rail to watch the port traffic in Puerto Rico, when a crisply uniformed Christine, pulling a large suitcase, had walked up the gangway to board the ship. She clearly was a new crew member. Several others had already come on board, but Tasos felt an instant, inexplicable attraction to her and decided to meet her as soon as he could.

The ship had nearly 500 crew members, but the resourceful Tasos had introduced himself to the new manager of the beauty salon by that evening. It was love at first sight for both of them. They spent a blissful six months cruising the beautiful Caribbean, working hard but also enjoying the good life during their time off. Tasos, being an officer, had a nice cabin with a window, a double bed, and a refrigerator.

As their work contract drew to a close, neither was in any doubt that they were meant to be together. Tasos promised to emigrate to Canada, where Christine was from, after returning to Greece for a few weeks to wrap things up there. They'd been married for sixteen years.

After dinner, we all sat out on the back deck while I poured liqueurs and made special coffees. I asked Tasos whether he'd had any particular adventures while working in the merchant marine industry, which he'd done for many years before switching to cruise lines.

As his eyes met mine, I could see his thoughts travelling far away. I shifted in my seat and leaned forward, sensing a good story.

"One time in West Africa, the ship that I was working on was attacked by pirates," Tasos said. Claire and I breathed in sharply, and even the kids stopped talking.

Tasos smiled. "Christine and Themis of course know this story, but it's a pretty good one, isn't it, you guys?" He raised his eyebrows and they both nodded vigorously.

"Please tell us about the pirates!" Brit and Jake clamoured.

Tasos looked at them with a smile, enjoying their anticipation.

"OK. Then I'll tell you about one of the most dangerous places I've ever been. At the time, I worked on a general cargo ship. And on this trip, we were delivering goods to Nigeria. After a two-week journey from Europe, we had to wait at anchor for about a month before we could go into the port and unload. We hadn't been at anchor for more than a week when pirates attacked our ship."

Claire, our kids, and I were hanging on his every word.

"They threw grappling hooks with ropes from small boats, then climbed onto the ship. About ten of them got on board in the early hours, around 2:30 a.m. They were huge Nigerian men with knives and automatic rifles. I was working a 4:00 a.m. to 8:00 a.m. shift, so I was sleeping when it happened. One of the guys on duty was able to hit the emergency alarm, and when those of us off duty opened our cabin doors to see what was going on, we heard rapid gunshots—bom! bom! bom!—and angry shouts in a foreign language.

"Before we could barely process what was happening, the crew were all herded at gunpoint into the mess hall. We were terrified, of course. I don't think any of us had been through a pirate attack before. I certainly hadn't. 'Who is the captain?' one of the pirates shouted. 'I am,' Captain Dimitris replied, raising an arm. The same pirate walked over and struck him so hard that he fell to the floor and lost consciousness for about ten seconds. 'From now on, this ship is mine, you got that?' the pirate barked, looking down at the captain, who nodded weakly. I remember he was bleeding from one ear. Then the pirate turned and look around at the rest of us crew, daring us to object. We were all frozen, fearing for our lives." Tasos looked around at our wide-eyed faces.

"Go on, Dad, tell them what happened next," Themis urged.

"Well, we got incredibly lucky. About two hours later, just before dawn, we heard sirens from far off. Remember, the ship was anchored off shore. The pirates had been so confident that they'd decided to relax and drink before taking the ship out into the open ocean to finish off the heist. The sirens were the Nigerian navy. Typically, they don't have time to deal with these situations, because piracy is so rampant there. But, this vessel had been returning to port, saw the tell-tale small boats alongside our freighter, and decided they'd give their new recruits a taste of what would soon become routine for them. The pirates fled the mess hall, and by the time some of us had reached the deck, they were already speeding away in their little boats."

"They let the pirates escape?!" Jake asked incredulously.

Tasos nodded. "They let them go rather than risk hurting civilians in an exchange of fire. But I heard that one of the senior naval officers told our captain he'd radioed another vessel, which would intercept them before they'd travelled very far. I learned later that half of the pirates were killed while resisting arrest, and the other half were thrown in jail. The police didn't even need witness statements from our freighter, because the pirates had charge sheets a mile long."

I let out a low whistle. "You were very lucky," I said.

"It was probably the scariest situation I've been in," Tasos said. "I'm not sure what would have happened if the navy hadn't shown up. Maybe I wouldn't be here now."

I reached over to offer him a top-up on his liqueur, but he politely declined.

"Tasos, what do you think of the epidemic?" I asked. "The health authorities are saying this is a different virus, something they've never encountered before, very difficult to control."

He squinted thoughtfully. "Tom, humanity has gone through these sorts of scares before. I'm confident that scientists will find a way to fight this new virus too. I trust science." There was something about his calm optimism in the face of this massive global threat that instilled confidence in me. This seemed irrational, given I hardly knew the man, but he had a unique aura about him.

The conversation shifted to happier topics, and we stayed up well into the evening, finally saying our goodbyes a bit after midnight.

Chapter 2

After that first get together, the two families became good friends. The kids played together every day, and we had dinner at each other's houses once or twice a week. Tasos was a very good listener, showing interest in my struggles at work and boosting my bruised ego on many occasions.

One day, for instance, I mentioned how my boss was treating me. At the time, I worked for the Surrey Post, a local newspaper. The chief editor, Mr. Callingham, complained that I didn't find interesting enough stories—as though it was my fault that in our small city, only minor things were happening, apart from new cases of AV. When I used the word "boss," Tasos looked at me intently, and I noticed for the first time that his right eye was green whereas the left was hazel. That right eye in particular sparkled in anger.

"Tom, I have a request," he said, calmly controlling his evident emotion.

"Anything, Tasos," I replied.

"Can you please never use the word 'boss' again?"

It struck me as an odd request, and I wanted to know what was behind it. "Well, sure, I can definitely try. Why? What would you call him?"

"Your employer," he said emphatically.

"OK," I said. "Would you like to elaborate?"

We were building a compost area in their back yard, and

Tasos put down the tool he was holding and crossed his arms.

"Tom, our society has created a whole system of wrong standards, so a small percentage of people can control the masses. Using the word 'boss' may seem small, but it's a very important example. Every time you say boss, you make yourself the slave. Every time you say boss, you are the dog. They love to hear you call them that. But you're putting yourself down, beneath them, without realizing it." He paused, looking off into the distance, absorbed in thought. "Your employer is not a good one, and the universe will eventually adjust the status quo." His words and tone sounded ominous. I had already gathered that he held strong beliefs about the working class and employers, passionately disliking most owners and managers. This conversation contributed to my growing understanding of his perspective.

A few days later, I was relating another run-in I'd had that day with Callingham He had peevishly denied a request I'd submitted for a day off to accompany my two children on a school field trip—as it turned out, the last one that would be held for a very long time. "He's a pathetic, bullying little tyrant in his tiny realm of our newspaper office," I fumed. I'd been struggling with hypertension for a while, and I knew that getting upset like this would raise my blood pressure, but I couldn't help myself. I hated the injustice and Callingham really riled me with his arbitrary authoritarianism.

"Having a petty tyrant for an employer is a common problem," Tasos said. "In the employer-employee relationship, there is such an imbalance of power. This always limits what employees can do when they're being treated unfairly. Because ultimately, the employer can take away the employee's job. This is how employers suppress the working middle class, and how the rich one percent continue to rig everything in their favour, from politics to economics to wars to science and medicine. The truth, though, is that the working middle class can live without the rich one percent, but the one percent cannot live without the labouring middle class."

I thought about this for a moment. "Do you think the one percent will be able to protect themselves from AV for much longer, Tasos?"

He shrugged. "Maybe. But like everyone else, they're still relying on scientists to come up with a cure, and scientists are workers, part of the middle class. And," he said, intensely looking me in the eye, "I don't know why, but I have a feeling that the cure will come from an unexpected source, and that this source won't be favourable to the selfish rich. Call me naïve, but I still believe in natural justice."

Shortly after that, we each went in for dinner, but I continued mulling over the implications of what Tasos had said.

For a little while longer, life continued almost as normal in our tiny corner of the world, and we had some good times. At our first gathering, the day Tasos and his family moved to the neighbourhood, he had described a treehouse that he planned to build. I soon learned that when he said he would do something, he did it…and to the highest standards. The treehouse was finished by the beginning of September, ready for the Labour Day long weekend so the kids could enjoy it before returning to school. They had been polite but relentless in asking when it would be ready, checking with him each afternoon when he returned from work. Most evenings, he used the long summer daylight hours to make progress. I would pitch in when I was around and he needed some extra help or simply wanted company.

When the treehouse was finished, Tasos and Christine organized an "official opening" ceremony, inviting me and my family to be the first visitors. The treehouse was magnificent! Elevated ten feet off the ground and made with steel for structural integrity, it was about twelve feet in diameter. Despite the size, it somehow looked and felt like a tree from the outside. There was a hidden door that opened via a voice-activated lock. Knotted ropes as well as a rope ladder offered other options for accessing the treehouse, which was hidden by a multitude of different flowers and vines in strategically placed containers.

Tasos demonstrated the voice-activated device, pointing to a spot on the trunk with two lights, one green, one red. The red one was lit. "Watch this," he said. "Oh Mama." A door slid noiselessly open, revealin g a space large enough for two adults or three kids.

"Cool, eh?" Tasos asked me, smiling.

"It is amazing, Tasos!"

"Let's go up," Tasos said, gesturing to a small vestibule. "This is the elevator, in case someone doesn't feel like using the knotted ropes or the rope ladder." I followed him into the small space, the door closing behind us automatically. He grasped a remote control with two buttons, hanging from a cable. "Are you ready, Tom?" I nodded. "For safety, if the door isn't completely closed, the elevator won't work."

He then pressed the top button on the remote, and the elevator rose silently. After about five seconds, it stopped. The doors opened onto a large room, with a two-seater couch, a couple of chairs, and a small kitchen area. Another door revealed a half bathroom with toilet and sink, and a third door led to a balcony about three feet deep, with glass sides and a solid guard rail. All around the balcony were flowers and small shrubs. A large PVC pipe at one corner of the balcony led down through a greenery-enclosed chute.

"See that, Tom?" he asked. "That's a slide, big enough and solid enough for adults to use too."

"Tasos, this is amazing," I said. "I wish I was still a kid!"

"Actually, Tom, I meant for us adults to use it too. You can go up there with your wife for a weekend, for example. It'll feel like you're camping. You'll have privacy from the kids but be close by to check on them or in case they need you."

We went back inside, and he gestured for me to take a seat, then poured us both a cold drink from the bar fridge that hummed quietly beside a sink and counter area.

"Tasos, this is the life," I said, grinning as I relaxed into the sofa and nodded my thanks as he passed me the drink. He called down to the others to come up when they wanted, and we then sat and talked. Being up in a treehouse is guaranteed to make anyone feel like a kid again, and for that afternoon, I could almost forget about the epidemic.

Tasos always seemed more interested in making other people happy than in pursuing his own interests. His compassion and caring for others was constantly in evidence, but not in an intrusive or self-aggrandizing way. He was mechanically inclined and could fix most things. With his welding machine and other power tools, he would help anyone in the neighbourhood. If someone needed their vehicle's engine oil changed, he'd do that for free. "Just a thank you is enough, my friend," he'd say. "I'm happy that I could help."

When I remarked on how unusual I found this to be, Tasos said he had started working at age fifteen, in a machine shop. This gave him the skills and economic freedom that most other young adults didn't have. He'd decided to experiment by sharing his hard-earned money with his friends, with no expectation of getting anything in return. "That's how I learned about the depths of their characters, who I really wanted in my life, and who were selfish and not people I wanted to continue with in friendship."

By seventeen, he had graduated from high school and set off on his first merchant marine ship, soon working as an assistant engineer. His thirst for learning made most things come to him very easily. His humility led him to avoid seeking recognition, preferring the quiet life. "Many people are intimidated by success," he told me, "while others are drawn to it but for the wrong reasons. I'd rather just get on with my life, meeting people and helping them when I can."

His generosity became increasingly useful for lowering our little area's chances of contamination, although the risk was still very real and rising. Each day, I was reporting on numerous new cases of AV. There had been no incidents at our kids' school or even in our small city, other than a few isolated cases that were quickly tracked down to exposure in other cities. The infected individuals had been reported and quarantined. But still, the mortality rate remained at 100%.

Even Tasos, with his solid faith in science, was worried, telling me there had been a few cases in a neighbouring city, where his workplace was located.

"Tom, I hope they find a vaccine or cure soon, because I'm starting to feel at risk." It was a Friday evening in early October, and we had just decided to talk with our kids about not trick-or-treating for Halloween this year, because the risk of infection was too high.

"I feel the same way, Tasos," I said. "Did you know that in China, there are millions dead already?"

"Really?"

"Yes," I nodded. "The Chinese government is hiding it, but social media is leaking the truth. People have started to think that humanity is heading for extinction. Every day I visit hospitals, Tasos." I rubbed my face. "I report on the dying. The devastation for the relatives is overwhelming. Everyone, sick or not, is wearing surgical masks and visors and gloves. Some have full face masks. It's like being on another planet."

"I would hate to do your job, Tom," Tasos said. "You must be terrified by so much exposure."

"I am," I said, "but it's what my job requires, and that's what's paying the bills. Thankfully, Claire can do all of her work from home." My wife was a clinical psychologist, and for the past several months, she had been conducting sessions entirely by video chat.

Tasos looked at me and said, "You're a brave and decent man, Tom. I feel privileged to be your friend."

I felt a bit embarrassed by his praise, so I shrugged awkwardly and mumbled my thanks. The truth was, I didn't feel brave at all. Even as a reporter for a small paper, I knew that the official estimates of deaths were frightening, and the real numbers were probably much higher. A few hundred thousand had been officially reported in North America, but I was skeptical.

That autumn, the protective measures in hospitals were extended to other public facilities and government buildings. Private companies had already brought in their own protocols, and soon, infection prevention clothing and equipment were apparent everywhere, from hand sanitizers to free surgical masks and gloves and glasses, to body temperature indicators at the main doors of buildings. Doctors appearing on news programs were sounding helpless and worried, despite their attempts to maintain a professional demeanour. Public confidence in government and science was breaking down, and the whole world was trembling with fear.

On the Internet, doom-laden websites were attracting record numbers of visitors. "The End" forecast the extinction of the human race within twelve months. "Prediction Time" purported to have recalculated the Mayans' predictions of the apocalypse and claimed that AV would destroy all but a select few, who would remain for a "rebirth" of humanity. The site "Nature's Time" stated that humanity had made nature angry, so it was punishing us. Some groups believed the epidemic would ultimately spare a tiny percentage of humans, and that alien ships would pick up the survivors as part of some huge interstellar experiment by super-intelligent beings.

It was easy to laugh at such nonsense, and I ended up writing a feature piece on these and other grim, sensationalistic, or just downright fantastical websites and movements. Mr. Callingham kicked up a fuss, saying it would "harm our readership base." But instead of following his orders, I published the piece in our digital edition then sent it to the printer at the very last minute, so it would also appear in the hard-copy version—as a two-page centre spread. My conversation with Tasos had emboldened me, and when Callingham predictably flew into a rage, I simply picked up my jacket and briefcase, and said calmly, "Until you can address me with politeness and respect, I won't be back," and walked out. Several of the other staff members actually clapped.

Coward that he was, Callingham sent me an email the next day that fell short of an apology: "Our recent exchange was regrettable. Your skills are required here at the office, so we hope that you will return to work this coming Monday." It was enough of a victory for me that I decided to return. I was optimistic about changing the environment at work, not just for myself but for my co-workers.

Chapter 3

Feeling better than I had in ages, I planned to spend a quiet, extended weekend at home with family and friends. Then all hell broke loose in our tranquil neighbourhood. Christine became infected with AV.

It was an early Saturday afternoon in November. Seeing Tasos in his backyard, I walked over to the fence to say hi.

"Tasos, how are you?"

"Tom, hi. How are you?" he replied, leaning his rake against a tree and approaching the fence.

"I'm doing well, thank you," I said, looking forward to telling him about what had happened at work. Our schedules had conflicted in the past couple of days, so I hadn't yet had the opportunity. But immediately, I noticed unease in his voice and worry on his face. "Tasos, is everything OK? How are Christine and Themis?" I felt a knot forming in my chest, as I'd never seen the usually upbeat Tasos look this way before.

Gripping the top of the fence, he looked into my eyes and said, "Tom, Christine is sick."

"What do you mean?" Although his meaning was obvious, part of me couldn't accept that our illusion of invincibility had finally been penetrated by the increasingly chaotic outside world.

"It's the virus." The words I had dreaded hearing.

"Are you sure?"

He nodded. "We'd hoped it was just a cold. Then she woke up this morning with a high fever, so we took her to emergency at Vancouver General. They ran the tests and said she's infected with the virus, Tom." Tasos was breathing shallowly. I'd never seen him this emotional before. "Tom, you should step back a bit. It's possible I'm infected. The three of us will have to quarantine ourselves."

"Oh, Tasos, my friend, I'm so sorry. Where is Christine now?"

"She's at home. The doctor gave her some medication to keep the fever from getting any higher. He said that younger people fight the virus more effectively. But he also suggested getting an oxygen tank and equipment, for the difficult times that will come. We picked it up on the way home from the hospital." Tasos bent his head, and I saw tears falling as his voice broke. "Tom, I don't know what to do. I'm numb. My beautiful Christine, the love of my life, is going to die!"

I began to reach across the fence, to grasp his shoulder in comfort, but he held up a warning hand to stop me. "Tasos, is there something we can do? Would you like us to take care of Themis for the time being so you can organize your thoughts, have one less thing to worry about?" "No thank you, as I mentioned, all three of us have to quarantine ourselves so we can verify whether we're infected or not. But thank you for the offer, I appreciate it. For now I have to disinfect the whole house. Christine will stay in our bedroom. The doctor said to use protective gear when I look after her."

We kept in touch with Tasos and Christine by video chat in the first few days, then by phone.

Once Tasos declared the house safe, he invited us over. "Don't feel obligated," he assured us. "We'll completely understand if you'd rather not take any risks." Claire and I decided to go, but we insisted our kids stay home. They were disgruntled but accepted our concern; the seriousness of the epidemic was starting to penetrate their innocent world.

I had purchased hazmat suits with built-in respirators for all of my family. "I'd rather overreact," I told Claire, and she agreed.

Feeling as protected as we could, we went over. Tasos—wearing the same kind of suit—ushered us into the house. It smelled like a cross between a hospital and a janitorial supply shop. He led us up to the bedroom and opened the door. Christine was lying on a large bed covered with soft blankets. The room was spotless. She looked better than we had expected, and we felt rather foolish in our hazmat gear, but I reminded myself: 100% mortality rate.

Themis immediately ran to his mother's side and hugged her, saying, "Mom, are you OK? I've missed you so much. Why aren't you wearing a costume like the rest of us?" We'd tried to lessen the kids' concerns by calling the protective gear a costume, but I don't think they were fooled.

Christine looked at Themis and said quietly, "I don't need the costume, honey." Themis started to ask more questions, but Christine said, "Let's chat about this in a little while, with your dad. Right now, I'd like to talk with Tom and Claire for a short time, before I get tired again. Why don't you go and check your room, to see if everything's the way you'd like it after Daddy had it professionally cleaned." Themis nodded and skipped away to his room, happy to be home and still fairly oblivious to the seriousness of situation.

After a short visit with Christine, spent mostly talking about the kids and whether we should stop sending them to school, her eyelids were evidently becoming heavy, so Tasos suggested we let her rest. "Let's go downstairs and have some coffee or a drink and some food." He squeezed Christine's hand and smiled. "I'll just be in the kitchen, my love. If you need anything, you just page your personal assistant!" He pointed to a call button device on the bedside table nearest Christine, explaining to us that if she pressed it, the pager on his belt would alert him immediately. It was good to see that despite his anguish, he still retained a spark of his usual humour.

Downstairs, Tasos said we were safe to remove the protective gear. We sat at the kitchen island and Themis went into the living room to watch TV, after Tasos offered to bring him some lunch. While making sandwiches and slicing fruit, Tasos explained everything he knew so far—how they thought Christine had contracted the virus (at her workplace), and how far the infection had progressed.

"Her lungs are already infected," Tasos said, speaking quietly so Themis wouldn't hear him. "For some reason, it reached them very quickly, so it seems the virus is multiplying rapidly." Tasos set down his knife and bent his head, no longer able to hold back his tears. Claire passed him a box of tissues, and I poured him some more wine, at a loss for words.

"I don't know how I'm able to work these days. I do everything in a daze. I look at the clock constantly, can't wait for the time to go home. I hate having to work to pay the bills; I'd rather be home with Christine. I've hired a nurse, Susan, who's going to look after Christine and take Themis to school and back. She'll be a big help when I'm at work. I don't see us having a merry Christmas this year. I feel so vulnerable, but I haven't lost hope. I still have faith in the scientists. Surely they'll have made some progress by now. It's been nearly two years since the virus emerged, hasn't it?"

"Yes," I replied. I hesitated, not wanting to sound pessimistic, but I also didn't wish to be dishonest. "Things basically don't look any different now, in terms of finding a vaccine or an anti-viral drug treatment. They haven't even found a way to slow the disease's progress. But," I continued, "there are so many brilliant minds working on this around the world that it seems impossible for them not to find something very soon."

He nodded. "Thank you for your optimism. I feel the same.

That's how I find the strength to continue, that and Themis," he said, glancing toward the living room and smiling sadly to himself.

Over sandwiches and coffees, we continued our discussion about the kids and school, ultimately deciding that for now, since Christine was the only known case in our neighbourhood and the elementary school had just a little over 200 students, the risk was very low.

Claire and I went home overwhelmed with sadness. Less than six weeks later, Christine died.

Chapter 4

Christmas was dismal. Tasos tried his best for the sake of Themis, but his pain was almost unbearable. For a few weeks, right after Christine's passing, he and I communicated only by text message or email. He said he was just too emotional and too tired to do anything but work and look after his son. Respecting his grief, I kept in touch when he wanted, and otherwise just observed him coming and going to work. Themis was also having a really rough time, missing his mother and worrying about his dad. He would spend a couple of afternoons each week with us, sometimes staying overnight.

By the new year, reports from around the globe were devastating. The most populous countries had deaths in the tens of millions, and their social infrastructures were struggling to cope. In all major cities, including Canada's, everyone wore surgical masks. Government offices were struggling to stay staffed. Most schools were holding classes only two days a week, as teachers either became infected or refused to come to work. Mail was delivered only three days a week. Long-haul truck drivers and other involved in the movement of goods were dying in greater percentages because their jobs put them at greater risk of infection. Consequently, there had begun to be shortages in food, clothing, medicine, and pretty much everything else we had until then taken for granted as always just a short drive or an Amazon order away.

I was still working at the newspaper, collecting information about what was happening in our city, as well as tracking and reporting on the desperate research worldwide for a vaccine or anti-viral drugs. Increasingly, I wondered whether those predicting human extinction were right. What chaos and violence would ensue before that happened, though?

My focus on the outside world came to an abrupt halt near the end of February when Themis and our two kids came home from school feeling unwell. The earliest we could get them in for testing was the following morning, and by noon, we knew they had AV. The drive home from the clinic was silent. Claire's face was expressionless and whiter than I'd ever seen it; she looked like a zombie.

Once we got home, we started the entire disinfection process. We put on hazmat suits and moved Brit's bed, other furniture, and clothing into her brother's room so they could be together. It felt horrible to be wearing protective gear when our children were ill. But we knew that if we too fell ill, no one would be able to look after them…or us. My parents were in Ottawa, Claire's were in Houston, and both domestic and international flights were running on drastically reduced schedules at prices only the very rich could afford. We were willing to take on whatever expense necessary, but when we called them, our parents refused to travel, too frightened about getting sick themselves.

Tasos came over the next day to talk.

"Tom, Claire, I don't know if I can take this," he said. "Themis is all the family I have here. I've decided to stay home with him rather than go to work."

I had been considering doing the same, especially as Claire was inundated with grief-stricken and panicked clients and wouldn't be able to look after the kids on her own.

"What have you heard, Tom?" asked Tasos. "You're the best informed of us. Is there any hope?"

"I wish I had something positive to say, but I don't, I'm sorry. The scientists still haven't had any success, and of course they're starting to die now as well. Half of the world's countries are on the brink of social collapse, and I'm afraid Canada will go that way too before this year is out."

For the next two months, the three of us took care of the kids. Fortunately, the progression of the virus was slower than it had been for Christine. Humans can maintain hope in the most desperate of circumstances, and we had begun to think that perhaps, despite whatever else was happening to other people, our kids would be spared. Then Claire got sick.

Initially, I was numb. I focused on making her comfortable and checking on the kids. After a couple of hours, all three were sleeping. In a daze, I pulled on some protective gloves, strapped on an air filtration mask, and staggered over to Tasos's house, pressing on the doorbell.

An upstairs window opened, and Tasos leaned out. "Oh, hey Tom, it's you. I'll be right down." Half a minute or so later, he opened the door, and at the sight of me his eyes flew wide open above the rim of his face mask. "Tom, what is it? Have the children gotten worse?"

"No, they're stable. But Claire is infected. We just got back from the clinic." I burst into tears and felt my knees buckle.

Tasos grabbed me before I crumpled on the doorstep, wrapping one of his powerful arms around my shoulders. He slung my right arm around his waist and helped me inside, seating me on a couch. "Oh my friend, I'm so sorry. This is devastating."

"Tasos, I don't know what to do," I said. "My whole family may be gone in a few months. They're what I live for. I don't think I'll want to keep going if they die."

We sat in silence for a short while, then it hit me. "Tasos, wasn't that Themis's bedroom window you were leaning out of?" He nodded. "But you weren't wearing any protective gear."

He looked at me wordlessly for several moments, then

said, "I feel the same way, Tom. I don't want to live without my family; that's why I wasn't wearing protection. I haven't worn anything around Themis since he got infected. I only wear it when I'm around others, to keep them safe. I didn't tell you and Claire because I didn't want you to know how depressed I am. For some reason, I haven't become infected."

"Tasos, you're crazy! Who's going to look after Themis if you get infected?"

"Tom, I've thought through the timing, and it's highly likely that even if I got infected now, I would die after Themis. And after he goes, the sooner I go, the better."

Realizing we were currently both too depressed to be of much help to each other, I returned home.

Claire was in the kitchen, mechanically preparing some food, still in shock. "I woke up soon after you left, Tom. I'm not sick enough to be bed-ridden yet. How is Themis? How is Tasos holding up?"

"Themis is almost the same, like Jake and Brit. Tasos took your news hard. Claire, he hasn't been using protective gear around Themis. He's in despair and wants to get infected so he can die too."

"Oh, my god," Claire said, mouth agape.

"Yeah," I said. "But he hasn't been infected yet." I sat down heavily in a chair. "Honestly, I feel the same way. I wouldn't want to go on living without you and the kids. But I can't give up hope yet. So I'll keep wearing the gear."

"Thank you, honey," she said. "You mustn't give up!" She gave me a small, tired smile.

"I invited Tasos for dinner. Susan, the nurse, offered to come over and look after Themis for a few hours. Please don't let on that I told you about his attempt to become infected, OK?"

"Of course," she said.

A few hours later, Tasos came over. I offered him a mask at the door; Claire was standing just behind me. Tasos looked at me solemnly and said with his deep voice, "I'm not going to pretend, my friend." He spoke to Claire. "I hope Tom has told you. Has he?" She nodded. He looked back at me. "Tom, you keep the mask on, OK?"

We went into the living room, as the lasagna in the oven wouldn't be ready for another few minutes. "Tasos," I said hesitantly, "don't you think it's strange that you haven't been infected yet? Maybe this is significant."

He shrugged. "I've hardly ever been ill in my life. Don't even get colds." He rubbed his face tiredly. "I don't know. I'll think about it tomorrow."

I didn't want to cause him more stress, so we started discussing our gardens and greenhouses, which had become much more important since food distribution networks had begun to weaken.

Chapter 5

A month after her diagnosis, Claire was deteriorating. The kids, infected for much longer, were by now in a similar condition. Themis and my three invalids all struggled to breathe without an oxygen mask. I had ceased to care about the outside world other than what was necessary to look after our two families. As more and more people understandably were functioning in the same way, society was falling apart. The chance of developing a cure or vaccine seemed impossible now, as even scientific laboratories could scarcely keep going for lack of staff and resources. Human extinction seemed inevitable.

It was a Sunday in early June, and I was in the kitchen, preparing nutritional drinks for Claire and the kids because they now had difficulty eating solid food. Birds were singing in great numbers—the natural world reaping the benefits of much-reduced human activity and destruction. Over their beautiful sounds I heard Tasos calling my name loudly outside the front door. He sounded different. Something was going on. I hurried to the door and opened it on a smiling Tasos, something I hadn't seen in many long months. Immediately, he engulfed me in a bear hug, shaking with laughter and evidently unable to contain his excitement. I thought, "Poor man, he's finally lost his mind!"

"Tasos, what's going on?" I asked. "Why are you laughing and hugging me?"

"Don't worry, Tom. I haven't gone crazy, and by tomorrow, you're going to be doing the same. Maybe sooner!"

"What do you mean, Tasos? What on earth has happened? Has a cure been found?" I spun around to the TV, which I kept on throughout the day, desperately hoping for good news.

"I know everything now; I understand everything. I know why it's me and I know why now." He stopped to catch his breath and said. "OK, Tom, in a few words: I can heal your family right now. And by tomorrow, the kids'll be playing in the treehouse again with Themis."

Now I was sure he'd gone crazy. "Tasos," I said slowly, and I hoped kindly, "you sound like you think you're God. How about sitting down, having a drink, doing some deep breathing. You're freaking me out."

Tasos grinned, and I started to worry about what I was going to do with a very large, very strong, delusional man who'd decided he was God.

Abruptly, he sat down on the couch and said in something closer to his normal voice, the one before the virus had struck our families, "I'll have that drink, and I'd like to join me by having one too, in celebration." He held up a hand. "I realize that I must be coming across as nuts, so I'll try to tell you calmly what happened and what I've discovered."

I opened a bottle of very good red wine—why not? I poured each of us a glass and sat opposite him in an armchair. "OK, fire away," I said.

"We are going upstairs to give Claire and Jake and Brit one drop of my blood each, and by tomorrow, they will be completely better—like new," Tasos announced.

I was frozen and mute. What he'd said was nonsense.

"No, my friend," he tried to assure me, "I repeat, I haven't lost it. Here," he got up, still holding his wine glass. "Come over to the window. Let me show you something—or I should say someone."

I followed him to a window that faced his house, providing a view of nearly the whole backyard, including the treehouse.

"Who do you see at the treehouse?" he asked.

I gasped and felt my heart do a double beat. Themis was climbing the rope ladder.

"Tasos, what's going on? How is this possible? Who and what has healed Themis?"

"I just told you, Tom. Your family will be well too, if I give each of them one drop of my blood," he said. "Here's the proof right in front of your eyes. You know that I would never do anything to hurt you or your family. So please give me the opportunity to restore Claire, Jake, and Brit's health." He paused, scanning my face for a reaction. "There is much more to this than you can imagine, Tom," he said. "Let me try this. And then, when they've recovered, I'll tell you when and how it happened—how I realized that I have this ability. But first, I want to see my dear friends, your loving family, completely healthy again."

I couldn't think of a reason to no…except I was worried that by agreeing to it would indicate I'd lost my mind too. "You know I want nothing more than to have them healthy and safe again. Do what you have to do. Let's go upstairs."

Tasos hugged me again, this time more gently. "Everything's going to be all right, Tom. I promise. Now, do you have something sharp, like a small, pointed knife?"

I went to the kitchen and pulled out a well-sharpened paring knife from a drawer. We kept a bottle of hydrogen peroxide in the kitchen, in case someone cut themselves. I poured some of the liquid over the blade to sterilize it, then handed it to Tasos.

We went upstairs to the kids' bedroom. Brit and Jake were sleeping, which they did most of the time now. Tasos look at them with love, then pressed the knife against one of the fingers on his left hand, piercing the skin just enough to draw blood.

He turned to me with a smile and said, "Come closer so you can gently pull Brit's lower lip out a bit."

Lowering his left hand to my daughter's mouth, he squeezed a full drop of blood out of the cut and made sure it dripped into her mouth. We then went to Jake's bed and repeated this.

"That's it, Tom," he said to me, smiling. "Let's go to Claire now."

Claire was awake and whispered, "Hello."

"Hello Claire," Tasos said with a smile, then waited for me to explain to her.

"Honey," I said, taking her hand in both of mine, "Tasos thinks he has found a way to cure you and the kids. He's already cured Themis—I've seen him with my own eyes, playing in the treehouse just now! I've already let him give the cure to Brit and Jake. Will you let Tasos give you the treatment that cured Themis? It's completely painless."

Claire's brow furrowed. "How is this possible? What's this treatment, Tasos?"

"It will seem a bit unusual," he said to her, "but will you trust me? It will take literally only a moment to administer to you."

She gazed at him, exhausted. "OK, Tasos. Go ahead."

Tasos said, "Open your mouth a little." Claire looked inquiringly at me. I nodded encouragingly and tightened my grip on her hand. "Trust me; this is safe," he continued. "Not just safe but life-saving." He squeezed a drop of his blood out of the cut and into her open mouth.

"That's it," Tasos said, looking at us both. "Claire, you will feel better by tomorrow."

She shook her head and closed her eyes. "This isn't possible. You've both lost your minds. Please go get some sleep; you're both so tired. It's understandable that you've got a crazy idea in your heads."

"Honey," I said, "I know it seems completely bonkers. But, let me help you out of the bed so you can come to the window to see Themis playing outside. Tasos gave him a drop of his blood yesterday, and now he's cured!"

Claire did as I suggested. At first, Themis was nowhere to be seen, and I thought for a moment that I'd been dreaming. My stomach clenched in fear. But Tasos slid open the window and called out: "Themis! Where are you? Can you come down into the yard for a minute? I want to show Tom and Claire that you're well."

Within a moment, Themis came down the slide and planted his feet on the grass. Then he got up and waved to the three of us, grinning.

Claire looked as dumb-struck as I had been downstairs. I held on to her, worried that she might faint. "This is wonderful!" she whispered, then began coughing. I gently helped her back into bed.

"I'm going to leave you two now and get back to Themis. Claire and the kids should get some nutrition into them, then rest and sleep until the morning. But I'll see you tomorrow. And then, a whole new world is going to open up for you!"

I smiled and shook his hand. Claire, still dazed, simply nodded and whispered, "OK, see you tomorrow, Tasos."

A few hours later, after preparing and bringing some hot cereal up to Claire and the kids, putting on a load of laundry, and tidying up the kitchen, I grabbed the bottle of wine I'd opened earlier for Tasos. I poured a glass and sat down on the couch to think through everything that had happened. I was mentally and emotionally exhausted, but underneath this was a calm that I hadn't felt for such a long time that I'd forgotten what it felt like. Heaving a deep sigh and scarcely daring to hope, I settled back in the couch and took a long sip...then another.

Chapter 6

"Dad! Dad!" Swimming up from the depths of a dream, I heard Jake's voice calling me. Once I'd registered the sound, my eyes snapped open, then squinted at the bright sunlight coming through the living room window.

"What time…?" I mumbled, realizing I'd fallen asleep on the couch after I don't know how many drinks. I reached down to the floor, where my smartphone had fallen, and checked the time: 10 a.m. Monday.

From upstairs, I heard Jake's voice again and bolted upright. How could he be calling me so loudly when only yesterday, he could hardly whisper? Then I remembered. Tasos. The miracle. His cure. I took the stairs two at a time and burst into the kids' bedroom.

Jake was sitting on his bed, a duvet still covering his legs. But he was smiling, and breathing normally without an oxygen mask.

"Hi buddy. Sorry, I thought you were still sleeping. How're you feeling?"

"I'm OK, Dad. And I'm hungry."

"Me too!" declared Brit, who was also sitting up.

"Are you both sure you're feeling fine?" They nodded. "Well, be careful when you get up. You'll be wobbly on your feet at first."

Jake stood up, looking thin and bony in his pyjamas. "Not me."

Brit nodded vigorously as she too got out of bed. "I feel fine, Dad!"

"Well, if you feel strong enough to shower, I bet you'll feel better after you've done that and put on clean clothes. I'll go downstairs and make you some bacon and eggs."

"Could we have French toast too?" asked Brit.

Their clear, steady voices asking for their favourite breakfast was music to my ears. "Coming right up, madam!" I said. "But first, I need to check on Mom. Want to come with me?"

"Yes!!"

I put a finger to my lips to shush them, in case Claire was still sleeping.

"I'm not asleep, you guys, come in!" called Claire. Her voice was loud and chipper.

As I opened the door, I held my breath, scarcely able to believe what might be true. There she was, sitting on the side of the bed, already dressed.

The kids and I ran to her, and we had a massive, laughing group-hug. "I'd love some bacon and eggs and French toast too," smiled Claire.

Leaving the kids and Claire on the bed, still hugging, I went downstairs to the kitchen. I'd never been happier in my entire life, thanks to Tasos and his amazing healing.

"Who is he really?" said Claire as we all sat having breakfast. "How can he possess that kind of power?"

I shook my head. "I don't know, honey. But I have a sense that something much greater than even this massive epidemic is coming."

Claire put down her fork. "What do you mean, Tom? That sounds scary."

"No, no, nothing to worry about. I don't know yet, exactly, but I think Tasos's mission is just beginning."

The kids ate seconds then thirds. Seeing them with healthy appetites again was glorious.

"I have to call Tasos," I said, "and thank him for saving our family. I don't know what I can do to show my gratitude. But I'll do anything for him, for the rest of my life."

Tasos picked up on the second ring. "Hey, Tom. How is everybody?"

"I think you already know the answer to that, my friend. They're fine, totally back to good health other than needing to put on a few pounds. How is Themis?"

"Oh, he's doing great. He's been in the treehouse since early this morning, as soon as he finished breakfast. He'll be very happy to know that Jake and Brit are feeling better too. Would they like to hang out in the treehouse with Themis? There are some things I wanted to talk with you about, so I thought I'd come over, if that's OK."

"Of course! I'll let the kids know Themis is waiting for them. See you in a minute."

My heart was pounding in anticipation. How could I properly thank the man who had saved my wife and children? The doorbell rang, and I flung the door wide and embraced Tasos. "You saved my family's life, Tasos, and mine too, because I wouldn't want to live without them. I don't know how I can possibly thank you enough or repay you, but anything you ask, I will do."

"Tom, you're my close friend! You would do the same for me if the situation were reversed, right?" He smiled. "How is Claire?"

"She's doing fine. Please, come in, she can't wait to see you."

As we walked into the living room, where Claire had quickly arranged some coffee, cream, sugar, and mugs. She rose from the couch and gave Tasos a warm embrace. With tears in her eyes, she thanked him profusely. "Tasos, Tom and I will do anything for you. How can we possibly repay you? Tell us!"

His smile took on a serious note as he said, "Well, OK. Anything, you say?"

"Anything," Claire and I said in unison.

"Then I want you to start believing in what I believe. Do you think you can do that?"

"Absolutely," I said.

Claire nodded in agreement. "Please, explain what you mean, what you believe. Is it part of how these miracles have happened?"

"I think so," Tasos said earnestly. "I want you to believe in the new religion." He looked at us both, but we remained silent, waiting to hear more.

"I want you to believe that we should be living in a world that has no armies, no pollution, and no 'boss' word."

Without hesitation, both Claire and I said, "Done. From now on, our family will embrace this new religion."

From his pocket he pulled out an envelope sealed with wax and held it out to me. "Yesterday, after Themis and I had breakfast, I wrote what is inside this envelope. Can you hold on to it for a few months? Four, five, six—I'm not sure how many yet."

"Absolutely." He placed it in my hand. "Now, can you tell us how you realized you have this amazing power?"

Picking up his mug of coffee, he began. "On Saturday, two days ago, I was gardening in the back yard. I don't know why or how, but a snake appeared. It had brown stripes with green and white dots, and it bit me on my arm." He showed us two little dots on his right bicep. "I didn't know if it was poisonous or not, so I ran into the house to tell Themis I had to go to the hospital for an anti-venom injection. I didn't want to die from a snake bite; Themis wouldn't have had me to take care of him.

"Themis suggested that he suck the poison from my arm, since I couldn't reach the wound with my mouth. So I said,

'OK, just make sure you spit it out each time you suck.' Then I went to the hospital, where they checked me over and said I'd be OK." Claire and I were leaning forward on the couch, listening carefully.

"I didn't think about it again after I got home. Then the next morning, about 11 a.m., I heard Themis calling me from upstairs, very loudly. Guys, I tell you, I had a feeling something big was happening. Themis sounded like his old self again. By the time I reached the stairs, he was already at the top, smiling and saying he was hungry.

"Standing at the bottom of the stairs, as Themis skipped back down the hall to have a shower, I had what I guess you'd call an epiphany. I realized that my blood had cured him. And I felt that I now know everything that matters. I understand why I'm a compassionate person, why I care about others, and why me—I mean, why I was given this kind of power. And I know what I have to do." Tasos looked at me intently. "Tom, I'm going to need your help to carry this out. Your connections as a reporter will be very useful."

"Anything, Tasos, anything you want," I said.

"Great," he said. "Well, why don't we leave it for today and just spend time with the kids? We can start making plans tomorrow."

Tasos texted me the next day while I was at work and asked me to come over to his place before dinner.

After work, I grabbed a six-pack and walked up his front path. Tasos already had the door open.

"Hi Tom," he said with a smile. "How are you doing today?"

"I'm OK," I replied. "Nothing that can't be fixed with a beer and the knowledge that the workday is over," I said, lifting the six-pack. "How are you? How's the saviour of my family?"

He smiled kindly and said, "Let's go into the back yard."

After we'd sat down on the deck, he asked, "So what's going on in our city and around the world? How bad is the pandemic now?"

I cracked open a beer for each of us. "Tasos, my friend, there's no end in sight. And my employer has become an even worse tyrant than before. His son is infected, and two more guys in the office emailed today that their wives are infected. Callingham is taking out his frustration on anyone who's still working."

"Tom, it's time for things to change. And we're going to start at your workplace."

"What do you mean, Tasos? What do you have in mind?"

"Remember all the times Callingham's kicked you in the balls and you couldn't do anything about it? Remember how many times you've been mistreated there?" His eyes sparked with anger.

"I don't have to remember; he was doing it again today."

"Well, my friend, imagine yourself having the power to go to work tomorrow, walk into his office, and say, 'From now on, this is going to be my office.' And he'll agree. Can you imagine Callingham down on his knees, begging you to keep working for him, offering you whatever salary you want?" Tasos smiled broadly.

"And do you care to explain how this will come about?"

"It's all been planned my friend."

"Who's planned it, and how?"

"Me," he said, tapping the side of his head. "I'm a foreman, remember? And organizing is my forte. Tomorrow, you'll go to the office and talk to your employer about saving his son's life."

"Oh my god," I said as the realization dawned on me. "You can use your divine blood to save Callingham's son's life, and he'll feel obligated to treat me well as a result."

"Divine blood," Tasos repeated. "Tom, you've got it. First,

you'll introduce them to the man with the 'divine blood' to save the boy's life, and after that, you will have the exclusive coverage of the divine-blood man's doings." He spread his hands wide.

"Wow," I said. "I'm going to be swimming in very deep water."

"And you're going to do it like a champion."

I breathed in deeply, then exhaled sharply. If Tasos had so much faith in me, I couldn't argue with him; maybe he was right.

"Tom, there's a lot to do, many plans to make, and I need your help."

"Tell me what you're planning. I've been dying to know since yesterday!"

"One thing at a time, my friend," he said. "First, get your situation at work sorted out, and we'll go from there. Call me to arrange the healing of Mr. Callingham's son and your co-workers' wives. And don't rush to choose your office or decide on a salary increase. Remember, you can have anything you want. I'm giving you all this power, so use it well."

We continued talking for the time it took to finish the six-pack. I tried to get more details of his plans without success.

"I told you, Tom, one thing at a time," he repeated with a smile.

It was dinnertime, so we said goodbye, planning to talk over the phone the next day.

Chapter 7

Wednesday morning, Callingham had a completely different Newman to deal with. I walked into his office without knocking, wearing a nice suit rather than my everyday reporter's garb.

"Mr. Callingham," I said to him with a smile.

"What's going on with you, Newman?" he asked angrily. "How dare you walk into my office without knocking! And why are you smiling when the world's going to hell in a hand basket?"

Something in his eyes and voice suggested he was becoming unhinged. "Mr. Callingham, I want you to pay very close attention to what I have to say. I promise you'll like what you're about to hear." I paused, then said, "I know the Divine Blood."

"Who's that?" he snapped.

"Tasos Perasmas. The man who's going to save your son's life."

"You must be crazy, Newman. You were always an idiot, but now you're nuts too. Get out of here!"

"No, sir, I won't get out, and I'm not nuts. The Divine Blood has already saved my wife and kids. I've named him the Divine Blood, and I have exclusive coverage of his actions and whereabouts."

"What will he want for saving my son's life?"

"For himself, he'll simply want you to believe in what he calls 'the new religion.' For me, he wants you to grant my requests."

"And what requests are those, Newman?"

"To give me whichever office I want, increase my salary to whatever number I say—and start treating me with respect."

Callingham crossed his arms and scowled. "Sounds like complete BS to me."

"Well, you can try at the hospital across the street. They claim to save lives there too—although they've had zero success with AV. Oh, but you'll know that already, because you're in the media." I wasn't usually sarcastic, but Callingham brought out the worst in me.

For a few moments, I thought he was going to fire me or physically attack me or perhaps both. But then, he seemed to deflate. His face, his whole body sagged, and for the first time, I saw Callingham as a man rather than a petty tyrant who thrived off my misery.

"Newman, if your friend the 'Divine Blood' can save my son's life, I'll do what you ask, and I'll believe whatever he says. Just don't ask me to kill anyone."

That last bit surprised me. Then I realized that despite his awful behaviour, he wasn't a monster. He was a bully, a mediocre man, and I probably would never like him, but at least now, I didn't feel twisted by hate for him. And very soon, he wouldn't be lording it over anyone, ever again, as a "boss."

"Mr. Callingham, you do realize that saying you'll believe in the new religion won't be enough, right? You'll have to do things differently from now on. For example, you'll have to stop being an abusive boss and start becoming an understanding employer. You'll have to personally make sure all your employees live comfortably, without struggling to look after themselves and their families. With respect to me, I'll let you know what I need once your son has been cured."

He looked up at me wearily. "I've been a bastard to you for

years, Newman. I imagine you'll want to ruin me financially, see me suffer. I can say I'm sorry, and I will mean it. But I don't expect you'll believe that."

"Mr. Callingham, after so many years, you don't know me at all. I'm not like that; I'm not a vengeful person. But right now, it's time to save your son's life. I'm going to phone the Divine Blood and tell him you're ready."

He seemed dazed. "Thank you, Tom. You're right. I don't know you."

While I was speaking with Tasos on the phone, Callingham was writing something down on a clean sheet of paper. I watched as he wrote the date at the bottom, then printed his name and scrawled his signature.

"Here, Tom," he said, handing me the paper. "You have it in writing what I've agreed to. I know you didn't ask for this, but it's the least I can do. You don't have much reason to trust me—yet. I hope that will change in the future."

Callingham's son Jonas was close to dying, so Tasos asked for the address and said he'd meet us there within the hour. I told Callingham that I needed a few minutes to speak with Ed and Jim, my colleagues whose wives had contracted the virus. Both were incredulous but desperate and agreed to meet me at their homes once I texted them with times.

As we walked into the Callinghams' home and down a hall to the boy's bedroom, we could hear his laboured breathing, despite the oxygen mask. Tasos stood close to the boy while I, the nurse, and the boy's father watched his every move. When the surgical mask was off Jonas's face, you could see he was a good-looking young man, despite being ravaged by the virus. He was scarcely breathing.

Tasos poked his finger with a needle he carried in a sterile container. When a drop of blood appeared, he squeezed his finger so the liquid dropped into the young man's mouth. And that was it.

"He will be better tomorrow," he said to Mr. Callingham with a smile. "And after that, everybody in this home will believe in the new religion, am I right?"

Callingham looked bewildered. "Is that all you need to do? Please tell me this isn't a terrible joke."

I gently laid a hand on his forearm. "Mr. Callingham, I know it seems impossible. I felt the same way when the Divine Blood did this for my son, daughter, and wife. But it worked! Please, believe in this. You'll see, Jonas will be better by the morning—a bit thin from lack of food, but you'll soon fix that. And then, you'll believe in the new religion."

After that, I texted Jim and Ed, then Tasos and I left for their homes. Each time Tasos performed his cure, the distraught husband was understandably skeptical; they were both journalists, after all.

"I doubted too," I told them. "But it worked. I'll FaceTime you when I get back to my house, so you can talk to Claire and my kids, and see that they're totally well." Although we didn't spend a lot of time together outside of work, our families would meet a few times a year at various functions organized by the newspaper or the kids' schools.

Tasos and I drove home in our separate vehicles, pulling into our driveways a few seconds apart. There was no rush-hour traffic these days.

I thanked Tasos again for what he'd done that day.

"We need these kinds of actions, Tom, for my plan to progress and succeed," he said.

"Tasos, I don't want to be pushy, but when are you going to tell me and Claire about your plan, so we can start helping?"

"You're already helping, Tom, and very soon, you're going to be very busy. But I understand your impatience to know what's going on, where I'm going with all of this. Tomorrow, when we have the confirmation that we expect from Mr. Callingham, Jim, and Ed, we'll sit down and talk more extensively about my plan and the actions we have to take." He smiled. "We can talk about it over a celebratory dinner at my place. You up for a barbecue?"

"You bet!" I laughed. "But text me what you'd like us to contribute, or else you know Claire—she'll bring enough food for an army."

Tasos laughed, then became serious. "Very soon, Tom, there will be no more armies. I mean it. Now, have a good night, and I'll see you all tomorrow."

At about noon the next day, I was at work, writing my first story about Tasos, when my phone rang.

"Tom Newman here," I said.

"Tom, have you decided which office you'd like?" It was Callingham, but I just barely recognized his voice; he sounded like a different person, warm and friendly.

"No, Mr. Callingham, I haven't decided yet. How is Jonas doing?"

"Tom, he's up and eating! Not even feeling weak after lying in bed for weeks. It's nothing short of a miracle!"

I smiled into the phone. "That's fantastic."

"I'm sorry for being a tyrant, Tom. I've been a real jerk, worse than that. I promise to be a far better employer from now on."

I thanked him, and after he said he'd be back to the office the next day, we said goodbye.

A quarter of an hour later, Ed and Jim called within a few minutes of each other, both to tell me their wives were also feeling better. Although I hadn't expected otherwise, I could feel my own conviction and excitement growing. I emailed Tasos to let him know about the cures and told him I was looking forward to hearing all about his plans that night. I hoped he wouldn't put us off any longer.

My hope was rewarded. After an excellent meal, Tasos made some strong Greek coffee, and the kids decided to play a board game in the treehouse while eating large bowls of ice cream.

Claire and I looked at Tasos expectantly.

"My friends," he began, "there are so many things that have to be done. There is a reason I have this power. It's because of the way I see things. The universe—or god, if you want—has given me an opportunity to reorganize human society and change the whole world for the better, by giving me such power at the right time." He looked at me. "Tom, get ready to start writing about the Divine Blood."

"I already have, Tasos," I smiled. "I haven't shown anyone though, except for Claire." She squeezed my arm in enthusiasm.

"OK. First, we'll visit two hospitals and heal some people in the presence of respected physicians. But I want to make sure that the physicians have integrity and agree to the new religion. I also want to screen people before deciding who to heal."

"What do you mean you want to screen people?" Claire asked.

"At this time, those who are struggling most in life take priority in my books." He explained that he would find out what they, their immediate family members, and their siblings did for a living. "Some people deserve to be a priority because of who they are and how they have survived in the face of terribly unfair societal standards. Most of these people are poor or middle class. After maybe three hours of meeting these people and learning about them, I'll go home and decide on the number of patients I'll save the next day, and who they'll be. Then we'll go back and I'll heal them."

"Middle-class people?" I asked. "I'm not criticizing—it's up to you who you save, Tasos—but why?"

"I understand your curiosity. I'm talking about middle-class people who earn their living responsibly, yet still have never had a break. I'm planning to save rich and powerful people also, and their loved ones. And you are going to record everything. So be patient and you'll see what I have planned."

We talked for another hour about what was to come. But

rather than relate what we said, I'm going to let the events of the coming weeks and months speak for themselves.

We visited the first hospital the next day and spoke to a Dr. Cliff Keyman, the physician in charge of the pandemic response. He'd had no more success than anyone else in our city and beyond. Anticipating difficulties in getting a meeting with him, I leveraged my position at the newspaper and gained us "five minutes," according to his beleaguered personal assistant, Berenice.

I began by introducing Tasos and letting him take it from there. "Dr. Keyman," he began, "as Tom has said, I'm Tasos Perasmas, and I've come here today to help some of your patients who've contracted AV. I have, what you might consider, an unorthodox way to cure them."

Dr. Keyman stood up from his desk and glared. "I was told this was a media interview. The last thing I'm going to tolerate is yet another crackpot coming in with a 'miracle cure.' Please leave my office immediately."

Tasos raised both hands in a pacifying gesture and said, "Dr. Keyman, please hear me just for a moment before you kick us out. I understand your wife is infected and doesn't have much longer."

The doctor froze. "Where have you heard that?" The information had been kept confidential, but I had a discreet, reliable source within the hospital who had kept the secret other than giving it to me; I had sworn not to disclose it publicly.

Tasos continued without answering the question. "Dr. Keyman, I have the ability to heal people infected with this deadly virus, by giving them one drop of my blood."

As the doctor opened his mouth to scorn Tasos, I said, "We know it sounds absolutely insane, Dr. Keyman. But we have recordings to prove it. Please, let us show you a couple of them before you dismiss us as cranks."

When Claire and the kids had been ill, we'd made some videos, believing there was no hope of them recovering. Claire had insisted that we create something for me to remember them after they had died. Then we'd taken some videos the previous evening at Tasos's place, showing the kids and Claire completely healthy again.

Dr. Keyman exuded exhaustion and seemed to have very little fight left in him. "OK, what'll it hurt now?" he said. "I know there's no cure. But if it'll make you leave my office sooner and quietly, go ahead. Show me."

So we did. He was surprised and bewildered, then regained his professional composure. "Well, whatever it is you've done here, this is a hospital, not some mumbo-jumbo healer convention. I can't allow you to go around giving blood from your finger."

"Those are my wife and children, Dr. Keyman," I said as the last video finished. "Perhaps you know who I am from reading my articles. I'm no crackpot."

"Yes, I know of you, Mr. Newman, and you seem like a level-headed man. But I still cannot allow that."

Tasos was listening quietly, arms folded. I wasn't sure what to do next, so I said, "Dr. Keyman, didn't you treat Jonas Callingham?"

"Yes, he was here some time ago. He became infected about the same time as my wife."

"Well, he's the son of my employer. And Mr. Perasmas cured Jonas. Here," I held out my cell phone to show him Callingham's number, "please, call Jonas's father and talk with him. Better yet, video call him."

"All right," he said reluctantly, shaking his head. "I can't believe I'm still having this conversation." He dialed on his tablet computer, then propped it against a large framed picture on his desk—a photo of his wife.

Callingham responded after three rings. "Hello?" He was smiling.

"Mr. Callingham, it's Dr. Keyman, Jonas's physician when he was at the hospital. I'm calling to ask how he's doing. I'd…like to compare the progress of the disease in him with what has happened for people infected around the same time."

"Certainly, doctor, happy to help. Jonas is absolutely fine, back to perfect health."

Dr. Keyman looked stunned and was speechless for a moment. "Are you…are you sure?"

"Absolutely," said Callingham. "Would you like to speak with him? He's in the living room here with me." He panned the phone's camera around to Jonas, who smiled and waved.

"Hello, Dr. Keyman! I'm all better. Isn't it amazing? I feel like I was never sick at all."

"That's…wonderful, Jonas. I'm very happy for you. Congratulations," stammered the doctor.

Callingham's face appeared again. "Doctor, this happened thanks to a kind, wonderful man whose identity I swore to protect. He put a single drop of his blood in Jonas's mouth, and by the next morning, my son was completely cured."

"It's OK, Mr. Callingham," I said, moving close so that he could see me on the screen, "you can tell him. You have Mr. Perasmas's permission." Tasos leaned over in his chair to make himself visible, and gave the thumbs up.

"Oh, hi Tom, hi Mr. Perasmas. OK. Yes, Dr. Keyman, Tasos Perasmas has divine blood. He saved my son's life. With my own eyes, I saw what he did. I didn't believe it was possible, but one drop of his blood healed my son in less than twenty-four hours."

I looked at the doctor. His face revealed an internal battle between a scientist's disbelief and a husband's desperate desire to believe.

"Trust this man, Dr. Keyman," said Callingham. "He wants

to do good, and he can."

The doctor thanked him for his time and information, wished him and Jonas well, and said goodbye. Then he sat back heavily in his chair. I could see we had him—perhaps not convinced, but definitely willing to try.

"Mr. Perasmas, before I let you do this in my hospital, I would like you to perform your 'treatment' on my wife. She is also a physician, and a research scientist, and I'm sure she would want us to take on any initial risk before using such a frankly bizarre treatment on the public. Will you agree to this?"

"Yes," Tasos replied briskly. "Let's visit your wife right now so I can give her one drop of my blood. After that, I'd like to meet each person in the hospital who's infected with the virus. Then I'll come back in a few days and heal the ones that I choose."

The doctor looked like he was about to object at that last part, but he closed his mouth. "I'll take you to my wife now. We'll talk about the rest after I've seen whether you cure her."

Dr. Keyman's wife was in a nearby ward, which we went to after the doctor had donned the requisite protective outfit. Tasos and I declined to wear one, at which the doctor shook his head and shrugged. Outside her door, he said, "Wait here, please," then knocked and slipped through the door. He came back about a minute later. "You can come in. This is Lauren, my wonderful wife."

She looked very bad, similar to Jonas. As Dr. Keyman gently lifted her oxygen mask, she rasped, "My husband says you think you've got a cure. I hope you're right."

After Tasos had treated her, we spent the next three hours at the hospital so Tasos could meet all of the infected in-patients. Everywhere we went, we garnered stares for not wearing any protective clothing. "Not even face masks!" I heard one person whisper to another.

Before leaving, we stopped at Dr. Keyman's office and asked him to call me in the morning, once he had checked on his wife. “I sleep on a bed in her room,” he said. “If there’s any change for the better, I’ll be sure to know right away.”

As we walked out to the parking lot, I asked, “How many people will you cure tomorrow, Tasos?”

“Fifty. And Tom, please make sure you have everything you need to record what I do. I’m counting on you.”

“I won’t let you down.”

Chapter 8

The next day, we arrived at the hospital about noon. I was worried because Dr. Keyman hadn't phoned. But Tasos waved away my concern.

In the doctor's waiting room, we were greeted by a transformed Berenice. Without a word, she picked up the phone, pressed a button, then after a few seconds said, "Dr. Keyman, they're here."

The doctor came bursting out of his office, strode over to Tasos, and engulfed him in a bear hug. "Thank you, Mr. Perasmas. Thank you so very much. My wife is healed! I can't believe I'm saying this, but it's true. You've saved her life."

Tasos extricated himself from the hug with a smile and said, "I'm happy I could help two good people with open minds."

"Do you want to see her?" Dr. Keyman asked.

Tasos nodded. "Absolutely, may Tom make a recording of her? It's important for us to document what is happening, as many people will understandably be skeptical at first, as you were." The doctor said he was quite sure Lauren would agree.

This time, we opened the door to a very different scene. Lauren was sitting in a chair by the window, reading a book.

"Lauren, my love," Dr. Keyman said, "you have visitors."

Her face lit up as she put the book down, stood up, and held out her hand to shake ours. Then she clasped Tasos's forearm.

"Mr. Perasmas, how can I ever adequately thank you?" she

said. Then turning to my smartphone, which I was using to record the event, she said, "I'm Dr. Lauren Keyman. Yesterday, I was infected with the apocalypse virus and had only a day or two to live. Then this man," she gestured to Tasos, "came and put a single drop of his blood in my mouth. Today, here I am, completely well again. I want this incident to be broadcast everywhere as proof. I'm a physician and a scientist, and I would never have believed this to be possible. But it is."

We left the two of them a few minutes later, Dr. Keyman having given his permission for Tasos to treat others in the hospital. Wanting to get a move on, Tasos and I didn't bring up the selectivity he would exercise. "We'll address that later," said Tasos to me when we were out in the hall again. "Once what's happened has completely sunk in for them both, you can talk to them, Tom, about the new religion. And they'll see that although they won't like me not curing everyone, they'll need to accept it as part of the larger plan."

He had asked Dr. Keyman to assign two more doctors to accompany us as witnesses. The doctor said he wanted to be there as well, so the five of us went around to various patients' rooms, Tasos consulting his list and me recording everything while Dr. Keyman explained to each patient what Tasos would do.

The first was a forty-year-old bricklayer, whose wife was sitting in a chair beside him. "Mr. and Mrs. Manning," Dr. Keyman said, "Mr. Perasmas is able to cure people infected with the virus. If you consent to a very simple, painless treatment—receiving one drop of his blood in your mouth—then by tomorrow, your health will be restored. I would not suggest this if I had not witnessed him do this already with my own wife. All you'll need to do in return is promise to accept his new religion."

The Mannings looked at Dr. Keyman, speechless. Then Mr. Manning nodded. "Please, if you can help, then do this, and I promise that we will."

Tasos smiled. "I'm glad to be able to help you, Mr. Manning. I admire skilled, hard-working people like you."

We did the same with forty-nine more people, some in a single-bed room, some in a four-bed room, some in a six-bed room. Tasos gave his blood only to those he had chosen the previous day. Out of discretion and sensitivity for those not receiving it, we drew the curtains around each person's bed and spoke quietly, using as few words as possible.

One of the selected was a university student who was the kid brother of a member of a prominent and powerful biker gang. The older brother and a couple of his biker friends were in the room when we arrived.

"Hello Mr. Boulen," Tasos said to the biker, shaking the man's hand.

"Hello Mr. Perasmas," he replied. "Save my kid brother's life and you'll have some very good and powerful allies." His two friends nodded.

Tasos smiled. "I like the idea of having your allegiance, Mr. Boulen. I think that will be very helpful." After administering the treatment, Tasos said, "He will be up and running in a maximum of twenty-four hours, probably by tomorrow morning. Please let Mr. Newman here know how to contact you, because I'll be needing your help soon."

Mr. Boulen gave me his number, then we continued to the rest of the lucky ones. Another crucial encounter for Tasos was with a twenty-year-old named Jonathan who had recently lost his dad to the pandemic and whose mom was now very ill too. We stopped at the mom's bed; the son was sitting next to her, holding her hand between both of his.

"Hello, Mrs. Messier," Tasos said. "How do you feel today?"

"Hi, Mr. Perasmas," she whispered. "Not very well, I'm afraid."

She was a cashier at the local supermarket, and Jonathan

was at university, studying computer programming. He had received several scholarships. "There's no way I'd ever have gotten to university otherwise," he'd told us yesterday. "The fees are impossible for families like ours."

"Don't you worry, Mrs. Messier. Tomorrow, you'll feel much better, like brand new." Tasos said to her with a smile. To Jonathan he said, "Once your mom is cured, I'd like to speak with you. I understand that your professors already consider you brilliant in your field, way beyond any of the other students. I need someone of your calibre working with me. Will you consider it?"

"Mr. Perasmas," Jonathan replied, "I can't wait to sit down and talk with you once my mother is cured."

By dinner time, we were back at our homes. The highlight of the day for me was when Tasos at last gave me permission to publish my article. "It's time for the coverage to begin," he said, his voice ringing with passion. "But we still need some more people. Yesterday, on my way back from the hospital, I stopped in to see a Superintendent Jim Cooper at the RCMP. I know him from some work a couple of years ago, and I found out through a mutual acquaintance that his son Gabriel was infected. He let me treat Gabriel. This afternoon, when I had to take a short call at the hospital, it was Jim, telling me his son was cured. So we have the superintendent completely on board. Trustworthy members of the police forces will be crucial for the plan."

I nodded. "So what would you like me to do?"

"We need the best lawyers on our side, Tom. Others as well, but legal matters are always crucial, and they're going to be vital as we roll out the new religion. First, I'd like you to identify the city's top lawyers, then find out which of them have family members who are infected. If any of the lawyers are sick themselves, then they'll be candidates for the cure too. You're going to need some help, so I've taken the liberty of hiring a personal assistant for you. Claire interviewed several today while you and I were at the hospital and has chosen the best one. I'll pay her salary."

My head was spinning a little with all of the information. "Lawyers…a personal assistant…OK, of course I'll do as you ask. This is all part of the plan, right?"

"Yes. We're going to convince everybody to believe in the new religion," he said, spreading his arms wide.

I was tired, as I'd been up late the night before, writing. A wave of doubt washed through me. Not doubt about Tasos, but about the rest of society. "But how, Tasos? Look at how people live, the mess our society is in, in so many ways. Will people really be convinced? It seems impossible." I rubbed my face, worrying that I might anger him but unable to withhold my concerns.

"Difficult, yes, but not impossible. Especially if you consider that this is what the Divine Blood wants." He winked.

"I have no doubts about your plan, Tasos. My doubts are about other people and their capacity to change."

He held up a hand. "I know, Tom. And there are so many things to line up in order to accomplish something this big. But don't forget, I'm a foreman—good at organizing."

I could tell he was trying to allay my fears with his confidence, and I knew I just had to go with things, believing, taking it all one step at a time.

We said goodbye. Tasos said he'd had a call on the way home, so there was something he needed to go out and do before settling for the night. Themis would be having dinner at our place.

I knew I'd be spending several hours online after dinner, researching the city's lawyers. During the meal, Claire told me about Karen, the person she'd chosen to be my PA.

"She's thirty-five with short brown hair, brown eyes, and a pleasant face. More importantly, she's very intelligent and a highly experienced researcher. Her job before the epidemic was at the university, but she took a leave of absence when her children became ill. Tasos is actually going to her home this evening to cure them." I was surprised. "He didn't want you to feel you had to come along, so he told me he wouldn't mention it to you."

"So that's what he was going out to do after I talked to him in the driveway."

Claire nodded. "Whatever information you find out tonight about the lawyers you can email her, and she'll start working on it tomorrow, once her son has been cured."

By 2:00 a.m., I had pressed send on a message to Karen. She replied shortly after 4:00 p.m. the next day, introducing herself and saying it wouldn't be difficult to find out more about the people on my list. By late that night, she had categorized them by salaries, experience, field of expertise, family status, and personal worth. She'd also found out who was either infected with the virus or had one or more family members who were.

Of the ten she had narrowed down from my initial list, I chose three for initial interviews, and Karen set up the meetings. Work in the law courts had slowed to a fraction of the usual volume due to the epidemic, so I was able to have all three meetings within a couple of days.

The first was Harold Thompson, a fifty-five-year-old lawyer specializing in national and global finance, whom I met at his downtown office on the fortieth floor of a glass-and-steel architectural masterpiece. His professional and personal record were outstanding. Four months earlier, his wife and son had both been infected, and they were now in an advanced stage of the disease. It surprised me that he was still working. When I mentioned this, he said, "It's how I cope. I work here part-time while a care team looks after them at home. My wife said my constant anxiety was driving her crazy." He smiled wanly, and I could see the strain of his burden.

In advance of the meeting, I had sent him links to the articles I had by then published about the Divine Blood. They also contained some of the videos proving the cure was real. When I first walked into his office, I said, "Mr. Thompson, I have a way to bring your family back to health."

"If my research didn't tell me you're a solid, sane, intelligent man, Mr. Newman, and the videos didn't check out as genuine, I'd think you were a quack coming to sell me snake oil."

I smiled and, after we had briefly discussed his wife and son's condition, I said, "Well? What do you think? Are you in?"

"I'm desperate to save them, so I don't think it makes any sense but to say yes. Still, I'd like to know what your friend, the 'Divine Blood,' will want in return. I don't believe in souls, so I can't sell him mine."

"He wants your professional help. But over and above that, he wants you and your family to start believing what he believes. He calls it the new religion."

"What does that mean exactly?"

"It's not a religion in the usual sense. There's no need to believe in a god. It's based on three core principles: no armies, no pollution, and no use of the word 'boss.' It'll bring fairness and justice to the world."

Thompson raised his hands. "OK, you got it. If I see my son and wife cured, your friend will have the full weight of me and my firm's expertise behind him—for free. And my family will follow this 'new religion' of his."

I rose and shook his hand. "Then I'll be in touch very soon to let you know when he'll come to your home to deliver the cure."

My meetings with the other two lawyers were broadly similar. Timothy Gilford was fifty and a renowned criminal lawyer who had become a judge a few years earlier. Prior to the outbreak of AV, his appointment to the Federal Supreme Court was expected to be announced any day. But with the epidemic ratcheting up to unprecedented levels, all such government business had been suspended. Mr. Gilford's two teenage daughters were dying, and he was swift to agree to work for Tasos and embrace the new religion if his children were saved.

The third lawyer was William Robinson, forty-two and already a highly experienced trial lawyer. His wife, Diane, was three months pregnant when she contracted the virus. His was the easiest agreement to obtain.

Phoning Tasos after I had left this final meeting, I arranged to stop by his place before joining my family for pizzas and a night of watching comedies on the TV.

"How are you, Tom?" he asked when he opened the door.

"My health is excellent, and my news is even better," I said. "The team of lawyers you want is ready. Here are their names, the names of their sick family members, and their addresses. Once you tell me when you'll be visiting them to deliver the cure, I'll let them know. They're waiting anxiously to hear back."

"Perfect," he replied. "I'll visit all of them tomorrow. It's time to start rolling out the new religion. Once I've confirmed that these lawyers and a few other key groups are on board, I'll be ready."

"Is there anything more you can tell me tonight?" I asked, hoping for more of a glimpse into what was to come.

"First, let me heal these lawyers' families. Then next week, we'll get everyone together at a meeting, to reveal the complete plans and how we're going to accomplish them. I'm not ready for that yet, though. Can you meet for breakfast tomorrow, Tom?"

I laughed. "Of course. Should I keep the rest of the day open as well?"

He nodded. "Yes. We still have more team members to recruit."

Chapter 9

The healing of the judge's and lawyers' families went without a hitch, as I'd expected. I also learned that while Karen and I had been researching the lawyers, and I'd had my initial meetings with them, Tasos had been busy with healing sessions with twenty-five more law enforcement personnel. "Superintendent Cooper provided me with more information about them, and I know they'll be very helpful for my plans," he explained to me over breakfast. Cooper has the list of their names, and you can use any of them as sources of information for your articles. But right now, their identities must remain concealed and unidentifiable to anyone else, to protect them and their families."

"Wow, my friend. I'm guessing those twenty-five people represent about sixty healing sessions, between them and their immediate family and friends," I said, after swallowing the last of my crêpes. Tasos nodded. "You were very busy last week!"

"I will need all these people, Tom, you'll see," he said with an enigmatic smile.

"Are you OK, Tasos? Have you noticed any adverse effects in yourself?"

"Oh, I'm feeling perfectly fine, Tom, but thanks for asking. Actually, after every healing session, I feel a boost of energy. I'm rejuvenated just knowing I've done something good."

"So, what's next?" I asked.

"Once I tell you that everyone I've given my blood to has been healed, I need you to set up a meeting for next week. The judge and lawyers need to be there, plus Superintendent Cooper and Jonathan Messier, the computer whiz kid. I also want to visit another hospital and heal another fifty people. So I need you to arrange that—the same way we did it last time. I'll go to the hospital to meet and screen people, then come back and cure them."

I nodded. "Leave it with me. Karen and I'll find out which would be the best hospital to go to next, then I'll let you know."

By that afternoon, Karen had found and put me in touch with a hospital that was treating many AV victims and was also the site of a research facility that now focused exclusively on AV research. The head of the hospital's Pandemic Recovery Section was Dr. Eric Procof, whose ten-year-old niece had been infected five months earlier. The young girl had very little time left, and the family was devastated.

I called Tasos to let him know, and he said to make the initial hospital meeting for 9:00 a.m. the next day. "Thank you, Tom. Everything you're doing is invaluable for our goals." His voice had a tone of honest appreciation. He had a way of making you feel good about yourself, even just by thanking you for something relatively small.

We took my car the next morning. Both of us were in a talkative mood, and I told him I had arranged the big meeting for the evening after next.

"Tom, I hope you're ready for what's coming up for you after that meeting." The hairs on the back of my neck stood up in anticipation. "You're going to be at the epicentre of the media coverage about me. Soon, we're going to be sending a shock wave across the world."

I nodded, thinking Mr. Callingham would explode with

satisfaction. We'll become a major newspaper overnight, with exclusive coverage of the Divine Blood, plus Tasos's plans. Wow…and I'll go from an insignificant little town newspaper reporter to the most famous reporter in the country—maybe the world. Everything Tasos had predicted was happening. And more.

"Tasos, this is big, really big! There's going to be a profound change that will turn the world upside down!"

"It will," he smiled.

A few minutes later, I pulled into the hospital parkade. Tasos stretched after getting out of the car and as we walked toward the entrance said, "At the meeting tomorrow evening, I'll reveal the rest of my plan and all your questions will be answered."

We walked to the reception desk and asked for Dr. Procof. A few minutes after the receptionist had paged him, he appeared, welcoming us and leading the way to a private sitting area to chat. He was young, maybe 40, a good-looking, tall guy with a friendly albeit exhausted demeanour.

"Dr. Procof," I said, "I'm Tom Newman. We spoke on the phone about the pandemic and something you'll be very glad to hear."

"How are you, Mr. Newman?"

"Very well, thank you, Dr. Procof." I gestured to Tasos. "This is Mr. Tasos Perasmas. He is the Divine Blood, if you will." Tasos smiled and nodded but remained silent. "You have a young niece who is sick, is that right?" I asked.

"Yes I do," he replied, "and she's very sick." His shoulders sagged. "I've lost any hope. I don't know what to do. My sister is devastated. She wants to believe I can come up with a miracle cure, but we're no closer to discovering one than we were six months ago."

"Dr. Procof," began Tasos, "that is why we are here. Your niece will be OK. I'm going to have her healthy by tomorrow."

He smiled gently.

"What do you mean, Mr. Perasmas? There's no medical cure for this virus yet."

"Oh, I know that," Tasos said. "But I can offer an alternative cure. I'm going to give her a drop of my blood and, before this time tomorrow, she'll be up and running around, the way a little girl should be."

The doctor looked very skeptical and rather angry. I quickly leaned forward, holding my laptop open towards him.

"Dr. Procof, we realize this sounds crazy, but if you just watch this, I think it will help." I pressed play to run a combined video I had created, showing several of the previous healing sessions. "This is my family. He healed my wife and two children. This is Dr. Cliff Keyman's wife, Lauren. And this is..."

The doctor watched with his mouth open. "I can't believe what I'm seeing," he said. "I'm friends with Lauren and Cliff, but I didn't know she'd gotten better. I'd like to call them right now."

Tasos smiled at him. "Please do, Dr. Procof. I entirely understand."

Dr. Procof pulled out his phone and called the Keymans. After a few minutes of talking, he said to Tasos, "Lauren is very well but says she cannot say how, out of respect for the healer's confidentiality."

"You can tell her that Tasos Perasmas is giving her permission."

The doctor spoke into his phone, then held it towards Tasos.

"Dr. Keyman," Tasos said, speaking to the outstretched phone, "this is Tasos Perasmas. Please go ahead and tell Dr. Procof how you were healed."

After further intense listening, Dr. Procof said, "Thank you Lauren. I'm so glad you're well! I'll talk to you soon."

He hung up and looked at Tasos, shock written across his face. "She said you have divine blood, and just one drop of your blood is enough the eliminate the virus."

"So is that enough for you to trust that I can heal your niece?" Tasos asked him.

"It seems unbelievable, but the evidence speaks for itself!"

"His healing sessions have had 100% success, Dr. Procof," I said. "We have recordings of every single one. Mr. Perasmas has saved over a hundred lives already."

"Maybe we can visit the research facility, then, to see whether we can create a vaccine to help others too," the doctor said excitedly.

"I certainly have plans to help others," Tasos said. "And I would like to speak with the scientists of your research facility to better understand what's different about my blood, from a scientific standpoint. But first, let's see your niece."

Dr. Procof took us to Ellie's hospital room. The little girl looked very bad. She was sleeping, her mouth slightly open, breathing shallowly. It was clear that scarcely any life remained in her. Tasos quickly, soundlessly let one drop of his blood fall into her mouth, then stepped back and nodded.

"All done, Dr. Procof," he said. "By this time tomorrow, at the latest, she'll be absolutely fine again."

Tasos then asked Dr. Procof to escort us to the rooms of about seventy other patients. While Tasos quietly conversed with them, I discretely took notes on my laptop.

These visits took nearly three hours, after which we thanked Dr. Procof for his help. "We'll be back tomorrow," I told him as we shook hands. "If you have any questions in the meantime, please contact me."

By noon the next day, Tasos had decided which patients would receive the cure. The drive back to the hospital took nearly ninety minutes. After letting them know we were en route, we picked up coffees and light snacks, and chatted pleasantly about the coming afternoon.

Dr. Procof was waiting at the reception desk, along with his sister Ingrid, and little Ellie—who looked as full of life today as she'd appeared empty of it yesterday. The two adults hugged Tasos and thanked him repeatedly, tears in their eyes. Then Ingrid bent down and said gently, "Ellie, what do you want to say to Mr. Perasmas?"

"Thank you so much, sir, for saving my life!" she piped in a small but firm voice.

"You're very welcome, Ellie, the pleasure is mine. I'm glad to see you feeling better," Tasos replied.

We then began visiting the patients who were to receive treatments. In each case, I requested permission to record the events before and after. No one declined. Dr. Procof watched, along with two other physicians. One of these, Dr. Christine Jekings witnessed her husband Terence being treated. He'd had been infected four months before, not long after they were married.

"Mr. Perasmas," said Dr. Jekings, "thank you so much for giving us the chance to have a future together. I'd like to be your personal physician. I could help you maintain your health while you save more lives."

"Thank you, Dr. Jekings," he said, smiling. "I appreciate and accept your offer."

On the drive home, we discussed tomorrow's meeting of "Team Tasos," as I jokingly dubbed the group. We were holding the gathering at Tasos's home, starting at noon. The anticipation kept me awake well past midnight. I used the time and energy to begin drafting some new articles.

Chapter 10

I was the first to knock on Tasos's door the next day.

"Good morning, Tom. How are you feeling, my friend?" Tasos asked, motioning me inside. We walked down to the kitchen, where pleasant aromas of cooking and baking made my stomach rumble.

"I'm very well, thank you, Tasos. How about yourself?"

"I feel energized, Tom. It all starts today, the big, overarching plan." He poured us both coffee and leaned against the kitchen counter. "You must be looking forward to getting your articles published."

"I'm definitely ready to go!" I said.

By noon, everyone had arrived: the judge, the two lawyers, Superintendent Cooper, the biker Mr. Boulen, Dr. Jekings, and Jonathan Messier. We all sat down at Tasos's dinner table, and everyone looked excited.

Tasos stood at the head of the table, smiled, and began. "I want to thank you for accepting my invitation to this meeting. I'm counting on your essential and invaluable help to advance my plan, which is to establish the new religion. This is a religion that has nothing to do with traditional religion, and will be one that everyone can believe in, regardless of their religious faith. I'm sure you all want to know more about this." Every head around the table nodded. Tasos then sat down.

"The new religion is where spirituality meets science for the betterment of humanity. It is based on respect and equality. It has three guiding principles: no army, no pollution, no use of the word 'boss.' For the first time, citizens will set the criteria that governments use to make laws, rules, and regulations. Citizens will dictate the directions and mandates that governments will follow—all governments, because their current political ideology is now irrelevant. Anything outside these criteria will be unacceptable. It will be in our constitution that this is how citizens want to live from now on." He drank some water, then continued.

"My plan is to change the world, make it a better place for all. And I will accomplish that by establishing the new religion to guide a new way of life, a new social order, a new status quo. Enough of incompetent governments, enough of those who control our societies with counterproductive laws, rules, and regulations. These have restricted honest citizens' freedom and given them only poverty, homelessness, and psychological suffocation. Citizens have had enough of governments that make laws, rules, and regulations to serve only their political and material well-being, to benefit only them and their corporate masters. Citizens have had enough of corrupt governments that have been in place for hundreds of years. And these corrupt governments exist across the entire political spectrum. Citizens have had enough of the abuse of power by governments and elites. Governments have allowed corrupt individuals and groups to get away with tons of social and environmental injustices. Enough of broken promises, enough of child poverty and homelessness."

Tasos's voice was controlled, but his eyes were fiery with conviction as they swept the table, looking at each of us in turn.

"Citizens want peaceful and respectful societies. We're not going to accomplish that by building armies. And after hundreds of years of rotten, diseased ideologies based on 'profit-any-way-you-can,' the only way to change is with drastic and significant actions in the direction of respect and equality. The universe—or God, if you wish—has given me the power of what Tom has called 'divine blood.' I had an epiphany about the use of this power, and the decision I've made is based on the knowledge that I've gained during my almost fifty years of living. I've carefully observed and learned about current affairs, politics, economics, and history. As an officer in the engine room of merchant marine ships, I visited dozens of countries on several continents, and many cities in those countries. So my beliefs are well developed and are a result of acquired knowledge and personal experiences. I am also aware that what I want to do will only be possible with the help of my friends—brave and loyal individuals in specific professions." At this, he spread his arms and hands in a gesture that encompassed all of us.

"My plan is to make myself very well known for my healing power. No level of promotion is too much. I want to create the general perception that I am absolutely precious, so any and all of my requests will be unquestioningly accepted, because I save lives when no one else can. I expect to be loved. And after we let everybody know what I want, the citizens will love me more, because I want to start by having nine of the twenty most economically powerful countries legally adopt the new religion as their way of governing. This," Tasos said with a broad smile, "is my plan."

Mr. Robinson raised a hand. "Is that why you want to do this, Mr. Perasmas, so that people will love you?"

Tasos look at him calmly for a second. "Yes, but not for my ego, Mr. Robinson, but because if my actions inspire peaceful and loving feelings, they will positively transform the world."

"I understand, Mr. Perasmas. The result is what counts," Mr. Robinson replied.

After that everybody began talking at the same time, asking

Tasos questions. It was chaotic. I looked at Tasos, and he seemed joyful, allowing the excitement to flood the meeting.

After several moments, he raised his hands to shoulder height, and the group quickly quietened. "I love your enthusiasm," he said with a smile. "I understand that you have many questions. Rest assured I'll explain anything you need to know. Each and every one of you. I like to keep things organized, so just give me a few more minutes to provide some additional details. First, though," he pushed out his chair and got up, "please help yourselves to some food and some more beverages." He gestured toward the kitchen. "Please—your brains will need fuel while we think and talk through many important things!" He laughed, then led the way so his guests wouldn't feel awkward.

Once we all had full plates and glasses and had taken our seats again at the table, Tasos resumed. "In the new religion, social order will be directed to social equality. The gaps between the rich, the middle class, and the poor will shrink until there is equality, because everybody has the same right to live comfortably. I want to start with help from a brilliant and honourable judge," here he nodded to Judge Gilford, "and brilliant counsellors, beginning with you two and the team you will assemble. The most significant change will be that citizens will direct the government rather than vice versa. Citizens will set the criteria for making laws. So the first thing for you three legal experts to do will be to form the Citizens Council Office. This will consist of nine honourable individuals devoted exclusively to protecting citizens' rights and interests from governments' mismanagement of their assets. Judge Gilford, I need you to head the establishment of the Citizens Council Office and handle the transition of power. We will talk about details later. I also need a council to handle economic matters—because I expect a lot of money to be coming in," he said with a smile.

"What do you mean, Mr. Perasmas?" Mr. Thompson asked. "I thought this wasn't about money."

"No, it's not about money in and of itself," Tasos said. "But money is an essential tool for pressure. I plan to sell my divine blood to the rich and famous, with a hefty price tag."

"How much will you charge them for a drop of your blood?" said Mr. Thompson.

Tasos smiled widely first, then said, "Everything they have."

"Everything?"

"Yes, Mr. Thompson, everything. If they want me to save their life or the life of somebody they love, they'll need to give me everything they have. And you, my legal team, will ensure that all of the legalities are covered."

Again, everyone started speaking at once, and again, Tasos savoured the energy pulsing in the room.

This time, Judge Gilford politely called for order, and the group was quiet. "Mr. Perasmas, I need to clarify something, if you will," he said.

"Please, go ahead. Transparency is essential to the new religion," Tasos said.

"You want to impose a new way of life in at least nine countries. Even if that new way will ultimately be democratic, you'll be forcing them—literally to 'do or die.' And in the case of the rich, you'll be charging money for saving a life. I see a lot of similarities with abuse of power here. I promise to help you; I owe you everything for saving my daughters' lives. But don't you think that you're proposing to do the same thing elites have been doing since time immemorial?"

"Yes, I do," Tasos replied with a smile. "I am one of them, Judge Gilford. They made me. But I am the best of them. And the last of them. We all grew up in a society that is based on the idea of profiting any way you can. And to follow this creed, to have this intent, you put aside any moral values. You do whatever is necessary to profit. I learned these societal standards well, and now it's my time to 'profit.' And the way I want to profit is by turning all these societal standards against them. Do you see? I'll take all the ugliness they represent and turn it against them." Tasos thumped the table, and I could see how much the thought of that ugliness angered him.

There was instant silence, and the judge gazed at Tasos intensely, as did everyone else. Then, they all began clapping.

Tasos breathed in and out deeply to calm himself, then he resumed. "Mr. Thompson, you'll be very busy. Very soon, you and your team will be handling hundreds of billions of dollars."

"What are you planning to do with all this money, Mr. Perasmas?" Mr. Robinson asked.

"I promise to do only beautiful things, in pursuit of the belief that everybody has a right to live comfortably," Tasos said with a smile. Then he turned to Superintendent Cooper. "I'll need your help with my protection, Superintendent. I'm expecting a lot of resistance to my plans from rich and powerful people, and governments as well, from across the political spectrum. None of these people are going to like what I want to do. And they'll try to stop me."

"Absolutely, Mr. Perasmas," Cooper replied with conviction. "You'll have a permanent security detail, and I know the best person to be in charge of that. His name is Callahan. I'll hook him up with you."

"And my people and I will handle another level of protection," Mr. Boulen added.

"Thank you, Mr. Boulen," Tasos said. "Tom," he turned to me, "the time has come for you to inform the world about me. I'm counting on you to promote me and my abilities, and to appoint a stellar team of media specialists to help you with that."

"I feel this is what I was born to do, Tasos," I said. His face radiated appreciation and anticipation.

"I will need you to coordinate with Mr. Messier," said Tasos, turning to the young computer wizard. "With your expertise, you can advise on the best ways to use the media and the Internet to promote me and my plans—and to protect them. I'm counting on you, Jonathan. We live in a digital world, and your talents will be invaluable."

"Cyber-security is my thing," beamed Jonathan, "and what you want to do is beautiful. I want to be a part of it."

Tasos smiled at him in satisfaction, then looked at all of us. "Power to the people. The citizens will set the mandate of those who want to serve their country. And those will be people the citizens choose. They will make laws, rules, and regulations inside those parameters. Judge Gilford, Mr. Robinson, and Mr. Thompson, I need you to help me draw up detailed benchmarks for the Citizens Council Office to measure each nation's progress towards implementing the new religion."

In his excitement, Tasos was speaking rapidly, and it was becoming difficult for us to follow. Even the judge and lawyers looked lost. Judge Gilford was the first to react.

"Mr. Perasmas, forgive my interruption, but I think we all lost you after 'power to the people.'" Tasos smiled broadly, so the judge continued. "You speak like a simple man, yet you're saying things of deep significance. Can you please explain how the citizens will set the mandate? What the Citizens Council Office will look like? And how each nation's progress will be measured?"

Tasos smoothed back his hair and breathed in deeply. "Judge Gilford, forgive my excitement. I'll try to explain myself more clearly. Implementing and establishing the new religion means changing the way of governing, so that government officials chosen by the citizens have no power over the direction of the laws, rules, and regulations that they draft. The citizens set the mandate. Each country's constitution needs to be restructured based on the principles of this mandate, and the governments must try to accomplish a hundred percent of the new religion's three principles. With your help, we will find a way to legally implement and establish the new religion. Maybe a referendum, or unanimous endorsement of a motion in the House of Commons—like when they vote unanimously to give themselves pay raises." There was chuckling around the table. "Now, consider what is a sure fact: everybody will very soon be in a hurry to get my blood. So the way I see things unfolding is that many politicians and government officials have somebody they love who is sick, or they themselves are sick. They'll need my blood to save their lives, which will put a lot of pressure on them. You'll represent me and express my expectations of payment for giving them my blood. The deal is that all nine of the twenty most economically powerful countries must legally establish the new religion as a way of governing. Then I will give each of these countries one test tube full of my blood. And I will give them tips on how to speed up the process of saving more lives.

"So the present governments' choice will be clear. They'll realize that all their money and power won't bring them happiness when they're dead from AV, and they'll find a way to establish the new religion. You will need to verify, every step of the way, that everything they do is legit and valid. We'll draw up the details, such as what must go into effect immediately as a new way of governing, and the time frames for the long-term changes that the new religion dictates."

Mr. Robinson was the first to react. "Mr. Perasmas, I have to admit your plan sounds brilliant. But also unrealistically optimistic. I will carry out your wishes, a hundred percent. But what you're planning seems impossible. You want to flip the world upside down!"

Everybody was holding their breath.

"Mr. Robinson, thank you for the constructive criticism," Tasos said with a smile. "Yes, you're absolutely right, I am planning to flip the world upside down. But I always bring rigorous logic to my plans and actions. My logic is simple: I would do anything to save the lives of my wife and child. I'm counting on that being the same for other people. Look at all of you—you're ready to do anything for me, right?"

We all nodded, but doubt was still etched on many faces.

"Look," said Tasos patiently, "we're living in a time when biblical-scale horrors are taking place: terrorist attacks, wars, invasions, severe weather conditions because of human-caused global warming. This pandemic is the latest and most devastating, threatening the destruction of all humanity. At least five or six hundred million people are dead already. And I'm the only person on this planet that can do something to save our species from annihilation. What do I ask in return? Just for everyone to be kind, to stop warring, stop being corrupt, and instead help others, bring a permanent end to homelessness and child poverty. So many beautiful aspects of life are being ignored right now because of people's thirst for power and materialistic profit. So, Mr. Robinson, I think they will run to do as I say." His confidence was unshakeable.

Mr. Thompson leaned forward. "Mr. Perasmas, may I ask you to review when you expect the nine governments to ask you to give them your blood, and when the money will start coming in? I'm concerned about the timing for accomplishing your plans."

"Thank you, Mr. Thompson," Tasos replied with a smile. "Of course, we need to be very organized, you're right. So after these two gentlemen," he pointed at me and Jonathan, "let everybody know who I am and what I can do, I will let you know when to communicate what I want. Tom's articles will be thorough in providing information and clear evidence about my healing power. I anticipate they'll attract many millionaires and billionaires. I expect the money will start coming within a week, at most, once we go public about the cure I can provide.

"In the meantime, I'll continue saving the lives of people I choose for free. This will generate more publicity. So I see no more than three to four weeks elapsing before governments contact you gentlemen." He nodded at the judge and lawyers. "Then we will tell them what I want and let them decide whether they're going to save the lives of the people they love, or whether they love their power and money more. I don't think any of them, with their backs against the wall, their lives at stake, will choose their old values."

Tasos stood up and began walking around the room. "You asked for more information about the Citizens Council Office. Well, I need you to find some additional honourable, totally trustworthy people to run the Citizens Council Office—let's call it the CCO for short—because when the new religion is established, the governments will be subject to the CCO's audits. This way, citizens will keep an eye on government operations to prevent abuse of power, and of course to make sure that governments do their job; which is to direct our society with superior management according to laws, rules, and regulations that ensure all citizens are equally respected. This is the foundation of the peaceful society that the new religion will bring about."

He paused and looked at a clock on the wall. "How are you all doing? How's your stamina? There's plenty more food in the kitchen. If you're game for me continuing, there's lots more I can tell you today."

Everyone was adamant that they wanted to continue, so I brought in carafes of coffee and tea from the kitchen, along with cream, sugar, and two platters of baked goods that Claire had made that morning.

"OK," Tasos said, rubbing his hands with enthusiasm. "Let's start with the no-army facet of the new religion. It dictates that we declare a war against war, meaning, against any and all lethal weapons. First, we must dismantle any nuclear capability, recall all military from foreign countries, and retire 10,000 of the highest paid and elderly military personnel, starting with the Minister of Defence. We'll take all lethal weapons from the police—they're not going to kill any more people regardless of skin colour, period. We'll start taking all lethal weapons out of circulation and destroying them. And we'll start dismantling all militaries—we're not going to need them. With the help of your brilliant legal minds and the people you recruit to your teams, I'll draw up the details for the long-term changes that the no-army stipulation means." He held up a hand. "Now, I know this is complex. But let me continue by telling you about the three main stipulations, acknowledging that each of them will require tremendous planning and effort?"

We all nodded.

"All right. Well, for the no-pollution component of the new religion, the immediate action will be to stop any permit approvals for businesses that have the potential to pollute until we establish a new Ministry for the Environment. After that, the permit approval process will be controlled much more carefully, making the environment the number one, non-negotiable priority. No more talking about protecting the environment. With the new religion, it is going to be written in the constitution.

"And my favourite facet of the new religion is that no one will ever be called 'boss' again." Tasos now had a look and a smile that made you think you wouldn't want to mess with him. I involuntarily shivered. "As I've said, social equality is the goal, and all citizens have the right to live comfortably. This includes not having people lording it over them as bosses. Government officials will reduce their gross income by fifty per cent until income parity is established throughout society; that should motivate them to work efficiently to accomplish this goal. Then they will start with 1.0 as the maximum salary throughout society. For example, a president or prime minister will earn 1.0, and that includes all of the perks. The rest of the people in government will earn a little bit less than that. When it's time for a pay raise, they can ask the Citizens Council Office for one, and if it believes they deserve one, they'll get it. It's that simple. All public workers will lose any extra privileges they have compared to private-sector employees. We'll install methods of monitoring the time government officials and employees work, because citizens will want accountability from their governments. Oh, and there won't be any royalty in the new religion; the titles and symbols they have will no longer be valid, and their estates will be returned to the rightful owners: the citizens."

As Tasos sat down, several people started talking at the same time. From looking very serious, even severe, Tasos's face was transformed by a huge smile.

"Tasos," I called, and the others became quiet. "My friend, you're going to set off a social, political, economic, and cultural bomb that will bring so much good. I can't wait to be part of this."

"Thank you, Tom. Now, don't think I'm criticizing your word choice, I know you meant it metaphorically, but since you said 'bomb,' I want to reassure everybody that the new religion is against any kind of violence. I will be terribly disappointed if somebody, in the name of the new religion, engages in violent actions. I want everybody in this room to make it a priority, whenever they're dealing with others, to make clear the new religion is against violence, period."

Everybody started clapping.

"That also reminds me to mention that initially, I will be in hiding, with the help of Mr. Boulen and Superintendent Cooper. This will be necessary to prevent me from being abducted to forcibly remove my blood. So," Tasos turned to the police officer and biker, "this is something we need to coordinate ASAP."

"Mr. Perasmas, may I bring up a point?" Cooper asked.

"Please do, Superintendent," Tasos replied.

"What if some of the useful or essential people for our plans don't pass the screening requirement—I mean the requirement that they or one of their loved ones has the virus?"

Tasos nodded. "That's a valid point. I'm willing, with your guidance about specific individuals' usefulness, to waive that requirement if necessary. And that goes for all of you." He looked around the table. "If you can explain the level of usefulness of somebody to me, I will accept them."

Everyone looked happy, satisfied, and empowered. I knew that feeling; it was what I'd experienced when I offered to save Mr. Callingham's son.

"I think at this point, we can close the formal part of the meeting," said Tasos. "You're welcome to stay longer to talk amongst yourselves, coordinate next steps, and so on. I want to thank you all for attending. Tom or I will be in touch with you very soon to arrange the date of our next full committee meeting. Between now and then, we'll have smaller meetings to deal with each aspect of what I've told you about here."

Everyone lingered for at least another half hour before leaving to join their families for dinner. Dr. Jekings stayed behind briefly to check Tasos's vitals to make sure his health was fine, then she too left.

At that point, Tasos turned to me. "Bourbon, Tom?"

"I'd love one, Tasos, thanks."

As we walked out onto the back deck, glasses in hand, he said, "Now, before you head home to get your articles ready for publication, I need to talk to you about something very important, something only you and I should know about."

Chapter 11

The three kids filed past us on their way to the kitchen. "We're starving!" they exclaimed. Each of them was still putting weight back on after their lengthy illnesses, and their appetites seemed even more bottomless than usual for children their age.

"Help yourself to everything," Tasos said, chuckling. "Dinner will be at about six, but I'm sure you'll be hungry again by then."

As we sat down on some patio chairs, I said to Tasos, "That was an excellent presentation and meeting."

"Thank you, Tom," he replied. "We'll still have to go over innumerable details, so the orientation will continue, especially with the legal team. You'll be present at every meeting, so you'll remain fully informed about the progress of my plans."

"I appreciate your trust and respect. So, what did you want to talk about just between the two of us?"

"Tom, I'm very concerned about the safety of the people we love," he said, a slight frown creasing his forehead.

I feel a shiver go through my body. "What do you mean, exactly?"

"You know that rich and powerful people tend to stop at nothing to accomplish what they want. I want to make sure we don't give them any leverage. They could try to hurt the people we love to get to us. My family and yours are very soon going to be in danger from the people who will see themselves as losing from my plan. I'm suggesting that we find some extremely competent and trustworthy professionals who will look after the safety of our families until everything is settled. I want Themis, Claire, Jake, and Brit to go somewhere away from us, totally out of the public eye, as soon as possible. Do you understand, Tom?"

I nodded as the gravity of his words sank in. "Yes, I do." I paused, then continued, "There's a small town a little over two hours' drive from here, where some acquaintances have a farm."

"Are these people relatives or close friends that you visit regularly?"

"Well no, not really," I replied. "We don't see John and Sherry very often, but they owe me a favour."

"What kind of favour? And how much do you trust them?"

"I saved John's life three years ago. I found him inside his car, which was overturned in a ditch—the deep kind they have in rural areas. I'd gotten lost coming back from an interview I was doing as part of research for a feature piece. Normally, I'd never have ended up on that road. He was unconscious and badly injured but I managed to pull him out of the car. Thankfully, emergency services were able to get there quite quickly, and John made a good recovery. From then on, John and Sherry have kept in touch a few times each year—calling to wish us a merry Christmas, that sort of thing—and they always say that if there's ever anything they can do for me, they will. They're very well off and have a big house on a private estate in the countryside."

"Tom, this sounds perfect." Tasos's eyes lit up. "You talk to Claire and the kids, and I'll talk to Themis. Then get in touch with John and Sherry to see whether we can visit them tomorrow. How does that sound?"

"Sounds great. I'll head home now and get going on this."

Claire was in the kitchen and the kids were in the living room, watching TV. I grabbed a phone and went into the backyard to call Sherry and John.

"Hi John, Tom here. How are you?"

"Tom!" I could hear the smile in his voice. "I'm very well, thank you. How about yourself?"

"Very good, thanks." After a minute or so of exchanging the usual pleasantries and questions about family members' well-being (during which I avoided telling him about our brush with AV), I said, "John, I'm going to be in your area tomorrow and was wondering if I could stop in for coffee."

"Oh Tom, I'd love to see you, and you know you're always welcome. But I need to warn you that our son Kevin is sick with AV." I heard him take a deep breath to calm the shaking that had come into his voice. "It's horrible, Tom, devastating. We're going to lose our kid. There's no hope, no vaccine, not even a hint. Sherry and I can't give up hope, but…we know that the only thing that'll save him is a miracle. And so far, I haven't heard of a single person not dying from the virus."

Now, I'll confess that although my first response was, of course, to express my sorrow to John, my second was to think, "Ah, this means Tasos can cure Kevin, and that will absolutely guarantee John and Sherry will do everything in their power to help protect our families." I knew, though, that it was essential to keep the Divine Blood secret until the news broke via my article.

"John, I'm so terribly sorry to hear about Kevin! As long as it won't be an imposition on you folks, I'll stop by tomorrow all the same."

"I assume you've got complete protective gear, Tom, especially given your line of work?"

"I do, yes," I said, "so please don't worry about me. I'll be fine. Is there anything I can bring you?"

The rest of our conversation was brief, and I said I'd see them the next day at about noon. "I'll text you when I'm half an hour away," I said, then wished them as peaceful an evening as they could have.

Before sitting down to talk with Claire and the kids, I sent Tasos a brief text message to let him know we had a noon appointment with my friends, and asking if it was OK to talk with him very briefly after dinner. He replied with a thumbs-up emoji.

Walking back into the kitchen, I said, "Claire, sweetheart, I need to talk to you."

She was sitting at the table, doing something on her computer, and looked up. "What's going on, Tom? You sound awfully serious. Did something go wrong at the meeting?"

"Not at all. It was great." I sat down with her and spent the next half hour telling her about Tasos's plan, the new team members, and the articles I'd very soon be publishing.

Claire was glowing with enthusiasm. "This is great news, honey. Of course, I have a bunch of questions, but...I have a sense there's something worrying you that we'd better talk about first."

I exhaled heavily. "Yes. Tasos thinks that for a while, all of us—him and Themis, you, me, Brit, and Jake—are going to be at risk of reprisals from the wealthy, powerful people who're going to lose out under the new religion. And I think he's right. So the way I see it, we need to get you and the kids to a safe, unknown place, and do that as quickly as possible. What do you think?"

Claire looked thoughtful. Slowly, she nodded. "It makes sense. Unfortunately, such people exist and will come after Tasos for his blood. And anyone he's close to will be targets—to kidnap so they can extort him into giving them his blood."

"Or even being taken captive himself," I added. "There are several possibilities, and all of them end badly for us."

"Is that why you were phoning John and Sherry?" Claire asked.

I had to laugh. "You're so perceptive and quick-thinking,

sweetheart. Yes, that's why I was calling them."

"Makes sense," she replied. "They've got that huge, private place out there, and I can't think of anyone who knows about your friendship with them. I think John would do anything for you, and Sherry feels the same way."

"Exactly. And there's more..." I then told her about Kevin being sick with AV. She immediately saw how Tasos could help them, and they in turn would be sure to do whatever possible to ensure our safety.

"Have you told Tasos yet?" she asked.

"No, but I'll go over after dinner to tell him."

"Well, I made lasagna, and it'll be another half hour before it's finished cooking. So I think I should start preparing for the relocation. How long do you think it will be for?"

I stretched and put my hands behind my head. "Hard to say, but I was thinking we should prepare for maybe three months."

Claire nodded. "Do you mind making the salad and garlic bread while I go upstairs and get started?" Then she kissed my cheek and headed towards the stairs.

After a lovely meal, Brit and Jake offered to wash the dishes and tidy up the kitchen. They could tell something was up, and I knew they were curious. All Claire had told them was that we were going on a small vacation. It was safest, for now, not to go into more detail with them.

Tossing on a jacket, I left the house and crossed the front lawn. Tasos opened his door before I had a chance to knock.

"Tom, c'mon in. Everything OK?"

"Just fine, although not for my friends Sherry and John. But thankfully, that'll change soon."

Tasos and I sat in the living room, and he looked at me inquiringly, waiting for further details.

"Their sixteen-year-old son, Kevin, has AV, so John was

hesitant about having me over. I didn't tell him anything about you or the cure, absolutely nothing. I just said I'd be sure to look after myself and would be fine to come over."

Tasos immediately perceived the big picture and grinned. "So first you save his life, and now you're going to introduce him to somebody who'll save his son's life," Tasos said. "John must be a good human being, Tom. He's certainly lucky to have had your paths intersect!"

I shrugged and smiled. "Well, chance brought us together that first day—or to be more precise, my terrible sense of direction and inability to read maps brought us together. I only wish we could get there before tomorrow, to relieve his and Sherry's suffering by putting Kevin on the rapid road to recovery."

Tasos was looking at me with genuine affection. After a few moments, he said, "This is one of the reasons I like you and am so glad to have you as a friend, Tom."

I looked at him, waiting for an explanation.

"You have high levels of empathy, my friend."

We only talked for another minute at most, as I was anxious to get back to my computer. I had to prepare some information and directives for Karen to finalize my articles for publication. She had excellent editing skills and was going to do a last check of each article before I sent them to Mr. Callingham.

Tomorrow night, we went to the press. By the day after that, the stories would be in hard copy and circulating online. Soon, things would become very, very interesting.

Chapter 12

"Hurry up, Themis! Everyone's waiting!" Tasos shook his head and laughed. "The only thing that kid's never late for is meals."

Themis came barreling out the door a minute later. "Sorry! I couldn't find my cordless headphones. Got 'em now!" and he waved them triumphantly above his head.

Everyone piled into our van—Tasos and I in the front, Claire and Britney in the middle seats, and Jake and Themis in the back. We hadn't been able to squeeze in everything for three months, so we'd left the remaining suitcases and boxes packed and waiting in the front hallway; I'd deliver them in the next day or two—or, if things had already become unsafe for me, we'd ask Superintendent Cooper for someone on his team to do that for us instead.

The trip took two and a half hours, but it went by quickly. Now that we were on our way, it seemed safe to tell the kids about the destination and why we needed to go there. They listened quietly, then bombarded us with questions, mostly about John and Sherry's house, and what it would be OK for them to share with the friends online. That was the toughest part, telling them that for a while, probably several weeks, they couldn't tell their friends anything about where they actually were.

"But Dad, Mom," protested Britney, "we'll have to lie to our friends!"

This was something we didn't want them to have to do; we'd always emphasized the importance of being truthful, and the kids took that very seriously. Claire turned to look at Britney and the boys. "Once we arrive at Sherry and John's, and get settled in there, how about I sit down with you guys and we brainstorm ways to keep what's going on with us private for now without having to lie. What do you think? I think we can do both things—stay safe and stay truthful."

The kids liked this idea, and glancing in the rear-view mirror at them all, I felt a glow of pride. This quickly combined with a surge of gratitude for Tasos, who had saved my beloved little family. I shook my head slightly in wonderment at the whole situation and smiled in anticipation of all that was to come.

A short while later, I turned from a quiet country road into a narrow, tree-lined lane, wide enough for only a single vehicle. "This is the start of their private road," I said, slowing to 20 kilometres an hour.

Claire lowered her window to breathe in the moist pine-scented air. "Look!" pointed Jake, "an owl!" Sure enough, a large, chunky-looking owl had launched itself from a branch and glided about ten metres ahead of the vehicle for a short while before flapping twice and landing on another branch, then swivelling its head to look back at us.

"Wow!" said Themis. "I thought owls only came out at night."

"Some can be active during the day," said Jake. He was already interested in zoology, especially birds, and had done quite a lot of reading about various kinds. "That's a barred owl, I think." He opened an app on his phone, tapped a few times to view a species profile, then nodded. "Yup, barred owl. They're sometimes diurnal."

"That's really interesting, Jake," said Tasos.

"Here we are," I said, as the lane ended at an open area, and the house and surroundings came into view. "You guys stay in the van until I explain a bit to them, because they're only expecting me."

To say it was a grand house wouldn't be an exaggeration. It was a massive two-storey log-cabin structure, with dozens of large windows, giving it a bright and airy interior that I'd noted on previous visits. The surrounding land was a mixture of cultivated gardens and meadows, some with long grass still growing and others recently mown.

John came out of the house as I drove the van up a circular drive to the ornately carved front door. He looked as city people might imagine a small-holding farmer would: blue jeans and a plaid shirt covering his belly, a canvas hat perched on his mostly bald head, and face and forearms slightly sunburnt.

I got out of the van to greet him.

"Tom!" he said with as much enthusiasm as he could through his evident sadness. "Welcome. But…" he looked in confusion at Claire and the others, who were still in the van.

"You brought Claire and the kids? And others?" He said. "Kevin's sick. They'll all be at risk. Did you bring enough protective gear?"

"John, it's OK. I've brought my friend Tasos Perasmas, who's going to heal Kevin."

John looked dazed. As he stood silent, Sherry appeared at the door and came out to join us.

"Hi there, Tom. What's happening? I thought John had told you that Kevin has the virus…"

John was still speechless with confusion, so I smiled at Sherry and said, "I know this is going to come as a surprise, and maybe even seem a little crazy at first, but I've brought someone who can make Kevin well. It's true," I continued as her jaw dropped in amazement. "He saved Claire and Brit and Jake. They were so far gone that I'd lost all hope, but our next-door neighbour and close friend Tasos Perasmas was able to cure his own son, then Claire and the kids."

"Tom, that's amazing," Sherry said, "but why haven't we

heard about this cure? We check the Internet constantly and we've seen nothing."

"No, you wouldn't have," I said. "But…you will very soon. For now, is it OK if we all come in? I have something very important to ask of you. First, though, if you'll allow it, Tasos would like to go to Kevin and cure him."

John and Sherry looked at one another, dazed, then they both said at once, "Of course, come in, please!"

I motioned to the others in the van, and they came out.

"This is Tasos Perasmas. Tasos, please meet Tom and Sherry. And here," I motioned for Themis to come forward, "is his son, Themis."

They all shook hands, and Tasos said, "I'm very glad that Tom got in touch with you and found out that Kevin is ill. By this time tomorrow, he'll be up and back to normal. I promise you this."

We walked into the house. "Is it all right if the kids and I take a look at your gardens?" Claire asked. "We can join you inside once you've taken care of Kevin."

"Of course," Sherry said. "Please, make yourself at home."

While we removed our jackets and shoes, John said, "What will this cure involve? Will it be painful or frightening for him at all?"

I shook my head and smiled gently. "When I tell you how simple and easy it is, you'll think it sounds insane."

"Go on," said Sherry.

"All that Tasos needs to do is put one drop of his blood in Kevin's mouth."

"What?!" John and Sherry looked at each other. "How can that work? You're right, it does sound a little crazy."

"Tasos has what we're calling 'divine blood.' We don't yet know what it is about his blood that can do this, we just know it's a fact. Not only has he cured Themis, Claire, Britney, and Jake—he's done so for a couple of hundred other people too, including doctors at our local hospital and the research hospital at one of the universities. I've video recorded everything. When I said you'll soon see it online, that's because today I'm publishing articles about this in the newspaper I work for."

Sherry turned to Tasos. "We know Tom would never lie to us, and he's one of the sanest people we know. And miracles can happen. So I believe you can cure Kevin. Will you need something from us in return?"

Tasos nodded. "I ask you to believe in the 'new religion.' But don't worry, this isn't a religion in the usual sense. There's no god or gods to believe in, no worship, nothing like that. It's a non-violent reorganization of societies all over the world, so that fairness, safety, peace, and preservation of the environment will finally be a reality."

I added, "Would you like us to go into more detail now?"

John and Sherry shook their heads. "No," said Sherry, "if you can save our son, and that's all you want in return, then I agree, and we can learn more later. I just want him treated as soon as possible; he's already at death's door."

"Yes," said John. "Please, shall we go upstairs to Kevin?"

It was a typical teenage boy's room, although tidier, no doubt because he'd been sick for many weeks. Pictures of rock stars and other celebrities decorated the walls, a few trophies were perched on a shelf. A very large computer monitor sat on a wide desk, along with a keyboard and wireless headphones.

Kevin was sleeping in his bed next to a large window that looked out onto a weeping willow tree by a pond and fields beyond. His dad touched his shoulder and spoke his name softly to wake him. On the way upstairs, John had told us that although Kevin had been infected about two months ago, he already looked at least four months into the illness. He opened his eyes and tried to smile at his parents. His breathing was shallow and raspy.

"Hey buddy," John said. "How're you feeling? Sorry to have

to wake you."

Kevin frowned. "I feel like I'm dying, Dad," he replied, a tinge of anger in his tone.

"Sorry, it was a dumb question," John said. "But look, I've woken you for a good reason—the best reason! Mr. Perasmas here is going to save your life."

Tasos approached the bed with a smile. "Kevin, I'm Tasos. I'm just going to put one drop of my blood in your mouth. Is that alright with you?"

Kevin looked at his parents, and Sherry said, "It's OK, Kev, it's safe. Mr. Perasmas has already done this for his own son, and for Tom, Claire, Britney and Jake.

"Tomorrow, you'll feel ready to climb mountains Kevin," Tasos said, then he poked his finger and squeezed a drop of his blood into the boy's slightly open mouth.

"Here's some water, sweetheart," said Sherry, offering him a cup. "Now rest, OK? We'll just be downstairs, talking. Dad or I will come up to check on you often."

For the next hour, we sat at their large kitchen table, drinking tea and coffee, munching on sandwiches, fruit, and cookies, and telling them about the new religion. They quickly saw the danger we'd be in.

"We can keep you safe here," said Sherry, and John nodded. "We have plenty of room, and the property is very private, as you can see. If you haven't told anyone you're here, then there's no easy way for someone to find out."

I exhaled with relief. "We were hoping you'd say that," I said. "Which is why we took the liberty of showing up all together like this."

"Tom and I will go back today, as we have some more things to take care of. But we'll return either tomorrow or the next day. We'll let you know as things progress, if that's all right."

"Absolutely," said John. "But before you go, let me put some snacks together for you to have on the journey home."

As I drove back, Tasos told me that Superintendent Cooper had arranged for security professionals to look after us and our families, as well as John and Sherry. We also talked about our next moves for promoting the new religion.

"Tom, we're going to have a few more meetings with the legal team, and I'll need you to be there to keep track of the direction I'm setting."

During the drive, he read through the articles that would be published the next day. He was pleased that I hadn't yet revealed the conditions we'd be setting for governments—just his abilities and his healing accomplishments so far.

I had something in mind for a front page that would make a big bang. I described it to him, and we talked about how Jonathan would be handling all of the online media side of things. "His genius is going to prove absolutely critical during this initial explosion of information," smiled Tasos. "We're very fortunate to have met him."

Back home after we parted ways, I had a video call with Karen to find out whether Mr. Callingham had approved the articles and the front page I'd proposed.

"He's incredibly excited, Tom!" she said, grinning. "He said we'll print three times the usual number of copies."

I smiled. "Thank you, Karen. You did a remarkable job. I'll see you in the morning."

"Bye, Tom. See you then."

Chapter 13

Holding the newspaper at arms' length, I gazed at the front page.

DIVINE BLOOD
He exists and he cures AV and he's Canadian!

"*Tasos Perasmas has found the cure for AV—or rather, he IS the cure*," began the lead article, which covered the entire front page, around a large colour photo of Tasos that I'd taken the day after he'd cured my family. He'd been in his backyard, beaming with joy as he watched the now recovered kids clambering on the treehouse.

It was 5:30 a.m. and I'd been at the newspaper's office waiting for the first printed batch to come in. I hadn't been able to sleep, between my anticipation and Claire and the kids being gone. Clutching several copies of the paper, I jumped in my car and drove home, parked hurriedly in my driveway, then bounded over to Tasos's front door. After I'd knocked loudly a couple of times, he opened it, looking bleary eyed.

"Tom, what…? Is everything OK?" He rubbed his face.

"Tasos, it's more than OK. I'm really sorry to wake you at such an hour, but I couldn't wait to show you the newspaper. Here!" I thrust it at him in my excitement.

He was instantly wide awake and said, "Oh, of course you were right to wake me. This is a huge day—the biggest day of your career so far, eh, my friend? Come in, come in. Let's get some coffee going and take a look at your masterpiece." He winked at me and we strode through to the kitchen, where he pressed a button on a coffee maker already set up to brew.

Sitting down at the kitchen table, Tasos smoothed out the paper and took in the front page, studying it carefully from top to bottom, side to side, as if it were a piece of art he was appraising. Then he began laughing.

"What…?" I began, wondering what was so funny.

"I'm sorry, Tom. No, no…I'm not laughing at this. It's beautiful, perfect! I'm laughing at the realization that it's happening, it's finally happening, the unveiling of the new religion!"

I began chuckling too, then got up to pour us some coffee. "So you like it?" I asked unnecessarily.

"Brilliant." He shook his head. "The media explosion this is going to create! The global explosion that's going to happen, for the good of humanity and the planet. Amazing." He turned to me. "When does it go online?"

"At 5:00 a.m.," I said. "I wanted to synchronize it as closely as possible with the morning paper delivery to shops, and the first deliveries go out at five. Jonathan is already awake." I showed Tasos my phone, where Jonathan's text messages to me were brief but punctuated with exclamation marks and decorated with emojis of shooting stars, comets, and round cartoon bombs with lit fuses. "He's practically exploding with excitement himself," I grinned. "Go ahead, read all the articles, Tasos."

He took his time going through the front-page piece, nodding at various times and smiling. Then he turned the page and saw that the third page was devoted to a profile of him. "*Who Is Tasos Perasmas?*" asked the headline. He leaned forward as he read.

Tasos Perasmas has the ability to instantly earn your respect, whether it's because of his perspective on life or the dynamic ways he chooses to handle any challenge.

His name, which is Greek, translates as "reincarnation of the passage." "Tasos" comes from anastasios, which means reincarnation, and "Perasmas" comes from perasma, meaning passage. So the fact that he has "divine blood" is an amazing coincidence—or perhaps not.

The Greek Orthodox community believes that someone with such miraculous abilities would be sent by God to redirect us in how we should be living. Looking at the world around us, it's clear from a massive amount of evidence that we've gone far off track—not just the pandemic, but so much else, including dramatic climate change.

Tasos looked at me. "So the Orthodox community believes I'm another messiah, Tom? Yes, my name happens to work perfectly for us," he said with a smile.

"Wait until they hear what Tasos Perasmas wants in return for his divine blood. They'll say, 'Only another messiah could ask something like that!'"

"Things are coming together even better than I expected," he said. "The bad and fearful days will also come, my friend. But we'll be ready."

His smartphone rang, showing an incoming video call. Tasos tapped on it, and Jonathan's face appeared. "Jonathan, hey, how are you? Just a sec, Tom's here, so I'm going to switch to the computer screen." He grabbed his laptop, which was already open on the table, and got the video call running on it.

"Hi, Jonathan," I said as his face appeared. "How're things going?"

"Mr. Perasmas, Tom, it's incredible! I've never seen or read or heard about anything like this. The story went live at 5:00 a.m., and by 6:30 a.m. the Internet had exploded. It's the time difference, with the East Coast of the States being three hours ahead of us, and Europe eight or more hours. In East Asia, the story broke at 10:30 p.m. their time but it's still taken off. It's too huge for anyone to ignore. I bet people there aren't even sleeping."

"Fantastic," I said. "How's the website looking?" Jonathan had suggested we create a basic webpage for when the story broke, as people would immediately want to learn more. Tasos had agreed, and I carefully curated the information that would appear there. The site had gone live at the same time as the articles had been published online.

"I think we've broken a world record in Internet history—seriously, I'm not exaggerating. We've already had several million visits to the site, and most of the visitors are now following us too. Plus, I've had fourteen private messages about money donations. We're not asking for donations on the site, of course, but these people are multimillionaires already wanting to know how they can buy your blood, Mr. Perasmas. And we've got more than a hundred requests for media interviews."

"OK, Jonathan," smiled Tasos. "Take a breath. You're doing an amazing job so far, young man. Thank you."

"You're welcome, sir. I'm quite pleased, actually," he said, looking a bit shy. "I don't want to brag or anything, but I anticipated basically the whole online world to hit the site within a very short time frame, and so far, it hasn't crashed, even though it would have crashed most high-end, powerful computers."

"Go ahead and give yourself due credit, Jonathan!" Tasos beamed. "You're a genius, and I appreciate your modesty but also want to acknowledge your brilliance. Now, have you directed those multimillionaires to our legal team?"

"Yes, Mr. Perasmas, I've done everything just as you and Tom instructed. Some of them are famous people."

"Keep up the good work, Jonathan. We'll talk again today." Tasos and I waved, then he disconnected the call.

He turned to me. "So, divine blood and messiah, eh?" He

poured himself another cup of coffee, warmed mine up, and sat down, exhaling heavily. "Tom, seriously, I couldn't have reached this point without you. Thank you."

"You're welcome, but nothing I do can be sufficient thanks for you healing my family. I didn't want to live anymore, but you changed everything, saved my world. Now," I continued, "I want to tell you about someone who I think could be helpful for us during the coming troubled and dangerous times you mentioned, while we need to stay safe from everyone who will feel threatened by the new religion."

"Do you mind if I make us some breakfast while you talk, Tom?" I gave him the thumbs up, and he began getting out ingredients, bowls, a frypan, and utensils.

"My friend Dan works in the movie business as a makeup expert—but not just basic makeup stuff. He alters actors' bodies and faces radically with prosthetics and things like that. Dan's wife has the virus. See where I'm going with this?"

"Yes. I'll need to be incognito, and your friend Dan could be very helpful. Tom, you are gold."

I smiled. "I took the liberty of seeing whether I could visit them this afternoon. He said anytime would be fine."

I got up and began helping Tasos with breakfast. Both of us were famished and probably ate more than we should have. Having been up all night, I went home to catch a few hours of before we went to see Dan.

"Text me when you're ready to go, Tom," said Tasos. "I'll just be here on the computer, watching how things are unfolding."

Alone in my house, I realized I wouldn't be able to sleep, so I lay down on the couch and switched on the TV. Simone Dickens, a seasoned, high-profile anchorwoman for the evening national news, was on. Evidently, they'd called her in to handle the breaking story rather than the usual morning and midday crews.

"—reports that one man, by the name of Tasos Perasmas,

has healing abilities and has already cured hundreds of the apocalypse virus patients all over the Lower Mainland. For those viewers just joining us, here is our correspondent Sheryl Omisky, reporting from University Hospital."

"Thank you, Simone. I'm joined here by the epidemiologist in charge of the hospital's pandemic recovery team, Dr. Cliff Keyman." The camera zoomed out to show the doctor's face, looking so different from when we'd first met him—relaxed, rested, confident, and optimistic. "Dr. Keyman, I have four words for you: Is it really true?" Dr. Keyman nodded. "So," the reporter continued, "there's a man healing people infected with the apocalypse virus. A man, in fact, whom you've met. Tell us what you know, doctor."

"Yes, Ms. Omisky, I've not only met Mr. Perasmas—he cured my wife Lauren, who is also a specialist here at University Hospital."

"Dr. Keyman, how is he healing people?"

"He is giving them one drop of his blood."

"Are they healed immediately?"

"No, it takes about twenty-four hours. But they are completely cured."

"When did he cure your wife?"

"A few days ago."

"And why haven't you let everybody know sooner, doctor?"

"Mr. Perasmas asked me to wait for his permission to make it public."

"But Dr. Keyman, don't you think that something so crucial should have been brought to light right away?"

"Mr. Perasmas saved Lauren, and I promised to do as he asked. I'm a man of my word."

"What is the success rate of Mr. Perasmas's healing?"

"One hundred percent successful."

The reporter turned to the camera and said, "I'll be continuing to gather information here as the story develops, Simone.

Back to you for now."

"Thanks, Sheryl. Now, we go to another hospital where Mr. Perasmas has also saved lives. From the Great Columbian Hospital, here's Sam Owens."

The camera then switched to another reporter, standing next to Dr Procof. The reporter began by asking the doctor to describe his first encounter with Tasos.

"Mr. Perasmas came to the hospital a few days ago to ask permission to cure some of our patients. He had videos proving that he could, in fact, heal infected people with one drop of his blood. I was hesitant at first, but given the complete absence of any progress in finding a way to treat AV, I was willing to accept even a completely unorthodox way of saving lives. So I gave him permission. He interviewed a hundred patients, then returned the next day with a list of fifty he would treat."

"Why did he screen the patients?"

"Mr. Perasmas explained to me that he wanted to meet and know about the person whose life he would save—their occupation, their spouse or other family members' occupations."

"So he has preferences?" the reporter asked.

"It looks like that," Dr. Procof replied.

"Is there any indication what category of people Mr. Perasmas prefers to save?"

"Not really. As far as I can see, there has been a mix of occupations, ages, ethnicities, and genders. Beyond that, I can't comment."

"Is there anything else you can tell us, Dr. Procof, to help us understand who Mr. Perasmas is, or how his blood has this ability?"

"Well, Mr. Perasmas generously gave us a small sample of his blood to test. It's early days yet, but Dr. Rachel Johnson and Dr. Christopher Cornish already have some very interesting findings."

The camera panned to a large screen on the office wall,

where two people in white coats stood smiling. "Dr. Johnson and Dr. Cornish," said the reporter, "thank you for speaking to us. Are you able to tell us anything about what makes Tasos Perasmas's blood so special?"

"Yes," responded Dr. Johnson, "we've already noticed a major difference between his blood and normal human blood."

"Can you tell us more?"

"There's something incredible in the DNA of Mr. Perasmas," Dr. Cornish said. "The simplest way to describe it is that his body is producing white blood cells that are like superheroes and have a seemingly inexhaustible capacity to multiply."

I felt a thrill go through me as the scientists described Tasos's uniqueness.

Dr. Cornish continued, "These cells instantly detect invaders, like the apocalypse virus, and attack those invaders. But instead of being destroyed in the process, they actually multiply and continue attacking. It's like hyenas when a pride of lions enters their territory. They start barking at the lions, even though they're much smaller and don't really stand a chance. After the lions kill a couple of them, twenty more hyenas appear that fearlessly attack the lions. A few of those twenty might be killed or injured, but so are some of the lions, and before they can rest, a hundred more hyenas appear, and so it continues until the lions are completely killed off."

"That's a remarkable image, doctor. Is there any way that we can use this knowledge to create a vaccine or antidote of some kind?"

"Not at this time," Dr. Johnson replied. "We'll need more blood samples to continue our research."

That was the last thing I recall from that particular report because at this point, despite my excitement, fatigue got the better of me, and I fell asleep.

Chapter 14

I woke to the sound of my phone alarm chiming. It was 1:00 p.m. Heavy rain was pelting the windows and thundering on the roof, and powerful wind gusts bowed the trees across the street. For a few moments, I was disoriented, not having woken up in an empty house for…I couldn't remember how long. Before getting married, I'm guessing. Soon, yesterday's and the morning's events came flooding back and I sat up, ready to embark on what I knew would be a very busy afternoon.

I decided to make some coffee first to recharge. Sipping a second mug, I sent Tasos a short text message: "*Good afternoon. Ready to go in 5 min if u r.*" He replied back with a single thumbs-up emoji. A moment later, a text came in from Jonathan, saying the website continued to "go nuts." I smiled and sent him my own thumbs up emoji.

On the way to Dan's, I asked Tasos whether he'd been watching the news.

He nodded. "Superhero blood cells—that's been my favourite bit so far," he chuckled.

"Mine too. Do you have any idea how you came by this unique blood?"

"I have a few ideas, yes. About why me and why now. I'll tell you about that later, once I've had more time to think. Hopefully, the scientists will gather more information too."

Dan and his family lived in a well-kept suburban area, close to a recreation centre and a public high school with an excellent reputation for its athletics programmes. The parking lots and fields around both of these were ominously empty. Dan opened the front door soon after I knocked. Unsurprisingly, his brow was furrowed and he looked haggard. Surprise then blanketed his face.

"Tom, hi. It's good to see you. But don't you have protective gear to wear? If not, just wait out here and I'll get you some; we have extra."

"It's OK, Dan, I don't need it, and neither does my friend. This is Tasos Perasmas. Tasos, meet Dan Patel, Hollywood North's makeup wizard." They shook hands, Dan hastily saying he'd just sanitized his before opening the door.

"Well, if you're sure," said Dan. "But it seems awfully risky."

I could tell from Dan's response that he hadn't been online or turned on the TV. Tasos's name hadn't registered with him at all.

"Dan," I said, "we came to see Liz as well as you. Tasos is here to cure her."

He stopped in his tracks halfway down the hall and spun around.

"What? Cure? What do you mean, how...?"

"Tasos has the ability to heal people infected with AV. I guess you haven't been following the news today?" I handed him a copy of the paper.

He scanned the headlines and looked at the front-page photo, then at Tasos, then at me.

"This is amazing. I'm awake, right? This isn't some dream? You're actually going to save my darling Liz?"

"Yes, Dan, that's absolutely right," I said. Tasos, standing beside me, nodded silently.

"Well, whatever it costs, I don't care. Please, can you do it now? She's no longer able to breath without an oxygen tank. I don't expect her to survive the night!"

Tasos said, "Take us to her now, and I will start the healing process."

As Dan led the way, I explained to him the simple cure and how long it would take for her to recover. "There's no fee for you, my friend," I continued. "But once Tasos has given Liz a drop of his blood, we'd like to sit down with you and explain how you can help us."

"Anything, absolutely anything," Dan said. "I can't believe this is happening. Liz, darling?" He tapped on her door, then went in first. After a few murmured words, he reappeared and motioned us to come in.

Tasos completed his task quickly and soundlessly, as Liz was in and out of consciousness. Dan asked us to find our way to the living room while he stayed with her for a minute to make sure she was comfortable.

Tasos and I sat in a couple of leather chairs and talked quietly while we waited for Dan. When he came in a short time later, he was carrying a tray of glasses, ice cubes, and several small bowls of snacks. Setting this on the coffee table, he gestured toward a sideboard displaying an array of liquors. There was also a bar fridge, which he opened. "Gentlemen, I hope you'll have a drink with me. I have non-alcoholic options too. Please, just let me know what you'd like, then you can tell me what I can do to repay you for this incredible miracle you've brought today!"

Once we had glasses in hand, I said, "Dan, we'll be brief as we have several more visits to make before dinnertime. Obviously, you can see that Tasos has a remarkable ability. With this, he's bringing a new way for the entire world to function, a system so that all societies will finally become peaceful and humanity can save the environment from imminent destruction."

Tasos leaned forward. "I call it 'the new religion,' although it's not a religion as we traditionally think of. There's no god involved, no need to believe in a superior supernatural force. We don't have time to go into the details right now, as Tom says. You can help us in return for saving Liz by accepting the new religion…and by creating a disguise for me. For the next while, my life is going to be in grave danger. You'll have to swear to absolute secrecy. No one can know that you've helped me, otherwise you and Liz will also be in terrible danger from the people who will want to get hold of me." He paused and looked intently at Dan.

Nodding, Dan said, "I accept all that you say. And as for the secrecy part, I'm used to doing that for my work. Usually, people's lives aren't at stake, but hundreds of millions of dollars are when I'm working in a big-budget film, and some of the people I work for value dollars way more than human lives. So keeping secrets is second nature to me. When will you need the disguise?"

"Very soon," Tasos said. "We have a meeting this evening, and I hope to know more at that point. Tom will keep you in the loop."

"In the meantime," I said to Dan, "let me know as soon as Liz is better—which she will be in no more than twenty-four hours, my friend." I smiled in what I hoped was a reassuring way, as poor Dan understandably still looked too afraid to be entirely hopeful, let alone optimistic.

We left quite soon after that. Tasos had received a list of people who'd be valuable for our growing team from Superintendent Cooper. They were all ill themselves or had AV-stricken loved ones. We were on our way for Tasos to deliver the cures—then recruit these people.

In the remainder of the afternoon, Tasos saved twenty more lives. Ten of them were police officers with special skills and two were high-tech professionals Jonathan had recommended. "Tom, these two techies are going to light us on fire!" Jonathan had practically shouted over the phone. "They taught me a lot of what I know. With them, I can do way more than I've already done. And they'll keep us as secure as the NSA. Even better, they'll keep us safe from the NSA," he laughed.

By dinner time we were both famished, not having eaten anything since the pretzels and other nibbles at Dan's. We demolished a large pizza between us, then headed for Mr. Thompson's office for a meeting with the legal team.

As we got out of the elevator on the forty-first floor, a receptionist ushered us into a conference room, where a large oval table was half-covered with legal folders and laptops. We shook hands with the three lawyers, then after everyone was seated we got down to business.

"Thank you again, gentlemen, for your valuable help," Tasos said.

"Mr. Perasmas," Judge Gilford responded, "there are so many things that we need to go over, and frankly, I'm very concerned about whether we can be prepared as quickly as you have in mind."

"I appreciate your candor, Judge Gilford," Tasos said. "I'm also confident that you gentlemen can handle this well. You are very capable. Hopefully today's meeting will provide the information, clarity, and tools you'll need. We're a team, and I will give you all the support I possibly can. Here," he pulled out a folder from his briefcase and handed out a thin stack of stapled printouts. "First, we'll talk about the Citizens Council Office and the authority they'll have. You'll find what we're going to discuss outlined in these papers, for your reference now and later."

Tasos stood up and began slowly walking around the room. "The Citizens Council Office will consist of nine honorable people. They might be retired or still working. I have in mind judges, lawyers, and scientists, but others are possible too, such as professors and investigative journalists. The main criteria are integrity and a total willingness to protect citizens' rights, freedoms, and well-being. I want you gentlemen to find these nine people to establish the Citizens Council Office, as well as nine equally suitable individuals as alternates in the event of unforeseen circumstances. These nine councillors will be the citizens' protectors, and the eyes for making sure that elected governments do their primary job, which is to reorganize our society 100 percent according to the principles of the new religion."

Mr. Thompson raised his hand. "Mr. Perasmas, will there be only one Citizens Council Office in the world, or will there be one for each country?"

"Every country will establish its own Citizens Council Office before full adoption of the new religion." He looked around the table. "Shall I continue?"

Everyone nodded.

"So…how will we measure progress towards 100 percent compliance with the guiding principles of the new religion? For the 'no army' criterion, the first ten percent will be achieved by retiring 10,000 of the highest paid military personnel and taking guns away from all police. The remaining ninety percent is something I'll outline in more detail once I've met with our military-dismantlement team."

"As for measuring progress in the 'no pollution' criterion, the first ten percent will be achieved by putting on hold any permit for a company that might pollute the environment, and having the Ministry for the Environment create thorough inspection policies and procedures. Again, the remaining ninety percent will be detailed very soon."

"For the 'no boss' criterion, 100 percent will be achieved when we have not even one child going to school hungry, not one person homeless, and all citizens living comfortably in terms of their residence, employment, and other aspects of their essential well-being. Banning the word boss from our language and reducing all politicians' earnings by 50 percent will constitute the first ten percent of progress. The remaining 90 percent of progress will be achieved by accomplishing all the other outcomes for this criterion."

"Mr. Perasmas," the judge said, "could you please go into a bit more detail about your expectations regarding reducing politicians' earnings?"

"Absolutely, your honour," Tasos replied. "Here's how it will work. Within six months maximum, we will determine what constitutes a 1.0 salary. This 1.0 will be what a professional needs to earn to live comfortably. For example, an iron worker will earn 0.5 as a beginner and 1.0 as a journeyman. The same goes for a carpenter, electrician, plumber, or any other professional. Once the dollar amount for the 1.0 salary is established, then the readjustment of the politicians' earnings will take place. Those at the senior levels of the civil service will earn 1.0 and the rest of the government and other politicians proportionately less. The absolute most that any government employee, including the prime minister and the ministers of the three top ministries, can earn is a 2.2 salary," Tasos explained.

He paused and looked at each of them. "The political ideologies of all, I repeat, all governments across the political spectrum are what has brought us to where we are now. Do you think there is any doubt about that?"

"If you are referring to the wars and the misfortune of millions," said Mr. Thompson, "yes, I agree. But the pandemic is God's will."

"Maybe. This certainly could be the way God or the universe has decided to eliminate the human race before the human race destroys the planet," Tasos replied, shrugging. "But ordinary citizens have suffered enough from mismanagement, corruption, lust for power, war mongering, complete disrespect for our planet, and the sick ideology that justifies anything in the name of profit. The governments have failed us. Our government leaders, those whom citizens trust to better their living conditions, are making things worse and worse. One after the other, the newest blames the previous one for everything. And the gross injustice of the rich getting richer and the poor getting poorer continues. But not for much longer," Tasos said with a confident smile.

"Mr. Perasmas…" The judge leaned forward. "Is the new religion ideologically left-leaning?"

"Not at all, your honour," Tasos replied. "The new religion is not communist, or centre, or any other of the ideologies on the political spectrum. The new religion is a completely new way of governing, a way that makes the government simply a manager with a mandate from the citizens. There will be no more sweet-talkers and liars abusing good, hard-working people. Citizens have lost trust in their governments, so every single person in those governments will have to start from the bottom and re-earn that trust. They won't receive increases in salary until they first earn complete trust. You see how this works?" He looked around the table, and heads nodded. "Now, the citizens will have brilliant people with high levels of integrity to protect them. The Citizens Council Office will appoint numerous inspectors who will determine whether the government is making decisions that are in the citizens' best interests. Because transparency and freedom of information are essential to the new religion."

"I'm going to play devil's advocate here," said Judge Gilford. "I think politicians are going to resent being paid the same as tradespeople."

"I am absolutely sure they will," Tasos said, arching an eyebrow. "So those individuals won't be welcome in government under the new religion."

"How will the new government be structured, and what will be its first task?" Mr. Robinson asked.

"There will be one person in charge—a prime minister—and

three major ministries: the Ministry for Peace, the Ministry for the Environment, and the Ministry for Social Equality. The government's first job will be to rewrite the constitution so we'll achieve 100 percent compliance for all three pillars of the new religion. The government will be obligated to accomplish at least ten percent of that task every four-year term."

"What about opposition parties?" Mr. Thompson asked.

"The citizens won't need opposition parties," Tasos replied, "because everyone will have the same goals. There might be some differences of opinion about which facet of the new religion to prioritize or emphasize, but these are differences that can be rationally and reasonably discussed, without the need for the wastefulness of opposition parties— which squander valuable public funds and other resources."

"Mr. Perasmas," said Judge Gilford, "if politicians and other government employees will earn the average 1.0 salary, how much will CEOs of big corporations get paid?"

"Like the very top government officials, the most any CEO will be permitted to earn is 2.2. No one, without exception, will make more than a 2.2 salary, and that will include everything—benefits, performance bonuses, and so on. This will be one of the government's earliest tasks: to determine how to reduce all CEOs who are over-earners down to the 2.2 salary level. And I doubt there will be many, if any, CEOs who don't fall in that over-earner category."

I was taking minutes of the meeting and raised my hand. "So just to make sure I have this right…when the government establishes the new religion as the new way of governing, politicians' earnings will be cut by fifty percent, and the already created Citizens Council Office will give them a maximum of six months to determine the 1.0 salary level. Then the government will find ways to cut all the excess salaries to the maximum 2.2 level."

Tasos nodded.

Sensing that the other three might be hesitant to ask this question, I said, "Can you explain how much other professionals will be paid, like doctors, lawyers, and judges?"

"Before answering that question, Tom, I want to clarify that all necessary services for citizens will be free of charge. People will be able to see the doctors they need, without worrying how they'll afford it. They'll be able to use the court system without being prevented by extortionate legal fees." He looked at the team members. "Please know that I mean no insult to your professions."

Judge Gilford laughed. "Oh, I'll be the first to criticize the ridiculous amounts of money that lawyers charge, and the incredible wastefulness of our present court system. In my view, it is criminal the way that for many, many centuries, the legal profession has devoted much of its energy to keeping itself in business. And that includes influencing lawmakers in government to pass laws that make the legal system more complicated—and therefore virtually impossible for ordinary citizens to understand, let alone navigate on their own."

"I couldn't agree more, your honour," chuckled Tasos. "Doctors of any kind will have a cap on their earnings, a 1.5 salary. Judges, as protectors of the laws, and our freedoms and rights, can reach the top salary of 2.2. Lawyers will earn no more than 1.4."

"What about sports stars?" Mr. Robinson asked. "They're used to earning millions."

"Another excellent question," Tasos replied. "The government will be mandated to make access to sporting events affordable. As a result, profits will no longer be humongous, and players' salaries will drop. The need for profit creates greed, and greed breeds corruption."

Judge Gilford said, "I think we now have a clearer understanding of what the government needs to tackle first, and therefore what the Citizens Council Office will be overseeing, measuring, and reporting on initially." His two colleagues nodded. "I'm sure you realize it will take significant time to make all these changes in our society."

"Yes, your honour, I know. In my estimate, it'll take about fifty years, and even then, it's not all going to be 100 percent. But we'll be most of the way there."

"Realistically, there is going to be resistance, including armed resistance," said Mr. Thompson. "How will we address that?"

Tasos looked grim. "Yes. The fact is, there will be guardians of the new religion, who will be responsible for external and internal safety. We have to be realistic."

"So there will be some sort of army after all," Mr. Thompson commented.

"Yes, a small organization with all the technological advances of the twenty-first century, including weapons. But these guardians will be completely invisible, and the weapons will be stored with security systems impregnable to all but a few key individuals. The citizens will not know about these guardians. And one day, that organization will no longer be necessary."

"Mr. Perasmas," Judge Gilford said, "why are you demanding that the police have their weapons taken away immediately?"

"Well, increasing numbers of police in recent decades have demonstrated escalating disrespect for civilians, and they've been allowed to get away with unprecedented brutal behaviour." I had rarely heard such passion in his voice, and I began to realize how profoundly he was affected by societal injustices. "There is no place for violence under the new religion."

Tasos held out his hands to the three men. "It must be written into our new constitution that we are fundamentally opposed to war. No longer will we lose sons, daughters, husbands, wives, brothers, sisters, and friends to war. No longer will veterans return with physical and psychological injuries.

The phenomenal amount of money we'll save by not supporting a vast military will be channeled into social programs."

"Will it be the responsibility of the Citizens Council Office to provide detailed direction to the government for the reallocation of these funds?" Mr. Thompson asked.

"No, Mr. Thompson, that will be the government's job. The council won't be engaged in that level of management." Tasos looked at his watch. "Shall we move on to how the government and council will start to address the second facet of the new religion?"

"Yes, let's do that," said the judge. "It's getting late, and I'd appreciate having a good overview of each facet before we stop for the night."

Tasos nodded. "All right, the environment. The new constitution will include the right to live in a clean, safe environment—and that means for the entire planet not just humans. The government will make laws to eliminate any kind of pollution. Timing is everything and strict deadlines will be essential for repairing the damage that the greed and profit-above-everything ideology has done to our environment. Scientists from all over the planet have said that we are rapidly destroying Earth. Fifty percent of wildlife has disappeared. Fish are dying in apocalyptic numbers from rising sea temperatures and massively polluted or acidic water." He pounded the table with his fist. "We must stop murdering the planet!" Eyes flashing, he said, "Just casually sitting here, we can brainstorm half a dozen ways that the government and Citizens Council Office will direct scientists and technologists to provide critical care and rehabilitation for our precious, unique Earth."

"How about eliminating all internal combustion engines within the next ten years?" said Mr. Thompson.

"And investing massively in solar, wind, and geothermal power production and conversion systems," offered Mr. Robinson.

"We also need to radically change food production and consumption," I said. "Raising animals for meat no longer makes sense, when the technology already exists to grow animal flesh. The introduction of this technology into general use and the rapid phasing out of animal farming would eliminate a third of all carbon emissions, according to reliable, recently released scientific studies."

"See?" said Tasos. "The five of us here already know that the solutions are there. They don't need to be invented. They already exist! But they've been suppressed by people who profit from the current methods, technologies, and systems, and who don't care about the planet. The new religion dictates that any decision the government makes must consider environmental protection as an absolute priority." He took a long breath. "I am a simple man, but I know our society has the technology to achieve all of this before it's too late for our beautiful Earth."

Judge Gilford said, "You may be a simple man, Mr. Perasmas, but you speak with great wisdom. We and our larger team will expand on and develop your directions for the government to follow."

It was dark outside now and as riveted as I was by the discussion, I had to stifle a yawn.

At that point, Tasos's cell phone rang. It was Jonathan requesting a video chat. Tasos had me display the call on the conference room's large wall-mounted screen.

Jonathan waved at us, a huge smile on his face. "Mr. Perasmas, your honour, gentlemen," he said, "I wanted to give you a quick update before the end of the day." He paused, then a graph appeared next to his face on our screen. "Here's a visual of our progress. We've broken social media records for likes and followers. We have more than 50 million followers, located all over the world, and we have about 50,000 applications from wealthy individuals asking for cures, amounting to over $25 billion. As you can see in the bar graph, about 10,000 of these are from China, and the rest are from elsewhere but primarily the US, Canada, Western Europe, and Russia."

I gasped. "Did you say 'billion,' Jonathan?"

He nodded. "Yup. I thought that for the very wealthy, I'd set an application fee of half a million dollars. That's nothing for such people. And the applications have poured in."

Tasos clapped his hands. "Bravo, Jonathan!"

"I made it crystal clear, sir, that this was only the application fee. I thought it would be a good way for us to more or less effortlessly attract some of the super-rich. I didn't give them a price for a cure, because that's of course for you to decide, Mr. Perasmas."

"Brilliant," Tasos said with a smile. "Either tomorrow or the following day, we'll let them know the price. Since you'll be gathering detailed financial information on them through their applications, please create a list of applicants ordered according to their wealth."

Jonathan nodded. "I had an idea, sir, and I hope you won't mind that I went ahead with it."

Tasos gestured for him to continue.

"To make sure that the super-rich disclose all of their assets, every last one of them, I put a clause in the application form that says: '*You must answer all of the questions on this application form fully and with complete honesty, and you must declare all assets without exception. Failure to do so will automatically disqualify you and everyone in your family from receiving the cure.*'"

At this, all five of us applauded. "It's the strongest motivator anyone could have," said Judge Gilford. "You hold all the power in this, Mr. Perasmas. You have what everyone wants."

Tasos said to Jonathan, "My young friend, you've done fantastic work. I don't want you to burn yourself out, so please promise me that after we end this call, you'll have a very good sleep. That," he winked at Jonathan, "is an order."

"Yes sir, Mr. Perasmas! I hope you all have a good night too," he said, then waved goodbye.

Tasos heaved a huge sigh of contentment. "Gentlemen, I am so grateful to you for helping me with this monumental task. And I don't want you to burn yourselves out either. So why don't we call it a day, as going into the third facet of the new religion in more detail is going to take more time than we should spend here tonight. I suggest we meet here again tomorrow at 6:00 p.m."

Mr. Thompson said, "I'll arrange to have dinner catered for us."

We all shook hands, then Tasos and I left first, as the other three said they wanted to discuss some work they planned to do together the next day prior to the evening meeting.

On the short drive home, Tasos and I discussed what information I could write about for publication the next day.

"I'd like us to do a short day trip tomorrow, Tom," he said, "and that will provide you with some excellent material for new articles. I'll tell you about it over breakfast. For now, let's get some rest!"

Chapter 15

When I got up the next morning, the first thing I did was text Claire to see how they were doing and ask about Kevin's health. While I was downstairs making coffee and some toast, she replied: *Kids and I r fine Kevin is GREAT! Back to normal but skinny like we were. Eating everything in sight LOL. When r u coming back? Miss u oxox*

I smiled and sent a quick response that I'd be there as soon as I could, hopefully by tomorrow. I also asked them to tell Sherry and John to make a video of Kevin, now that he was well, and email it to me for my growing database of cure histories.

As I was finishing my message, one came in from Tasos: *When ur up and ready come over. We're going on a short plane trip.*

Checking the weather forecast, I hoped it would be similar wherever we were heading. I grabbed a warm jacket and hat, put my boots on, and headed out the door.

Sitting at Tasos's kitchen table enjoying some sliced fruit with him, I waited to hear where we were going.

"Tom, there's a small town about four hours' drive north of here. The community is about eighty percent First Nations, and they've been hit very hard by the pandemic. There are only two general practitioners in the community, and they're both ill. The other medical professionals in town—nurses, paramedics, midwives, a physiotherapist—have been coping as best they can, because the hospital can't spare any of their specialists. You get the idea. They're really struggling in that community, and I want to help."

"Is this Eagle Run you're talking about?" I asked. He nodded. "I was reading about them a little over a week ago. It's a terribly sad situation."

"Not for much longer, my friend! Let's get going. I've chartered a float plane and let the pilot know we'll be there within the hour."

On the way to the float plane dock located on the Fraser River, Tasos explained that he wouldn't be screening the infected people in Eagle Run, he'd simply cure everyone. I was glad that my camera battery was fully charged and I'd brought two backup batteries so everything could be filmed.

I parked the car in a mostly empty lot that before the pandemic would have been packed with commuters' vehicles. As we walked down the dock, Tasos waved to someone at the far end. The man saluted, and I could see a broad smile beneath his jauntily angled hat. Drawing closer, I saw a grizzled man in his mid-fifties with a piercing, intelligent gaze.

"Al, this is my dear friend Tom," said Tasos. "Tom, Al and I go way back." He glanced sideways at the pilot, and they both laughed. "I'll tell you the story another time. Let's get going."

The flight to Eagle Run was less than an hour. It was located on the west side of a beautiful lake. A small cluster of people wearing surgical masks and elbow-length rubber gloves were on the dock as we taxied in. "Probably hoping that we're bringing the doctors they've urgently requested from the government," I said. "But the government has turned a deaf ear to them."

After Al had stepped out, so did Tasos, and I followed. We agreed to reconvene on the dock in three hours.

Tasos then turned to the gathered people and said, "Could you please direct us to the hospital?"

A swarthy man who appeared to be in his forties removed his mask and said, "Walk about 100 metres up that road," there was a single-lane track leading away from the dock, "then turn right, and you'll see it. How come you guys aren't wearing surgical masks?"

"We don't need them," I said.

"But how come?"

The rest of the people on the dock came closer and removed their masks as well. They were all First Nations, four women and two men.

"Have you been watching the news at all?" I asked.

"Of course," said one of the women. "What's that got to do with it?"

"So you've heard there's someone who can cure people infected with AV?" I continued.

"Yes. Dave," she said to the man who'd spoken to us first, "what's the guy's name?"

He immediately said, "Tasos Perasmas. It's a Greek name."

"Well, I would like to introduce you to the divine blood, Mr. Tasos Perasmas," I smiled, gesturing to Tasos.

Everyone froze then began speaking at once. Tasos held up a hand. "Please, can we talk while walking to the hospital? Tom and I have a lot to do, and we have only three hours."

Of course, the question each of them wanted to ask was essentially the same: Would Tasos please cure their family and friends. Tasos looked at me, inviting me to speak on his behalf. I cleared my throat and said, "Mr. Perasmas will cure everyone in this town who is infected." They all gasped, and one of the men began to cry.

"This is amazing, a miracle," said one of the women. "There are many sick people in our town. What can we do to help make this more efficient for you?"

"Once we get to the hospital," I said, "could you make a list of every address in the town where someone is ill, and provide us with a detailed town map so we can find the homes easily? I'm not getting any signal here for my cell phone, so I can't use my mapping app."

She nodded, told us her name was Marjorie, and said she'd be in charge of doing that while we visited the hospital's in-patients.

As Tasos entered the hospital, the receptionist got up hastily and offered us masks.

Tasos refused with a smile. "I don't need it, miss," he said. "I am Tasos Perasmas."

She gasped and pulled off her own mask, revealing the smile of a radiant young woman, about thirty years old.

"Mr. Perasmas, I'm so honoured to meet you! Are you here to help us?"

"Yes, I am, with the assistance of my friend Mr. Tom Newman," he nodded toward me. "He's the journalist who broke the story, and he'll be recording the events."

"I'll call Dr. Fining now. He's the head of the medical team today."

In less than a minute, a tall man in his sixties wearing a lab coat was striding toward us. "Mr. Tasos Perasmas?" he said with incredulity. "And you must be Tom Newman," he said, extending his hand to shake each of ours. "I can't believe I'm seeing you in our humble town's hospital!"

"We heard how Eagle Run is struggling, so we've come to cure everyone who is infected," Tasos said.

"This truly feels like a miracle," gasped Dr. Fining. "My wife is infected, and I've begun to show symptoms too."

"Do you feel well enough to take us to all of the infected people in your hospital, doctor?"

"Oh, absolutely! I feel like I've been totally recharged and cured already, just seeing you here and knowing what you've come to do. Please, come with me. There's no time to waste."

He led us to a large, open ward that contained over forty

beds. The patients ranged from toddlers to the very elderly, and most were in a very advanced stage of infection. Almost everyone was sleeping.

I began recording, first panning across the room and providing a brief introductory narration. Tasos quickly began dispensing the cure, while Dr. Fining looked on. He had declined receiving Tasos's blood first. "No, my patients must come first." The last two cures were delivered to Dr. Fining's wife and him.

Back in the hospital reception area, Marjorie was waiting with the list. She had her car outside and offered to drive us to every home on the list. We agreed. "Then let's stop at the coffee shop first," she said. "One of the guys at the dock this morning owns it and would really like to give you some coffees and sandwiches to take with you, since you have only about two hours left."

For the remaining time in Eagle Run, we visited home after home after home, creating what Tasos called "a tsunami of happiness." When he said this during our drive from the last home back to the float plane docking area, I laughed and said, "You've just given me the headline for tomorrow's front-page!"

Chapter 16

After landing, we went directly to Mr. Thompson's office for another meeting with the legal team. The caterers had already delivered a delicious spread for dinner, so everyone helped themselves, then sat down, ready for a productive session.

Tasos remained standing. "I'd like to propose a toast to all of you," he said. "Although there is a vast amount yet to do, I believe we're off to a spectacular start. Thank you all," as he raised his glass.

Everyone smiled, clinked glasses, and took generous sips of their drinks.

"How has your day gone, gentlemen?" asked Mr. Thompson.

"It's been very productive and uplifting, thanks," said Tasos. He briefly described our outing to Eagle Run. "Now, we still had a lot to discuss when we finished yesterday evening's meeting, so let's get down to business, shall we?"

I opened my laptop, ready to begin.

"Yesterday," continued Tasos, "Jonathan reported we'd already received $100 million. I heard from him on the way here, and we're now at $250 million." There was a small gasp around the table. "Yes, a quarter of a billion dollars. So who will be handling the economic side of things at this point?"

"That will be me, Mr. Perasmas," Mr. Thompson replied. "Judge Gilford and Mr. Robinson will be handling the establishment of the Citizens Council Office and the transition of power."

"Thank you, Mr. Thompson. I need you to hire a manager to create and run an organization that will look after all less privileged people. This organization will be called 'Brothers and Sisters,' and its first priorities will be kids in poverty, and the homeless. The $100 million that came in yesterday is earmarked for Brothers and Sisters. Once the new religion is established, the government will take over management of the organization. It will be the most important portfolio of the Ministry for Social Equality."

Mr. Thompson nodded. "What will the manager's salary be? I already have a few individuals in mind and can contact them right after this meeting."

"They'll be at the 1.0 level," responded Tasos. "Anything above that would be hypocritical, given the people they'll be mandated to help. And of course, the same criteria will apply for the rest of the people to be hired for Brothers and Sisters. If you're uncertain at any point, please consult with me."

"Since we're starting with a discussion of finances," said Judge Gilford, "can we talk in more depth about how the new religion will be handling the incomes of people who are now very highly paid?"

"Of course, your honour," Tasos replied. "First, I want to be clear about a fundamental principle: There is no place for profit in the new religion. This will be retroactively applied to some extent; we'll require people who took money from citizens by overcharging them for products and services to surrender it for use by the Ministry for Social Equality. Going forward, there will be a cap on the difference between companies' expenditures and revenues. They'll be allowed only what is required for future improvements for the company—with employees' welfare being the first priority.

"Mr. Perasmas, what do you propose for those who possess

high-value properties?" Mr. Robinson asked.

"As you know, part of the government's mandate will be to shrink the gigantic gap between the upper class and the middle class, and to eliminate the lower class, so no one is living in poverty. Everybody has the right to live comfortably," Tasos said. "So the government will heavily tax those with high-value property until their assets are reduced to a fair, socially healthy level."

"Can you define healthy, Mr. Perasmas?" Mr. Robinson asked.

"Certainly. It's very simple: Healthy means citizens will no longer live in a world where the one percent own more than the rest of us. Nobody is going to live like a king or queen. The current social situation is totally unacceptable. It's diseased, unhealthy. That there are hungry or homeless people is a complete disgrace in a prosperous country like ours." Tasos's eyes had taken on the fire that was apparent whenever he spoke about the injustices visited on ordinary people by the obscenely wealthy.

"Mr. Perasmas, since you mention royalty," Judge Gilford said, "how will they be dealt with?"

"Royal assets will be confiscated and returned to the rightful owners, the citizens. There is no room for royals in the new religion. Historically, they have brutally and ruthlessly abused their citizenry in order to amass untold riches. They can now go to work like the rest of us to earn their living and contribute to society. Instead of a hereditary royal family, the Citizens Council Office will nominate one family from the general population each year to have higher honour and recognition."

"So," said the judge, "you mean this family will be treated like royals currently are?"

"Yes," said Tasos, "with red-carpet treatment and all the other formalities. The media will report on what this family likes to do, eat, wear, and so on. And of course, their photograph will be displayed in government buildings, with their names and their family number, so the government will be reminded of who their employers are."

"What do you mean by family number?" I asked.

"For example, Mr. and Mrs. Fleming and their kids, John and Clarisse, will be citizen family number one, indicating the first year after the initiation of the new religion. The next year it will be citizen family number two and so on."

I nodded then got up to get a carafe of coffee and began pouring some for each of us.

"Mr. Perasmas, what do you predict will be the reaction of all these rich people when these 'bad' things happen to them?" Mr. Robinson asked.

Tasos beamed. "To be honest, I hope they get out in the streets and protest." He laughed. "Given how few of them there are, the sidewalks should be big enough. There won't be any need or cost to police their protests, and if they get loud, I'll be the first one out there saying, 'Oh, you're upset because now you'll have to wipe your own assess? Too bad. You should have been decent citizens when you had the chance.'"

The rest of us chuckled at the image.

Mr. Thompson then got us back on the topic of finances. "Is it possible for us to go through the current list of cure applicants, Mr. Perasmas?"

"Of course, Mr. Thompson. How many have you processed?" Tasos asked.

"Two hundred. Most are multimillionaires, and several are billionaires," Mr. Thompson replied, giving Tasos a binder then displaying the same information on the large wall-mounted screen for the rest of us to see.

The list included name, contact information, nationality, gender, age, amount of money ready for transfer to Tasos's account, and duration of infection.

"It will take me a few minutes to make a selection," said

Tasos. "Please, won't you get yourself some dessert while I do this?"

For the next twenty or so minutes, Tasos was absorbed in reading through the list and circling entries—I counted about sixty. He then looked up.

"Mr. Thompson, is my account ready and secure?"

"Yes, Mr. Perasmas, it's all set. The money transfers are already in, waiting to be accepted for deposit. I have access to any transaction you wish."

"Excellent," Tasos said. "These first sixty names don't require me to travel far. So you can start taking their money, Mr. Thompson. When the money is in my possession, we'll begin setting up meetings for the healing to begin."

"Mr. Perasmas, half of the applications are from the States. Are you willing to travel there?" Mr. Thompson asked.

"Hmm…it's risky," replied Tasos. "Surely these people are wealthy enough to get themselves here, if they want my help."

"How about we get the American applicants all together in one place here in Vancouver?" I suggested. "Have one healing session for all of them? That'll be very easy and efficient for you, Tasos."

"Excellent idea, Tom!" said Tasos. "Mr. Thompson, after we finish tonight, could you please start that ball rolling?"

Mr. Thompson nodded, but it was evident he wanted to say something else. "Mr. Perasmas…" he cleared his throat, "A couple of the wealthy Americans are actually too sick to travel. Fortunately, they're in Washington state. Are you willing to consider crossing the border?"

Tasos looked thoughtful, then turned to me. "Tom, I think this is where your friend in the film industry will be able to help us. Mr. Thompson, can you please coordinate with Superintendent Cooper to make the necessary security decisions and preparations? I'll be seeing him tomorrow, but I'd like you to work with him directly to arrange the border crossing.

Tom has introduced me to someone who can make me a disguise, so we'll take care of that." Mr. Thompson nodded and typed on his laptop.

I raised my hand. "Tasos, I just want to remind you that Dr. Jekings would like to see you before you begin these healings, to make sure you're taking care of yourself."

He smiled. "Very well. You're right. Tom, could you please see whether I can come to her office first thing tomorrow morning? I'd like to get under way with the cures as soon as possible."

Mr. Thompson had quickly done a rough tally of the funds from those sixty applicants. "Mr. Perasmas, after healing these people, you'll have about eight billion dollars in assets. Some of this is cash, but in some cases, people have pledged real estate, buildings, or other material assets. Do you want these liquidated, or...?"

Tasos looked thoughtful. "Hmm. Land and buildings could be very useful."

I looked at him inquiringly.

"The new religion is all about equality and establishing the right of everyone to live comfortably," he explained. "The money I take from the rich I was planning to return to the rightful owners, the citizens. I haven't yet thought it all through, but clearly it will be beneficial to have some housing immediately available for individuals and families in dire need. Thank you, Mr. Thompson, for posing that question. Could you please take me through those who've pledged materials assets?"

"Certainly," Mr. Thompson said. Using the cursor, he pointed to a name. "Mr. Jim Logani was infected three months ago, and the virus has progressed very rapidly. He owns a high-rise in Vancouver with 150 rental units. He also rents out a dozen large houses and two estates. Then there's the mansion where he lives with his family. In addition to all this, his other investments and accounts total two billion dollars. He pledges to give you all of this if you'll cure him."

"Perfect, Mr. Thompson, thank you," Tasos said. "In this case, I want the real estate as is, all of it. The other investments can be liquidated for immediate use."

"So you'll even take the house he lives in with his family?" Mr. Thompson asked.

"Yes, Mr. Thompson. I recognize his name as someone who heartlessly 'reno-victed' hundreds of people in Vancouver. Now, he can see what it's like to be without enough money to rent, panicking about where he and his family will live." Tasos shook his head. "I don't feel sorry for them. It's a fair deal—he gets life, after all. This is what it will cost him."

Looking at the deep anger and vengefulness etched on Tasos's face at that moment, I couldn't help but think that on the surface, he might resemble other abusers of power. I remembered what he'd said a few days earlier about being the last of them and the best of them. What a complex and fascinating person my dear friend is turning out to be, I thought.

Pointing to another name, Mr. Thompson said, "Are you interested in becoming a yacht owner? This billionaire you've chosen has a luxury 300-foot yacht valued at $158 million. It can carry twenty-two passengers and crew. And it's already moored in Vancouver, ready for use."

Tasos narrowed his eyes. "Ye-e-e-s," he said, drawing out the word. "I'd like to be a yacht owner, Mr. Thompson. What other assets does this person have in his name?"

"His total worth is two billion, mostly in the food-manufacturing business."

"Then liquefy everything but the yacht," Tasos replied, making a note in his binder.

Judge Gilford cleared his throat. "I apologize for interrupting, but I've just received emails from the four individuals I'd selected to fill the Citizens Council Office chairs. They've all accepted with great enthusiasm. So once we've received confirmations from the three that Mr. Robinson has proposed, we'll have that task completed. My four are all retired judges and they consider becoming a council member of the first Citizens Council Office the greatest privilege of their lives."

"This is great news, your honour," Tasos replied. "I'd like to meet all the council members individually and then as a group once the Citizens Council Office is established."

After that, Tasos returned to the list of sixty applicants and spent another hour discussing with us the potential uses for their material assets. We also covered a few other financial topics. By then, even Tasos was feeling tired, and he said, "Well, gentlemen, I'd better get a proper night's rest, or Dr. Jekings might scold me in the morning." We laughed and began tidying up our personal items, grateful that the catering company would be coming in soon to take care of the rest. "I think this meeting was very productive," Tasos continued. "Thank you for following me into this social tornado that I'm creating. Very soon, we'll have to start taking security precautions. Once I set up a meeting with our security team, I'll let you know, as it would be wise for you all to attend."

Both of us were quiet on the drive home. It had been an exhausting but highly satisfying day. Claire had messaged me earlier, so once I got home, I spoke with her and the kids on Skype for a little while, then pleaded exhaustion, said goodnight, and fell asleep on the couch. I dreamed we were going on a month-long vacation in Europe, which we could finally afford thanks to the new religion.

Chapter 17

The next morning, I called Karen to see whether she needed any clarification on the footage from Eagle Run or my accompanying article. She said Mr. Callingham had already approved the article and footage overnight. I was so used to him being either lackadaisical or overly critical about my work that I was surprised by his energy. Then I realized that perhaps he really had been transformed by this experience. Smiling as I ended the call with Karen, I hoped that this change would become the new norm.

I then texted Tasos to see whether he was ready to go to Dr. Jeking's office.

She gave Tasos a clean bill of health but cautioned him about getting enough sleep and eating properly. "Given the social upheaval that you're planning, and the danger this is going to put you in, Mr. Perasmas, I want your cognitive functioning to be top-notch. One mistake could be very costly to you and the people you care about."

The count of infected people globally had reached 1.2 billion, with about 60% of those in China. News about Tasos had led to the formation of numerous groups on social media, generating hundreds of thousands of posts begging Tasos to heal them and their loved ones.

After Tasos's show of vengefulness the previous night, I admit it was a relief to see tears in his eyes as we watched the news coverage in a café near the doctor's office.

"Tom, since the doctor says I'm fine, I want to visit one of the suburbs today to do some healing."

"Don't you want to rest for a couple of days, to be ready for some billionaire healing?"

"I will this evening, Tom. I appreciate your concern." He smiled.

"Where are we going?"

"A friend called last night and let me know that a mutual friend of ours is infected, as well as his two daughters. And his wife, who barely speaks English, is devastated, completely lost. They're originally from Ethiopia."

The traffic was always light these days, so it took us less than an hour to reach the apartment building where his friends lived. The neighbourhood was sketchy, and the building looked like it hadn't seen any maintenance in over a decade. I glanced at Tasos. "I envision your friends living in a much different place not too long from now, Tasos."

He nodded. "They're exactly the kind of family I have in mind. People who are being screwed over by the current system. Both parents have two jobs, but most of their income goes to paying an exorbitant rent and for overpriced food that isn't even nutritious. But…it's all they can afford. Not for much longer, though!"

The young woman who opened the apartment door was wearing a traditional Ethiopian habesha kemis.

Tasos introduced himself and me mentioning that he had worked with her husband in the past. "Your friend Ramo is also my friend, and he told me about Anthony and your daughters being sick."

"Please, come in. Ramo call, say you come. Thank you, thank you!" She told us her name was Martha, then went to tell Anthony we had arrived. When she came out of the bedroom, she said, "He is so sick. Our girls too, so sick. What medicine will you use?"

Tasos smiled and said, "Madam, by this time tomorrow, they will all be well. And we bring no medicine, except my blood." He then explained what he would do.

Martha hesitated. "Please," I said, "if you have any questions or concerns, don't hesitate to ask. We understand how strange this must seem."

She then told us that since coming to Canada, her husband had left their Ethiopian Orthodox Christian faith and become a Jehovah's Witness. "They do not allow blood transfusions," she said.

It was a difficult situation that we hadn't foreseen.

Martha began pacing the floor, evidently in great distress about the predicament. "Do you have videos?" she asked. "Videos of cured people?" When I told her I had several right there on my laptop, she said, "I will show Anthony now. He must decide. He is awake now. Will you please come with me?"

The three of us entered a tiny but meticulously clean and tidy bedroom, where Anthony lay rasping on his bed. When I asked whether they had an oxygen tank for him, Martha said their employers didn't provide extended medical insurance that would allow her to buy one.

I saw Tasos's jaw clench at hearing this. "Madam," he said in a low voice, "could you please write down the names of your and Anthony's employers? I will be paying special attention to them after this."

For the next twenty or so minutes, the three of us spoke to Anthony, telling him about the cure and answering the questions he put to us in a faltering voice, punctuated by struggles to catch his breath. At his and Martha's request, we showed him numerous videos of people who had been cured. Finally, he looked at Martha and said, "My dear, we must decide about our daughters together. It's not right for me to be the only one to decide. What do you wish to do?" He then spoke to her in

Amharic, and she answered quickly and fervently.

Anthony said a few more words to her, then looked at us and said, "Our daughters must live, and I cannot abandon my wife and my daughters. They may receive the blood, Mr. Perasmas, and I will too."

It took Tasos only a few moments to deliver the cure to Anthony and the two daughters, who were sleeping in a second bedroom. As Martha escorted us to the door, she thanked us repeatedly through tears of relief.

Since the previous day had been quite taxing for both of us, we agreed to head back to our neighbourhood and spend the rest of the day on various tasks that could be taken care of from our homes. It was lunchtime by this point, so I suggested we make something to eat at my place and watch the news. I was sure there'd be coverage of our previous day's trip to Eagle Run.

We settled into chairs in the living room, munching sandwiches and sipping coffee, and within about five minutes, the news anchor began reading the story.

"We have reports that yesterday, Mr. Perasmas performed numerous healings in the small town of Eagle Run, which has been hit particularly hard by the apocalypse virus. In just a few short hours, he saved the lives of over fifty people including two doctors. Eagle Run is a tight-knit community and has asked the media to respect their privacy, but one of the doctors agreed to speak with us on behalf of the town." The screen switched to the head and shoulders of a smiling Dr. Fining. "Dr. Fining," said the anchorwoman, "thank you for taking our call."

"You're very welcome, Gwen."

"Please tell us about Mr. Perasmas's visit to Eagle Run yesterday. I understand it was completely unexpected. What impact has his surprise visit to Eagle Run had on the community?"

"Well, Gwen, I've been a physician and surgeon here for over twenty-five years, and nothing has had such a devastating impact on our community as the apocalypse virus. As it happens, my wife and I both contracted the virus last month, and until Mr. Perasmas walked into the hospital yesterday, I was sure that we and a significant percentage of Eagle Run would soon succumb. Yet here I am, talking to you, and I can tell you that every single person in Eagle Run who had AV yesterday is no longer sick. Each of us received one drop of his blood, and within twenty-four hours or less, we were fine."

The interview continued for several minutes longer, interspersed with footage from the previous day which some of the people had given their permission to release to the media.

I looked at Tasos, who was sipping his coffee and nodding his head slightly.

"So, how's that for publicity, my friend?" I asked him.

"Exactly as I was expecting." He stretched, then looked at me. "There is so much to do, Tom. Do you have the stamina to do a bit more work today, but from the comfort of your living room? I'd like to check in with Jonathan, Mr. Thompson, and Superintendent Cooper. We can use video chat."

"Absolutely, Tasos. Let me make another carafe of coffee, then I'll be ready."

When I came back into the living room, Tasos was poring over the list of names Mr. Thompson had given him the previous day, circling a few, crossing out others.

"Ok, we're set," I said.

"Let's call Jonathan first for a quick social media update. While you were making coffee, I texted him, so he's ready for us to call."

Jonathan's face appeared on my laptop screen after two rings. "Mr. Perasmas, Mr. Newman, hello! How's it going?"

"Hello, Jonathan," said Tasos as I waved. "We're doing well, thanks. This won't be a long meeting. I'd just like a quick update about our online presence and the money that's come in so far."

"For sure, Mr. Perasmas," beamed Jonathan.

He began speaking quickly, rattling off a bunch of numbers and using so much technical jargon that Tasos held up both palms and said, laughing, "Whoa, whoa, Jonathan. I love your enthusiasm, I truly do. But how about taking a deep breath or two, then slowing down to the speed of mere mortals who don't live 24/7 in the digital world?"

Jonathan blushed and said, "Sorry, Mr. Perasmas, Mr. Newman. I'm just so excited. I've never been involved with something like this, the new religion. It's amazing."

Tasos and I smiled and waited for him to continue.

"As of a few minutes ago, there is ten billion dollars in your account. You had two more combined deposits, one and a half billion and the second 900 million, plus the donations that keep coming. The website now has 100 million followers, and we've received 100,000 applications for healing from ordinary people who say they don't have much, but they'll give all they have if you'll help them. Oh, and the Minister of Health wants to see you. Sir, he was really arrogant, treated me like something nasty on the bottom of his shoe."

I looked at Tasos, who now wore that predatory smile I'd seen at last night's meeting with the legal team.

"Well, the minister will just have to wait, Jonathan," he said. "And if he's unpleasant to you again, I want to know about it, OK? I won't tolerate any of our team being treated like that." He paused, then shrugged as if wanting to shake off something bothering him. "Have you been in touch with Mr. Thompson, who's heading up our finance team?" Tasos asked.

"Yes, sir."

"OK, Jonathan, keep up the good work, and we'll talk to you again soon," Tasos said.

"Thank you, Mr. Perasmas. Bye for now, bye Mr. Newman!"

Next, we video-called Mr. Thompson's office. Elizabeth, his assistant, appeared on the screen and smiled. "Hello gentlemen, how are you?"

"We're very well, Elizabeth, thanks," I said. "May we talk to Mr. Thompson, please?"

"Right away, Mr. Newman. He's expecting your call."

The screen switched to show Mr. Thompson's face, and we all exchanged greetings.

"Mr. Perasmas, I've made arrangements for you to heal two of the wealthy Canadians you circled on yesterday's list. They're going to be in one place, both of them, at noon tomorrow. I'll text you the address. They have a combined worth of about $1.5 billion."

Tasos and I nodded, and he said, "Excellent. I'm glad we're proceeding promptly."

"I've also spoken with Superintendent Cooper, and we've begun the arrangements for you to go across the border. I'm coordinating the gathering of the wealthy American patients. It turns out that in addition to the two in Washington state who can't travel at all—they're both in Seattle, fortunately—there are a few in nearby states who can be in Seattle within twenty-four hours. If you're OK with this, I'll arrange for several to gather in the same place."

Tasos looked at me inquiringly. I shrugged and said, "I don't see a problem with it. We can go see Dan again tomorrow and get the disguise under way."

"OK, Mr. Thompson, text me the address and the names of all the Americans who'll be in Seattle." Tasos said.

"One more thing, Mr. Perasmas," said the lawyer. "The Minister of Health wants to see you. Jonathan told me the minister was a real jerk to him, so I said I'd take over to save Jonathan having to deal with more of that nonsense. What's your response to the minister?"

"As I said to Jonathan, the minister can wait. Tell him I'm

very busy right now, saving lives, which is more than he's ever done in his fiscally irresponsible tenure as health minister."

Mr. Thompson smiled. "Understood, Mr. Perasmas. The delay can only work to our benefit."

"We'll be speaking to Superintendent Cooper in a few minutes," said Tasos, "then I'll have him get in touch with you to continue coordinating the cross-border trip."

The three of us said goodbye and ended the call. I got us some cookies from the kitchen, as the sandwiches hadn't quite sated our hunger. Then, we buzzed the superintendent.

To our surprise, he appeared on the screen rather than his assistant. "Gentlemen, hello," he said. "You were probably expecting my assistant, Ben, to answer the call. He's been working extremely long hours, so I sent him home early for some down time."

Tasos smiled and nodded. "Superintendent, we need to talk with you about me travelling across the border."

Before he could continue, the superintendent held up his hand. "Sir, I apologize for interrupting, but we need to talk using much more secure software than you've used to call me. Mr. Newman, can you write down the instructions I'm going to give you for installing some software? I've just emailed you the secure links."

It took about fifteen minutes for us to follow all of the instructions he'd sent. I then texted him a single emoji, as he'd instructed: 👍

A video call immediately came through via the new software.

"OK, sir, now we're ready," said Cooper.

"Thank you, superintendent," said Tasos. "Let's get right to the point. How do you propose to get me across the United States-Canada border and back safely?"

"Mr. Perasmas, we've arranged a temporary alternate identity for you."

Tasos nodded. "Please tell me more."

"I will provide you with the passport of someone who has died but for whom no death certificate has been issued. I understand that Mr. Newman has a friend who can make you a mask. I'm now sending you a high-resolution image of the person in the passport, so your friend can make sure you look like this person."

"Excellent," said Tasos. My email pinged, letting me know a new message had arrived. It was the image file from the superintendent.

"We will, of course, have an undercover security detail. Mr. Boulen is coordinating with us to provide secondary security. He'd like to know whether he can send you a short list with the names of some of his close friends in the United States who are presently affected by the virus. He says he would trust them with his and his family's lives, and having them indebted to you would prove invaluable in expanding our security network in the US as well as worldwide."

Tasos wore a huge smile. "That sounds ideal. Yes, please have him send the list as soon as possible"

"May I deliver the list and passport to you in person this afternoon, sir?"

"Please do."

"OK. I'll see you shortly, Mr. Perasmas. We can discuss additional details then. You might have questions, and I want to make sure I leave nothing unanswered."

Exchanging cordialities, we ended the call.

Tasos looked at me and said, "Tom, I know I proposed that we rest a bit today, but…how do you feel about visiting Dan, if he's available? I'd really like to get him started on that mask."

I arched one eyebrow and began humming the theme tune for Mission Impossible. As Tasos broke into a grin, I said, "Light the fuse!"

Chapter 18

I saw a dark silver car with tinted windows pull into Tasos's driveway about half an hour later while I was on the phone with Dan. Superintendent Cooper got out and walked briskly up to the front door, where Tasos was already waiting to welcome him in. I looked forward to hearing more about their conversation later on.

Dan picked up on the third ring. "Hey Dan, it's Tom. How are you, my friend and how is Liz?"

"We're both excellent, thanks, Tom. Still in happy shock at this miraculous turn of events! Is there anything I can do for you and Mr. Perasmas yet?"

"Yes, Dan, we're ready for your help. Would it be all right if we come by in the next hour or two?"

"For you and Mr. Perasmas, anytime works. I'm at your disposal," he replied.

"Great. I'm going to email you a photograph now, so that you'll see ahead of time what we need. I'll text you when we're leaving my place."

When I saw the superintendent's car pull away next door, I phoned Tasos to let him know we could head to Dan's right away. By the time I'd texted Dan, put my coat and shoes on, and headed through the front door, Tasos was already next to my car.

During the short drive, he told me he would be taking on

the identity of a thirty-two-year-old man named Greg Smith, who had died from AV but whose death hadn't yet been officially recorded. In face and hair colour, he bore no resemblance at all to Tasos.

Dan also bore little resemblance to the exhausted, disheartened man we'd seen a few days ago. Now, he was beaming and had a healthy flush to his skin. He greeted us enthusiastically and said Liz had gone out for a run. He invited us to come through to what he called his lab.

We walked through the door and were met by dozens of faces staring back at us. I was totally unnerved for a few seconds, until my brain caught up with my instincts and said, "They're masks, dummy!" Fortunately, I didn't say it out loud.

Dan stood quietly smiling, enjoying the effect, as Tasos too had stopped in his tracks.

"Wow, these are the real deal!" Tasos said. "I'm sure you're not going to have any problem helping me, Dan."

"Tom sent me a photograph ahead of time," Dan said, "and you're right, it's going to be easy. I have a 3D printer here. Once I've taken measurements and imprints from your face, I can put that data into the printer, make a few adjustments, and have an initial prototype for you to try on. In the meantime, let's have a couple of drinks and talk about any other temporary body modifications you may need."

"Fantastic," said Tasos. "As it happens, the man whose identity I'm assuming had a few tattoos. I have the details and high-res photographs of them on my iPad."

"I can make you tattoos that the people at border security won't be able to tell from the real things, Mr. Perasmas."

While the two of them worked together on getting the additional information for feeding into the 3D printer, I worked on one of the articles I planned to publish in the next day or two. When they'd finished, Tasos said to Dan, "My talented friend, there's no need for you to rush to get a prototype ready for us right now. Much as I appreciate your offer of drinks, there's one more place I need to take Tom today. I hope you'll forgive us for having to take a rain check on your kind hospitality."

I didn't know what Tasos was talking about, but I knew the lightning speed at which his mind could work, so I simply rolled with it, expecting he'd fill me in once we were back at the car.

But he had a mysterious little smile on his face and simply said, "Tom, can you take us to the hospital?"

"Sure. Is there someone you want to cure, Tasos?"

"No, no, not today." I couldn't get any more information from him.

At the hospital, he spoke quietly to someone at the information desk, who got up and escorted us to an elevator in an area normally restricted to employees. Thanking her, Tasos got into the elevator and I followed. We went up to the top floor, then down a hall and through a door, emerging on the hospital roof. A helicopter was on the helipad, and a woman I assumed must be the pilot was standing next to the aircraft, waving to us.

"Tasos, what—?" I began.

"Don't worry, Tom, nothing's wrong! Don't be alarmed. This was the nearest helipad to Dan's place, so that's where Superintendent Cooper sent the chopper to pick us up."

"Where are we going?"

"Let's enjoy the flight, and we'll see how long it takes you to figure out our destination," he said with a playfully sly smile.

I'd never been in a helicopter before. It was exhilarating, and for several minutes I even forgot to wonder where we were going. By this time, we were no longer over the city, and I struggled to identify any familiar landmarks. As I've mentioned, I have a terrible sense of direction, so that didn't help. All I knew was that we were flying over a mixture of farmland and forest. Twenty minutes after takeoff, we were landing on another helipad. There was a car, again with tinted windows, ready and waiting to take us somewhere.

By this point, Tasos was struggling not to laugh at me. "I'm sorry, my friend," he said, "but do you really have no idea where we are?"

"None at all, " I said as we climbed into the car.

Five minutes later, the car turned into a narrow lane, and recognition finally dawned on me. "John and Sherry's!" I exclaimed.

Tasos was beaming like a little kid. "I wanted to surprise you, Tom, so I asked the superintendent whether he could arrange this on short notice. It was no problem, so I texted John to confirm with him and Sherry. Claire and the kids don't know. I wanted to surprise them too."

I laughed and shook my head, amazed that amidst everything else he was orchestrating, Tasos had arranged this thoughtful surprise for me and the others.

Chapter 19

We spent that evening and most of the following day with Sherry, John, and our families, before taking the helicopter back to the city in the late afternoon. In two days' time, Tasos would travel across the border, so we needed to spend all of the day before that preparing.

Sitting down with a coffee at about 9:00 a.m., I made a few calls to book healing sessions for Tasos, and arrange for his mask fitting later that day with Dan and his assistant, Lucy. After emailing Tasos with the details, I had a video call with Superintendent Cooper to talk about security details for the trip. I was more than a little nervous about what might happen at the US border, and so to the superintendent.

"Tom, I understand where you're coming from. But let me assure you that Mr. Boulen and I have been working together closely to get everything coordinated for the operation. Given the nature of his activities, and the nature of mine, we know a lot about how each other's organization works."

"I'm guessing that the police have had the bikers under surveillance for many years," I said.

"You guess correctly," he said, looking a bit chagrined. "Frankly, it's not an alliance I would ever have dreamed of before the pandemic and the appearance of Mr. Tasos. But as the saying goes, 'Desperate times call for desperate measures.'"

I nodded. "I can imagine that given their control of the

illegal drug trade and other criminal enterprises, it's a bit of a shock to be working with them."

"Well, nothing shocks me anymore, Tom. But it is surprising. On the positive side, they have excellent connections and a staggering amount of intel about every aspect of border security in Canada, the US, and beyond."

"Good to know for future reference," I said. "So what are the plans for tomorrow?"

"First thing in the morning, you'll take Mr. Perasmas to the mask-maker's place, allowing plenty of time to get him completely disguised. A van will pick you up from there at quarter to noon, to arrive at the border by 12:30 p.m. There will be five of you in the van: you, Mr. Perasmas, Lucy, and two security personnel—one driving and one sitting with you in the back of the van. There will be security vehicles carrying additional personnel both in front of your van and behind it. At the border, you'll identify yourselves as a reporting crew that is covering pandemic conditions across the border. You're famous now, Tom, and no one will question that you're leading the coverage on this story."

We talked for a few more minutes about logistics, then I said goodbye and went over to Tasos's house. We didn't need to leave right away to get to Dan's, so Tasos suggested we watch a bit of the midday news beforehand. "You can fill me in on the details for tomorrow's trip while we're on the way to Dan's."

Much of the initial news report was more of the same we'd been seeing for months on end—dire statistics about the pandemic, the most shocking being that almost a quarter of the human population had now died. Mention was made that two leaders of countries were infected and ten more leaders had family members who were ill.

"And yet there is hope," the announcer said. "Tasos Perasmas, a Canadian, is saving lives daily. We have reports from the scientists studying his blood that there is a significant chance they will be able to create a vaccine, with further testing. But Mr. Perasmas is not currently willing to give any more of his blood for further testing, stating he has other plans, although there is no word yet on what those plans may be. In the meantime, Mr. Perasmas has been saving the lives of individuals from all walks of life. Apparently, he is healing some people for free, but from others he is requiring all their wealth."

An image appeared on the screen, next to the newsreader, showing the home page of the New Religion website. The newsreader continued, "The website for his 'new religion' displays the amount of money his organization has raised in this way and through donations, as well as the number of followers, and how to apply for an interview with Mr. Perasmas. According to the website, within ten days, Mr. Perasmas has become worth more than $10 billion. Wealthy people are giving him everything in exchange for saving their lives. We have reports that Vancouver International Airport has experienced higher than normal volume, mostly due to private jets, as all other air traffic has decreased significantly."

I looked at Tasos. "You're going to be busy, my friend," I said with a smile.

"Yes," Tasos replied, "and so are you!"

The news now switched to coverage of a large crowd of people, some holding signs, most chanting. They were assembled outside of what looked like a city hall building. The newsreader continued, "And outside Surrey City Hall, we have Lynne Semoo reporting on what appears to be a protest. Lynne, can you tell us what's going on?"

The image on the screen switched to a vivacious reporter with vibrant red lipstick and startlingly white teeth showing behind a clear face mask. "Dan, several hundred people have been here outside Surrey's City Hall for the past hour, in what appears to be a demonstration rather than a protest. The people I've spoken to say that they're here to show their support for Tasos Perasmas, the Lower Mainland resident who is allegedly curing people of the apocalypse virus. They claim to be embracing Mr. Perasmas's 'new religion' and are pledging their support for the new world he promises to bring. There is a police presence, but no violence has occurred. Officers have told me they're simply here to ensure that everything remains peaceful and adheres to public health and safety requirements."

"Thank you, Lynne," said the newsreader. "We'll check back with you in a little while. Now," he continued, "I have the Minister of Health with me here in the studio to answer a few questions. Minister," the camera shot widened to show a middle-aged man in a dark blue suit, white shirt, and light blue tie, "thank you for joining us here today."

"It's a pleasure, Dan," said the minister.

"The name Tasos Perasmas is on everyone's lips these days, for obvious reasons. His remarkable healing abilities are desperately needed. What does the government, and your office in particular, have to say about the situation?"

"Well, Dan, the virus continues to spread rapidly, and there's been no progress in developing a vaccine or in halting the virus once it has infected someone. The government is doing everything it can to provide assistance to affected communities."

"What about Tasos Perasmas? Have you been able to talk with him?" asked the news anchor.

"Scientists have confirmed that Mr. Perasmas has what they're calling 'kamikaze blood.' His white blood cells attack the virus and multiply and continue to attack until the virus is completely gone. Mr. Perasmas's method of giving one drop of his blood to an infected person has had 100 percent success so far. I have reached out to him, but so far he has refused to speak with me."

"Is it true that scientists believe it's possible to make a vaccine using Tasos Perasmas's blood?"

"Yes, they're cautiously optimistic that if they had more of his blood, they would be able to develop a vaccine. My office has been trying to reach him for a number of days now. He's humanity's only hope, at this point."

"Is there anything you'd like to say to him today, Minister? Perhaps Mr. Perasmas's is watching right now."

"Yes." The politicians looked directly into the camera, which zoomed in on his face. "Please, Mr. Perasmas, we'd like to talk to you. Whatever your plans are, my government would like to enter into dialogue with you and negotiate a plan. So please get in touch with us. Every minute is vital."

The camera panned out again to show both men as the news anchor said, "Minister, thank you for joining us today. Hopefully you'll hear from Tasos Perasmas very soon."

I looked at Tasos and said, "Everything seems to be falling into place. The government will be on their knees to you soon."

He nodded. "It is the right time and the right place, and I am the right person to initiate something like this."

"You mean it's the right time for you to change the world?"

"Yes, Tom, exactly that."

"If somebody else said that to me, I'd think it sounded arrogant and impossible. But not you," I shook my head. "Imagine, though, if this power had fallen into someone else's hands."

"It could still happen, Tom, unless we're very careful about security. But I have great confidence in the superintendent and Mr. Boulen, and their organizations."

His phone chimed at that point, indicating an incoming video call from Jonathan. I glanced at my watch and said, "We have time for a quick update from him before we leave for Dan's."

Tasos nodded and took the call. "Hey, Jonathan, how is my genius friend doing today?"

"Very well, thank you, Mr. Perasmas."

"How are the things in the digital world?"

"Very exciting. The applications for healing are at 200,000, and 2,500 of these are billionaires. At this rate, in a week you'll reach $100 billion, maybe more." Jonathan was grinning.

"Thank you, Jonathan. You're doing an excellent job. I don't want you and your team to be overwhelmed by all these applications, so just process the people with the most money," said Tasos.

"OK, Mr. Perasmas. Thank you. Can I mention something about your trip tomorrow?"

"Please do."

"I've given Superintendent Cooper a phone for you to use while you're travelling there and back. It has several additional layers of security to make sure that nobody other than me and the superintendent will know where the phone is at any point in time."

"That's a lot of trouble to go to, Jonathan. I could have just left my phone at home," said Tasos.

"That might raise suspicion, sir," said Jonathan. "Everyone has a phone these days. And as a photojournalist," he shrugged, "it would just look weird if you didn't have one."

Tasos smiled. "This is one of the many reasons why I'm so glad to have you on my team, Jonathan. You show initiative and take necessary steps to help me even before I know those steps need to be taken!"

Jonathan looked pleased and shy at the same time. "It's an honour to make myself useful, Mr. Perasmas."

"You're more than useful, Jonathan," I said. "You're essential!"

It was time to leave for Dan's, so Tasos ended the call and we left the house.

During the drive, he was very talkative, asking loads of questions as I filled him in on my conversation with the superintendent. The mask fitting went well, with only minor adjustments necessary. We were done in a little over an hour. Knowing the next day would be long and would require us to have our wits about us, we went directly home. Tasos wanted to write down ideas for discussion with the legal team. And I had a couple of stories that I wanted to finish off and send to Karen, so they would be circulating online by that evening. We agreed to leave by 8 a.m. the next day.

Chapter 20

I had trouble getting to sleep that night. Although not a worrier by nature, I knew that what we were undertaking—crossing the border using false documents, lying to immigration officials—was illegal and could land us in jail. The superintendent had told me his professionals were prepared "for every eventuality," including us being arrested. I had also spoken to the legal team, who had assured me that one of them would be with the superintendent all day, in case we were taken into custody. I trusted them all, but I couldn't shake the thought that while the rule of law normally could be relied on, everywhere around us were people desperate to save themselves, save their loved ones. Law enforcement officers were also human beings, and I couldn't shake the worry that if Tasos's identity was revealed, he would be abducted by people wanting either to use his blood themselves or to sell him to the highest unscrupulous bidder.

I finally drifted off at about 3 a.m., slept fitfully for a couple of hours, then tossed away the crocheted blanket I'd used to cover myself and sat up, bleary eyed, on the edge of the sofa. Glancing at the blanket, I felt my stomach knot with apprehension. Claire had made it several years ago, during her first pregnancy, and its pastel colours and soft texture brought her and the kids to mind. I ran my hand over it and smiled, then frowned as I slipped back into apprehension. If Tasos is abducted, will I be taken too? I felt guilty for hoping that I wouldn't, as though this was a betrayal of my friend.

Shaking my head impatiently, I stood up, determined to set aside my dread. During my conversation yesterday with the superintendent, he had emphasized the importance of not appearing nervous. "Border guards can pick up on fear like bloodhounds on a scent, Tom. Don't give them any reason at all to think you're doing anything more than coming to cover stories in Seattle. Keep your answers brief. Don't give them any more details than they need. Answer their questions, that's all. If you talk too much, that could tip them off."

"I'm a terrible liar," I'd said to the superintendent. "My wife says even Pinocchio was a better liar than I am."

"Then don't lie," he responded. "Just be economical with the truth. You'll be telling them that you're going to cover stories in Seattle. We've arranged for you to visit three of the city's main hospitals and interview people in their infectious disease departments. I'll email you the details after we finish talking. So if you're asked where you'll be going, that's what you'll say. Nothing more is necessary."

I was glad to see that Tasos had no such qualms. As he sauntered over to my driveway when we were due to leave, he looked relaxed and well rested. "Ready for 'Mission Impossible,' my friend?" he joked while fastening his seatbelt. He glanced over at me and winked. "I've renamed it 'Mission Everything's Possible,' and I have a feeling that great things are going to happen today."

In Dan's studio, Tasos rubbed his hands and exclaimed, "Good morning, my magicians! I'm ready to be transformed." He paused before sitting down in the chair that Dan offered him. "How is Liz today?"

At that moment, Liz walked into the studio, carrying a tray of snacks. "I'm doing great, Mr. Perasmas," she said. "Even better now that you're here. Would you like something to eat quickly before Dan and Lucy get started? You won't be able to do that once they're working."

Tasos polished off a couple of croissants in record time and downed a latte that Dan had made using a portable espresso maker he kept in the studio. He then sat back in the chair and said, "I am ready for you to make me into Mr. Greg Smith."

I had brought my laptop, of course, and to stave off my nervousness, I tapped away at a draft of the story I anticipated writing after the Seattle hospital visits. "You must go and do the interviews," the superintendent had told me. "That way, you'll have told the border guards the truth—just not all of the truth."

Over the next ninety minutes, I watched as Dan and Lucy changed my handsome, olive-skinned, clean-shaven, curly-haired friend into a younger man with long, straight, dark hair and a pale, acne-scarred face. When everything else was done, Tasos had to put in contact lenses that changed his eye colour to a muted shade of brown. Over top of the plain white undershirt they'd told him to wear under his own well-fitting clothes, they had him put on a baggy linen shirt, then a loose, casual coat, concealing his muscular torso. He wore his own jeans but changed his boots for a scuffed pair of basketball shoes.

When they were finished, he looked at himself appraisingly in the full-length mirror and said, "Dan, Lucy, this is great. My own son wouldn't recognize me."

Our driver and her colleague arrived to collect us a few minutes later. Tasos, Lucy and I got into a van that prominently displayed the name of the newspaper I worked for. The vehicles in our security detail were going to join us after we left Dan and Liz's place, so as not to draw any attention in the residential neighbourhood. As we came within a mile of the highway that led to the border crossing, I noticed a couple of nondescript vans join the light traffic in front and behind us. So far, things seemed to be coming together as planned. I tried to relax.

The three of us chatted, but the security personnel remained quiet for the most part, occasionally exchanging a few words with one another. As we neared the Peace Arch crossing, I overheard one of them comment that the wait for the border was longer than usual. It took us about fifteen minutes to reach the booth, where a uniformed border guard wearing a severe, suspicious expression stared into the vehicle, unsmiling.

"Travel documents," he barked. We all promptly handed our passports to the driver, who passed them through the window. The officer only glanced at them before handing them back, saying, "Park over there, to the left, and go into the office."

Our driver said breezily, "Anything wrong, officer?"

He gave her a hard stare and said, "Should there be? Is there something you'd like to tell me, young lady?"

Unruffled, she said, "No, sir."

"Then do as you're told."

I felt my stomach clench.

No one said anything until after we had pulled away from the booth, then Tasos said, "What's going on?"

"I'm not sure, Mr. Perasmas," said the driver's colleague, "but I've just alerted my commanding officer." I saw a smartphone in his left hand. "In the meantime, we do as we're told. Please remember not to say any more than you need to." His voice was calm.

As we got out of the van, I mentally rehearsed what I was supposed to say in response to "routine questions." Glancing at Tasos, I could see no trace of anxiety on his features.

There were about ten people ahead of us in line, so we had more waiting to do. Standing at the counter at last, passports in hand, we were told that the equipment they used to scan travel documents had "encountered some problems" that morning, so they would be manually entering our information into their computer system. This was much more time-consuming than scanning the barcode in each passport and it explained the unexpected delay.

Everything was going fine and five of us seemed to have been cleared for entry, when the young officer's eyes narrowed as he stared at the computer screen. He looked at us, and his eyes settled on Tasos. "Greg Smith?"

"Yes," said Tasos, showing no nervousness.

"It says here that you were charged in 2005 with possession of marijuana."

I could feel the blood leaving my face and hoped the officer wouldn't notice.

"That's ridiculous," said Tasos. "I've never even smoked a cigarette let alone marijuana. There must be some mistake."

"Are you calling me ridiculous?" said the officer, standing up.

"Not at all," said Tasos. "I'm just saying that your information can't be right."

"I don't like your tone," growled the man, and I saw his right hand move toward the holster at his hip.

This is bad, I thought, really bad. How could the superintendent have missed something like this? I felt sweat break out in my armpits.

Behind the officer, I saw a woman stand up from a desk and walking toward the counter. "Is something wrong, Officer Nelson?" she said.

The young man pivoted around to look at her. "Yes, ma'am. This guy," he pointed at Tasos, "was charged with drug possession fourteen years ago. And now, he's getting lippy with me."

I couldn't believe how quickly this seemed to be spiralling out of control. I felt panic tightening around my throat like an invisible hand.

A name tag identified the woman as Sergeant Willifred. She looked at the computer screen, then picked up the passport for Greg Smith. After a few moments, she said, "Officer Nelson, take another look, please."

"Ma'am?" he said quizzically.

"Take. Another. Look," she said.

He did, then said, "What am I supposed to be seeing, ma'am?"

Sergeant Willifred sighed. "Tim, the dates of birth don't match." She held the passport in front of him and pointed at the screen. "Look, see?"

The young officer's ears went bright red, and he mumbled. "Oh, um, I, uh—"

"The words you're struggling to find are, 'I'm sorry, sir, I made a mistake.'" She stared at him. "Go on, you owe this gentleman an apology."

Rather than looking apologetic, the young man scowled, as though it were somehow Tasos's fault that he'd made such a rudimentary mistake. "I'm sorry, sir. I made a mistake."

Tasos waved a hand in a don't-worry-about-it gesture.

The sergeant said, "Tim, go get yourself a coffee and then step into my office." Turning to us, she said, "I apologize for my staff member's behaviour, Mr. Smith. There's no excuse for it, and I'm sorry to have held you up."

"That's OK," said Tasos. "He's young, maybe a bit too keen. No harm done."

"I appreciate you being so understanding. The problem with the scanning system is that people get used to the machines doing all the thinking for them. So when the system malfunctions, like today..." She shrugged, then looked at me. "Tom Newman. You're the Canadian reporter who broke the story about the Divine Blood, aren't you?"

I relaxed a bit and smiled. "That's right, yes."

"Are you coming down here to cover what's happening in Seattle's hospitals?" I nodded. "That'll make for some very sad reporting." She shook her head. "Especially at the children's hospital. When you're next talking with the Divine Blood, please tell him that the world is waiting for his help." She took a deep breath. "Two of my kids are lying in that hospital right now, dying. I'd give my own life in exchange for theirs, in a heartbeat. It doesn't seem right, having your children die before you do." The sergeant shook her head. "Not right at all. Entirely wrong, in fact." I could see moisture forming in the corners of her eyes. She stood up straight then and said, "You have a safe journey now. Here's my card, in case...well, in case there's any way this Divine Blood friend of yours can help my kids."

The five of us were silent until we were back in the van and heading down the slip road that would reconnect us with the highway. Then Tasos said, "Well, that was interesting."

Our driver glanced in the rear-view mirror and said, "No kidding, sir. That's the sort of scenario that can throw a wrench into even the best planning. Still," she said, glancing at her colleague, "the superintendent will want to know about it."

"I just sent him a short text," he said, "confirming we've cleared the border. Our security detail ahead and behind us were starting to worry, but I couldn't risk trying to send a message while we were being grilled by Tim-Bits."

I chuckled. "He definitely needs to fine-tune his customer service techniques. I hope the sergeant gave him a good telling off. It's no joke having someone like that make mistakes, especially when he's got a gun."

"His days of being an armed US law enforcement officer are numbered," said Tasos. "This is an excellent illustration of why I hate guns and have no use for people with an inflated sense of their own authority. That young fellow is a potential time-bomb."

I waved Sergeant Willifred's card before tucking it into an inside pocket. "She could be a very useful person to have on our side, Tasos."

"That's Mr. Smith to you," he said, winking. "But I agree, Tom. And I'll now be coming with you to the children's hospital."

Chapter 21

It took us two more hours to arrive at a large estate with a big house, a few miles beyond the outskirts of the greater Seattle area. Mr. Thompson had arranged for all of the patients to be there. For security reasons, only one family member per patient had been allowed. Also for security reasons, Tasos stayed in disguise. "It only takes one drone flying over, taking pictures of Mr. Perasmas out of his disguise, and then his safety could be compromised," the superintendent had told me the day before.

The staff Mr. Thompson had hired to take care of the patients before, during, and after our visit had prepared them and their family members so they weren't expecting to see Tasos's face. As a compromise—for these people were, after all, paying phenomenal amounts of money to be cured by the Divine Blood—we had voice-recognition software on my laptop. So for each patient, we would play a video of Tasos at one of the healing sessions from a few days ago, then he would speak to them and the voice-recognition software would confirm him to be the same person they were seeing in the video.

No one objected, and in each case, there were many tears shed and innumerable expressions of gratitude and love for the Divine Blood. By the time we had finished with the last patient, I suspected Tasos was getting a bit uncomfortable with all of the emotion and the outpourings of adoration.

The whole process went so smoothly and quickly that we were finished before 5:00 p.m. We headed to Seattle and checked into our hotel. After a surprisingly delicious dinner delivered by room service, Tasos and I were both yawning…it had been a long day.

"Tom," Tasos said to me, "I need to get some rest, especially if I want to be up at 6:00 a.m. tomorrow. Could you please let the superintendent know that I'll be going to the children's hospital with you tomorrow, so he can make the necessary adjustments to our security arrangements?"

"Of course, Tasos. You go and rest. I've got a few things left to do, then I'm going to get an early night too. My interviews start at 8:00 a.m. but the first stop is the children's hospital."

"See you in the morning, Tom. And thank you again for everything you're doing. I think today's excitement at the border was just enough to keep us on our toes, eh?" he winked and laughed.

Less than an hour later, I was nodding off in front of my laptop, so I took the cue from my body and hit the sack.

Despite us having turned in early, the morning seemed to come far too quickly for my liking. Stumbling to the bathroom, I turned on the shower and let the powerful spray pummel my scalp until I felt a little less foggy-headed.

Within a few minutes of emerging from the shower, there was a knock on the door and a voice saying, "Room service!" I was glad that we'd pre-ordered breakfast the previous evening, and the aroma of dark-roast coffee, French toast, sliced strawberries, and vanilla whipped cream did almost as much to wake me up as the shower had. Stomach rumbling, I began pouring the coffee, hoping Tasos would come in soon.

He emerged from his room a few moments later, looking cheerful but a bit tired. As I poured a coffee for him, there was a knock on the door. Tasos opened it to Lucy, who bustled in cheerfully, ready to help him don his disguise again once we'd had breakfast.

By quarter to eight, we were in the van and our driver was heading to the children's hospital, which was only five minutes from the hotel. My phone beeped, indicating the arrival of a text message. It was from Jonathan and said simply "*ward C2B ask 4 nurse frank.*"

I smiled. Before going to bed the previous night, I'd contacted Jonathan to see whether he could find out where Sergeant Willifred's children were being cared for in the hospital. He'd gone one better, not only determining their location but arranging for me to interview their nurse. The idea was that while I distracted the nurse with interview questions, Tasos would slip a drop of his blood into each child's mouth without being noticed. I would then contact the sergeant the next day to ask about her children's health. I had to check with the superintendent about how exactly to handle disclosing to her that the Divine Blood had cured her kids, but this was a relatively minor detail. I wasn't yet sure what value there would be in having Sergeant Willifred's allegiance, but my intuition told me this wasn't an opportunity to be missed.

Everything went perfectly. I couldn't wait to make that call the next day, and hear the relief and joy in a mother's voice. We finished up at the children's hospital, then went on to the other two hospitals, where I conducted the necessary interviews. By half past twelve, we were back at the border crossing, and this time, it took us only a few minutes to deal with the Canadian immigration officers.

Tasos shook his head as we drove away. "What a difference compared with yesterday's rigamarole." After checking with the driver that we were far enough away from the border, he removed the wig and started to peel off the mask.

My phone rang. It was Mr. Thompson requesting a video call.

Tasos nodded, so I accepted the call. "Hello, Mr. Thompson," I said. "We just got across the border back into Canada a few minutes ago. What can we do for you?"

"Good morning, Tom, Mr. Perasmas." Tasos waved and smiled. "I have some interesting news." He cleared his throat. "The President of the United States is requesting a video conference call with you."

Tasos laughed out loud, and the sound was so infectious that Lucy and the two security personnel started laughing too.

"The President of the United States of America wants to talk to Tasos Perasmas," he smirked. "Some Greek Canadian he'd never even heard of two weeks ago. And I bet, Mr. Thompson, that he wants to talk with me 'with immediate urgency,' is that right?" Tasos arched an eyebrow and crossed his arms.

"With immediate urgency" was one of POTUS's favourite phrases to toss around whenever he felt like showing what an important person he was…which was pretty much anytime he made a public appearance. The president was a vain, idiotic bully of a man who seemed incapable of rational thought and couldn't make it through even a short interview without uttering something racist, misogynistic, or otherwise ignorant and narrow-minded. He was an embarrassment both nationally and internationally. Since taking office three years before, he had engaged in one corrupt practice after another, unchecked by a federal government that had lost control of its chief executive, and by a citizenship that had lost its moral compass.

"I wonder what he'd say right now if I told him I'd just returned from visiting his country incognito and converting some of its wealthiest citizens to the new religion." Tasos rubbed his hands.

"You'll be able to tell him soon enough, Tasos," I said, "if you wish. Mr. Thompson, what reason did the president give for his request?"

"Both of his sons are sick with the virus," said the lawyer.

"He wants Mr. Perasmas to cure them."

I looked at Tasos and saw on his face the wolfish smile that slightly unsettled me every time it appeared. The look of a ruthless predator.

"What do you want to do, Tasos?" I said.

"Oh, I'll talk with him," said Tasos. "Mr. Thompson, may we use one of the boardrooms at your firm's office?"

"Of course."

"Excellent, thank you. Could you get in touch with Superintendent Cooper and tell him of this new development so that he can adjust his security plan accordingly?"

Mr. Thompson nodded. "I took the liberty of giving him the heads up before calling you, Mr. Perasmas," he said, "to give them maximum preparation time."

"Please don't hurry," said Tasos. "I have every intention of keeping the president waiting. The more desperate he becomes while he waits, the better it will be for my plan. And if he's offended by the delay, then that's a bonus, as far as I'm concerned." Tasos paused, then continued, "Tell him I want our conversation to be broadcast live on all major national and international stations. And he needs to be in the Oval Office for it. He can have two of his henchmen with him, if he wants, but that's it."

Mr. Thompson nodded, then said, "Would you like me to arrange for some lunch to be brought to my offices beforehand?"

"How very thoughtful of you. That would be excellent, thanks," said Tasos. "I'd certainly rather not talk to that revolting man on an empty stomach."

We arrived at the firm's offices about ninety minutes later and enjoyed a very nice Lebanese lunch. While we ate, we had a brief video call with Jonathan, who said that he'd arranged to keep Tasos's location during the video call with the president hidden. He would record everything and save it on a secure server. "We're up against the most sophisticated cyber-security organization in the world, sir," said Jonathan, "the US military. And I'd bet my last Bitcoin that they'll be trying to detect where Mr. Perasmas is, so they can abduct him."

It was nearly 2:00 p.m. when Tasos said, "OK, let's get this conversation with the world's biggest ego started." He interlaced his fingers, then stretched his arms over his head. "This is going to be fun, Tom."

Mr. Thompson had arranged for the British Broadcasting Corporation to be the only ones in the Oval Office recording and broadcasting the interview. All the other networks had to receive their broadcasts via the BBC's feed. "That'll annoy the president," I chuckled.

The BBC World Service's logo appeared on the wall-mounted television screen, accompanied by intro music. Tasos crossed his arms and smiled in anticipation.

"And now, breaking news from North America. The President of the United States will be speaking live with Tasos Perasmas, the Canadian who is believed to possess unique blood that can cure anyone infected with the apocalypse virus. The BBC has been given exclusive access to the Oval Office, where we will be filming and broadcasting this conversation. Here's our Washington correspondent, Kaylee Tam."

As the reporter briefly introduced the impending conversation, Tasos's face appeared in one half of the screen, with "Tasos Perasmas, the 'Divine Blood'" displayed underneath. A few seconds later, the other half showed the Oval Office, with the president seated at his desk and two men—one in military uniform and the other in a dark-blue three-piece suit—standing to his immediate left and right. A ticker-tape of text now ran at the bottom of the screen, identifying the two men as the chief of staff of the US army and the secretary of state.

"Hello, Mr. President," Tasos said.

"Mr. Perasmas, you're a difficult man to find," the president replied in a loud, brash voice.

"I've been very busy," Tasos responded, "but as you see, I've found a little bit of time even for you." The sarcasm in his voice was unmistakable.

The chief of staff and the secretary of state looked outraged, and a cloud of displeasure came over the president's face. His entire life, he'd surrounded himself with sycophants who were too afraid to stand up to his bullying. I smiled to myself. Oh, you won't like Tasos one bit, Mr. President. You've met your match.

"Mr. Perasmas, I need you to do me a favour, a personal favour. I'm sure your people have already filled you in on what I want from you, and I'm sure you understand the importance of this and the benefits of helping the President of the United States." He flashed a smile that reminded me of shows I'd seen on the Discovery Channel's during *Shark Week*...except I like sharks.

Tasos answered in a slow, measured manner. "So you're making me an offer you think I can't refuse?"

"Something like that."

Tasos turned around to look at me. I was just off screen, so all that could be seen on the television was his back as he said, "See that? He's trying to play the Godfather with me while the world watches. I knew this was going to be fun." Tasos's smile made the hairs on the back of my neck stand up, even while I laughed with him.

Turning back to the screen, Tasos said, "I'll tell you how this is going to go, Mr. President." He paused for three long seconds, then commanded, "Stand up!" Everyone in the boardroom froze, and the shock on the faces of the president and his cronies was unmistakable.

Then, "How dare you!" spat out the uniformed man.

But the president stopped him and stood up.

"It's OK, General. I don't mind standing up and talking. And I like a man who's got some guts." That was a lie; anyone, man or woman, who challenged the president hadn't lasted more than a few weeks in the White House.

Tasos continued, "Now, come around in front of the desk so I can see all of you."

Ever the narcissist, the president strutted around to the front of his desk, puffing out his chest and smiling like he'd just been voted sexiest man alive. His two officials glanced at each other, then reluctantly joined him.

Pausing for dramatic effect, Tasos then dropped the bomb. "On your knees!"

The president's mouth dropped open.

"You heard me," barked Tasos. "If you want me to cure your precious sons, get down on your knees."

This time, the chief of staff began to protest, but the president raised his hand, then silently began lowering himself to his knees. Partway down, he had to grip the general's arm to avoid his outsized belly throwing him off balance.

"Good boy," Tasos said. "Now tell me how glad you are that I've agreed to talk to you."

There was fury in the president's eyes, but he swallowed hard, then said, "Thank you very much for agreeing to see me, Mr. Perasmas. I appreciate it."

My smartphone vibrated at that point, displaying a text message from Jonathan that said simply: "*1.5 billion viewers... world record...website numbers exploding.*"

I looked back at the big screen, then at Tasos.

"OK," Tasos said after about ten seconds, "you can stand up now." The president struggled to his feet, again with the general's help. "Now tell me about this personal favour you're asking."

The president was shaking, although I suspect it was with rage rather than fear. He'd never been publicly humiliated like this, let alone on global television.

"Mr. Perasmas, my two sons are infected with AV. I need you to save their lives."

Tasos rubbed his face, rumpled his hair, then put his hands behind his head, elbows outward, and swung his crossed legs onto the boardroom table. "Well, to be honest and completely clear with you, Mr. President, your kind are the last on my list for curing." The president's face was blank. "But I understand how you feel, with your kids on the verge of death. You must be feeling devastated and completely helpless. Is that right?"

"Yes, I am."

"You've got them the very best, most expensive medical care in the world, and that isn't making a damn bit of difference. They're still dying. You're massively wealthy and you're the world's most powerful man, yet here you are, unable to do anything. Hmm?"

The president nodded.

"And here I am, able to cure them, and all you can do is beg and hope." Tasos paused, savouring the situation. "Well that's how more than ninety percent of the world's population feels every single day, while you and your fellow monsters play your power games and amass insane levels of wealth. Will they be able to feed their children? Will their homes be blown up in an air strike? Will rising sea levels put their village underwater with the next monsoon? Will another foreign-owned corporation burn another thousand hectares of irreplaceable forest to raise cattle for McDonald's burgers while the local people are displaced and pushed into starvation? Ordinary, decent people around the world face these and a thousand other forms of suffering every single day because the top dogs like you only care about feeding your appetite for possessions and slaking your thirst for power. And that's why I won't help you."

The president inhaled sharply and panic showed on his face.

"Unless." Tasos stopped. "Are you listening to me very carefully?" The president nodded mutely. "Unless you do exactly what I tell you, and you keep on doing it. No double-dealing, or I'll make sure your sons become re-infected—and that you get the virus as well."

"Anything," gasped the president. "Name your price."

"The United States and eight more of the world's most economically powerful nations must adopt the new religion. Then I'll save your sons' lives. Do you think that you, with all of your charm, can accomplish this? Or will you need to tell your sons that their dad's a second-class politician and a failure as a father, not to mention as a world leader?"

The president looked like he'd sucked a lemon, and I had to stifle a laugh. I'm sure no one in his seventy-something years of life had ever spoken to him like this. "Who the hell do you think you are?" he shouted. "I can have someone come and pick you up and throw you in jail just like that!" and he snapped his fingers.

Tasos's face darkened with anger. "Don't kid yourself, Mr. President. You hold none of the cards here and I hold all of them. Now, are you going to play ball or do I hang up?"

The president was breathing heavily, and his face was a strange mixture of red and orange. "I—I—," he panted. "OK. You win. What's this—new—religion?" He had to lean backward on his desk at this point while he caught his breath.

"Good," said Tasos. "Now listen. The new religion is a totally new way of thinking. It will become the status quo. The three principles it's based on will be what we teach our kids in school, so they grow up to be decent, kind members of society. The new religion is society organized and run according to what the citizens want. The new religion is power to the people."

The president looked lost. "What are the three principles? And what do you mean power to the people?"

"The three principles are no army, no pollution, and no use of the word 'boss.' This is the society citizens want to live in. This is the mandate all future governments will have to adopt, no matter what their political ideology. They're finally going to do what the citizens want them to do, rather than getting elected and then breaking their promises and ignoring citizens' best interests. This is power to the people." Tasos's voice rang with passion.

"Mr. Perasmas, this is big stuff," the president replied. "I'm gonna need time to negotiate with my—."

"There won't be any negotiations. You do what I say, or I don't cure your sons. Is that crystal clear, Mr. President?"

The president's mouth hung open for a few seconds, then his shoulders sagged, and he said, "Yes, very clear, Mr. Perasmas."

"Good. And as I've said, don't even think about double-crossing me. You'll be hearing from people in my team who will arrange for the cures to be carried out. Your sons will be in my care and control while you make the changes in your country. Don't—" Tasos held up his hands as the president began to protest, "I told you there won't be any negotiations, with other people and especially not with me. It's my deal or no deal. You understand the art of the deal, don't you, Mr. President?" Tasos winked.

The president looked at his two henchmen, who shook their heads slightly and whispered something to him.

"Fine," he said. "My people will be waiting to hear from your team, Mr. Perasmas. We'll follow your instructions."

"First on the list," said Tasos, "will be a public apology for all the misery you've caused in citizens' lives. And you'll announce massive pay cuts for you and all the other corrupt politicians in your country who've been feeding like wolves on their flocks when they should have been protecting them like shepherds. I already have the salary amounts drawn up. You'll receive them shortly. So get ready to tighten that oversized belt of yours, Mr. President. And start packing your bags. Your days of social and economic dictatorship are over, forever. Now if you'll excuse me, I have more important things to do. Goodbye."

Tasos hit a button on the laptop in front of him, ending the call. Then he swivelled the chair around to face me and grinned, "I think that went very well."

Chapter 22

When we got home that night, Tasos was a little off—he looked concerned about something.

"Is there anything you want to talk about?" I asked. We were sitting in my living room, sipping snifters of brandy.

"Yes, Tom," he nodded pensively. "I'm concerned that the near future is going to be not only hectic but dangerous."

"What specifically do you think might happen?"

He ran his fingers through his hair. "I don't feel safe crossing the border again, at least not in the near future. And I have to be prepared for a hunt—with me as the prey."

"I understand what you mean, and I think you're right. You're wanted by the world now, for good reasons but also for bad ones." Pouring us both another inch of brandy, I said, "You can do your healing here in Canada. I'll let Mr. Thompson and the superintendent know. Who do you anticipate hunting for you?"

"The government, plus powerful people who want my blood, either for personal use or for personal gain." He laughed a bit ruefully. "They're literally 'out for my blood' although not for revenge. But I'm not naïve. Some of the people whose fortunes I demand in exchange for cures might become resentful once they no longer have the threat of death hanging over them. Who knows—they might decide they want to get their fortunes back by holding me hostage or by selling my blood."

I shook my head. "I wish I could disagree with you, but I think that's definitely a possibility, my friend. Do you have anything in mind in terms of steps you'd like to take?"

"Well, we've taken the most important first step, which is getting our loved ones out of Dodge. And I know I need to keep a really low profile in order to continue with the plan."

"The whole team is ready to help you in every way possible, Tasos."

"And I'm very grateful for that, Tom. I believe Superintendent Cooper and Mr. Boulen will already be anticipating all the angles and putting plans in place, as will Jonathan on the digital side of things—making sure we have untraceable communication devices and so on. But I'd like us to check in with them tomorrow, to get a complete rundown on what they have in place now and what they'll be doing as we go forward."

I grabbed my phone. "I'll text them and Mr. Thompson now to let them know. It's a new kind of situation for me too. I'd also like to get a list of security do's and don'ts from them, to make sure I don't inadvertently do something that would jeopardize your safety and security."

Tasos took another sip of his drink. "For tonight, I'd like to stay here at your place, if you don't mind."

"Of course! You're welcome to stay here as long as you like."

"Thanks, Tom. I'll grab some things from my house."

"Let me go with you, just to be extra-safe," I said. Finishing up my text, I hit send and said, "Ready when you are."

It took Tasos only a few minutes to get what he needed, then I showed him to the guest room, and we said good night.

As the aroma of coffee drifted up the stairs the next morning, I opened my eyes, stretched, and prepared myself mentally for another taxing day. Walking into the kitchen, I greeted Tasos, who was already drinking coffee and had the morning news on the TV. A reporter was interviewing people on the street in downtown Vancouver. Many were just walking by him, but some would stop to talk and express their concerns and complaints.

One middle-aged man in a tired-looking suit stopped and removed his surgical mask to respond to the reporter, who asked, "How do you see the future unfolding, with the pandemic continuing to rage? Do you think this is the end of humanity?"

"Well, I don't know about the end of humanity, but the future sure isn't going to be rosy. I think a few of us will survive."

"Do you have a relative or friend who's infected, sir?" asked the reporter.

"Yeah. A cousin of mine died a month ago, and a friend was diagnosed three weeks ago."

"Are you on your way to work today?"

"Yes."

"Aren't you worried about getting sick?"

"Of course I am! But if I don't work, I don't get paid. And my wages are already barely enough. I just have to hope I'll be one of the lucky ones who survives." He shrugged.

"Thank you, sir, and good luck," said the reporter.

As the man walked off, a young, well-dressed fellow stopped in response to being hailed. Pulling off his mask, he said, "Hi, what can I do for you?"

"Thanks for stopping. What are your thoughts on the pandemic?"

The young man crossed his arms and said, "I don't think the government's doing enough. And I think the way it looks, humankind is in big trouble. I don't know why the government isn't making this divine blood guy give them more of his blood so they can develop a vaccine from it."

"Do you think the human race will become extinct? Or will some survive?"

"Yeah, I think some people will survive. Like the ones who've been given his blood already. If enough people survive, I bet somebody'll make a movie about it one day and make millions of bucks." He laughed, and it was hard to tell whether he was being serious or cynical.

"Thanks for your time," said the reporter. At this point, a woman, who was standing nearby waiting to talk to the reporter, stepped forward.

"Hello," said the reporter, "would you like to tell us your thoughts on the pandemic? Do you think this is it, what some people call the End of Days?"

"Yeah, it's gonna be if this guy with the blood doesn't start helping more people soon!" she said, visibly angry. "He's blackmailing the whole world, telling governments he won't help them unless they adopt his crazy ideology. It's criminal."

"So you believe Tasos Perasmas should forget about his philosophy and give his blood freely?"

"Absolutely," she nodded. "He's being totally selfish. He sounds to me like someone who'll become just another dictator like dozens of other megalomaniacs throughout history."

I looked at Tasos, whose face wore an expression of great sadness. "What are you thinking?" I asked him.

He sighed. "I was hoping I wouldn't encounter this sort of thing, but realistically, I knew some people would feel this way. I'm a hundred percent sure that what I'm doing is the right thing. But, it doesn't make it any easier to feel OK about not giving more of my blood for research right now."

"I think I understand," I said. I could tell he wanted to say more, so I remained quiet while he organized his thoughts.

"You know me well, Tom," he said, "so I think you'll realize I'm not bragging here." He frowned, thinking. "I find pleasure in pleasing and helping others. I always have; it's how I've been my whole life. When someone's in need, I've always been the first to react and try to help. More than a few times, people have taken advantage of me. But I've continued to put my personal interests second to help someone else. This time though, I've decided to put what I've developed as my philosophy first. I know it will benefit the most people, in the long run. And that means, in the short run, not pleasing a lot of people."

The TV had switched to a newsreader reeling off the latest horrifying statistics about infection rates, total numbers dead, and how many people were thought to be dying each minute. Tasos was clearly distressed.

I glanced at my phone to check the time. "We're scheduled to have a video call with Mr. Thompson, Superintendent Cooper and Jonathan in a few minutes," I said. "I'm going to have some toast before it starts. Would you like some?"

Tasos smiled and gave me a thumbs up.

At 9:00 a.m., I hit send on an email to Karen, checking on the news pieces we were getting ready to publish about the interview with the president. Then I brushed crumbs from my shirt and initiated the video call to the other three.

After we'd exchanged greetings, I got right to the point. "We need to talk about safety and security, gentlemen. Specifically, Tasos's but also our families'. Now that the plan is underway, it's clear that many people will, for various reasons, be motivated to abduct him. Some of them might also try to use our families as leverage to force him to give his blood. Also, for the time being, Tasos has decided that it's too risky to travel across the border again."

At this point, Tasos interjected, smiling. "I suspect that by putting the President of the United States on his knees, I may have…annoyed a few people, starting with the president."

Mr. Thompson, Superintendent Cooper and Jonathan all laughed.

"Mr. Perasmas," said Mr. Thompson, "many people want to shake your hand for what you did yesterday. Right now, you're the most famous person in the world. Even if the new religion movement fails, you've gained a permanent place in history."

"Fame and glory aren't my goals, Mr. Thompson," Tasos responded, frowning slightly.

"Of course," said the lawyer, looking somewhat embarrassed.

For the next several minutes, we learned from each of them what digital, physical, and legal security measures were already in place and what would very soon be put into place. Everything seemed under control, and I hoped Tasos would now feel less concerned.

"How are things going with getting other governments on board?" asked Tasos.

"Very well," said Mr. Thompson. "We've finalized the necessary information and guidelines for the governments to make a smooth transition to the new religion. I've just emailed you both the complete document and the executive summary."

Jonathan jumped in at that point to add, "By the way, the emails of everyone in the team are totally encrypted now. The code is incredibly hard to crack." He looked both proud and shy as he declared this.

"Excellent," smiled Tasos.

Mr. Thompson continued, "We've also arranged for five more wealthy people to be healed, three days from now. In total, they'll bring you a billion dollars."

"We're identifying a secure site and making the necessary arrangements for you to get there, do the healings, and leave safely," said the superintendent.

"And I'll be jamming the signals around the location," said Jonathan, "to make sure no one can transmit information to or from there, except for our security team members."

"That all sounds good," said Tasos, nodding.

Mr. Thompson cleared his throat. "I've also received another request from the prime minister and the minister of health. The PM is in Vancouver right now and is hoping to meet with you. The Minister of Health can fly in tonight to be at the meeting too, if you agree to it."

Tasos paused for a moment before answering, then said, "OK, I'll meet with them both at noon tomorrow. Please make the necessary arrangements and let Tom and me know."

"Mr. Perasmas, I'd like to escort you to the secure location where we've arranged for you to stay until further notice," said Superintendent Cooper. "If I'm there in about an hour, would that be all right?"

Tasos looked at me. "Does that work for you, Tom?" I nodded. "Sure," he said.

We all wished each other well and ended the call. As Tasos got up to refill his coffee, a text message came through on my phone. It was from Judge Gilford, asking whether Tasos and I were available to video chat with him.

"Tasos," I said, "the judge would like to speak with us."

"Excellent," he said.

I texted a reply and a few minutes later, the judge's call came through on Zoom.

"Hello, Mr. Newman, Mr. Perasmas," said the judge. "How are you after yesterday's interesting conversation with POTUS?" He was smiling broadly.

"Very well, your honour, how about yourself?" said Tasos.

"Fine, thank you. I sure wish I could have been a fly on the wall of the Oval Office, especially after the conversation ended. I wonder what words were said then."

"Well," I said, "maybe Jonathan was somehow able to hack in and record their conversation." I shrugged. "He's got a lot of initiative. I wouldn't be surprised if he had."

Judge Gilford chuckled. "I'll be sure to ask him." Looking at Tasos, he continued, "Mr. Perasmas, I want to thank you for your great strength in the face of toxic social and political systems, and for restoring my belief that good is stronger than evil."

"It's easy to be strong if you believe in something beautiful,"

Tasos replied.

"Well, you'll be happy to hear that I have great news."

Tasos raised his eyebrows expectantly.

"I've been contacted by four of the twenty countries, confirming they'll comply with the requirements of the new religion—Germany, the Netherlands, Sweden, and Iceland. And they gave me their assurance that they will try to convince the rest to accept the new religion."

"Wow, four already?" Tasos beamed.

"Well, it's not every day that you see someone make the President of the United States go down on his knees. That made a huge impression. He…isn't very popular in the international community, as you know."

"That was one of my reasons for doing it," Tasos replied. "More importantly, he deserved it."

"You won't find me disagreeing with you on that! Now," the judge continued, "the other good news is that the first Citizens Council is ready to start work. They're inspired by your ideology."

"That's wonderful," said Tasos. "The beliefs that I have are very different from the status quo. But people are ready for a drastic change because the old ways have failed horribly and have caused tremendous suffering."

"I want to shake your hand, Mr. Perasmas. When can I see you?"

"Would you like to come with Tom and me to meet the prime minister tomorrow?" Tasos asked.

"I'd like that very much, thank you."

"Okay, then. Mr. Thompson is making the arrangements."

"I'll get in touch with him," said Judge Gilford. "That's all I had to report to you today, gentlemen. So I'll say goodbye for now."

In the time we had before the superintendent's arrival, I caught up on some email while Tasos had a shower.

Shortly after, the doorbell rang and I opened the door to Superintendent Cooper, inviting him in.

"Very happy to see you, Mr. Perasmas," he said as he walked into the living room and extended his hand to Tasos.

"Thank you, Superintendent, same here," Tasos replied with a smile.

I motioned to a chair, and he sat down. He began, "There are a number of things I need to go over with you, Mr. Perasmas. We've arranged for a dozen cell phones, five more identities with all of the requisite paperwork and credit cards and so forth, and five lock-ups around the city. And there will be a personal guard with you at all times from now on."

"Wow, this is amazing. Thank you, Superintendent. I really appreciate your help," Tasos said.

"It's my pleasure and honour," he replied.

For about twenty minutes, the Superintendent reviewed the details of the undercover requirements that would be in play from now on. Everything seemed highly satisfactory, but I detected a shadow of worry in Tasos's features.

"Is something on your mind, Tasos?" I asked.

He looked intently at me and then the superintendent. "It's not just me who's in danger, it's my son Themis, and it's Tom and his family too. I know we talked about this a bit in the video call this morning, but I want to be absolutely sure that everything's being done to protect them too, Superintendent. If anything happens to one of them, it'll be due to me."

"I completely understand. Please believe me, sir, that Mr. Boulen and his team along with me and my team have triple-checked every plan, leaving nothing to chance."

Tasos sat up a bit straighter and loosened his shoulders.

"Thank you, but I'll still worry."

A few minutes later, Tasos and the Superintendent got up to leave. "Please keep an eye on my place, Tom," said Tasos. "I hope to be back there soon, but...who knows?"

Chapter 23

I had writing and other tasks to take care of, but first I wanted to chat with Claire and the kids. I contacted Jonathan who confirmed that it would be safe to make the call. "Mr. Newman, it's all hugely encrypted and it's being monitored 24/7. About twenty of those hours, by me personally," he said with his usual gusto.

"Are you serious?" I asked. "What about sleep?"

"I'm kinda weird that way. If I sleep more than three or four hours a day, I feel really sick, the way 'normal' people do when they're sleep deprived. Something to do with my hardwiring," he said," and I'm a bit obsessive about computer stuff, as you've probably noticed. It's actually awesome for me to be able to devote myself to this all the time. I feel like my life finally has purpose!"

With that reassurance, I went ahead and called my family. Claire and everyone else were doing well out on the farm, which was reassuring. I really missed them. After the call, I felt a weight of sadness settle in my chest. So, I immersed myself in work until late afternoon, when Superintendent Cooper called to talk about the next day's big meeting.

"It's going to be in a community centre in one of the suburbs," he told me. "The building stands in an open landscape which makes it easier for our security people to control the site and the surrounding area, including the air space."

"Who's going to protect Mr. Perasmas?" I asked.

"The only security in and around the building at the time of the meeting will be police officers who are friends of Mr. Perasmas, and some of Mr. Boulen's bikers. The prime minister will have only two security agents with him, with no guns. Mr. Perasmas insisted on this, and the PM has agreed."

I was impressed and told him so. "This is just the tip of our security iceberg, Mr. Newman. If there's anything else you want to know, just ask. Tomorrow morning, I'll be sending two escort vehicles to bring you to the meeting venue. One will drive ahead of you and the other behind."

By the time we finished talking, I felt good about the next day and decided to see what was on TV.

Not surprisingly, Tasos's meeting with the US president was on every news channel. I was also pleased to see that the government guideline document Mr. Thompson had told us about had also been released to the media and was being discussed and analyzed. Tasos will be pleased, I thought.

A political affairs program was starting in a couple of minutes, so I quickly made myself a sandwich and sat down to watch. The program started with footage of the president going down on his knees, while a voiceover introduced the day's topic.

"There's a new man in town, one so powerful that he even put the President of America on his knees. In an unprecedented, live-broadcast interview—at the president's specific request—Tasos Perasmas, the so-called 'Divine Blood,' made it clear what he wants from the US and any other government that wants to use his blood to develop a vaccine and to cure those already stricken with the apocalypse virus."

The screen switched to the program's presenter, a striking woman in her early fifties with a piercing, intelligent gaze. "I'm joined in the studio today by political analyst and University of Toronto law professor Alexis Honing, who has obtained a copy of the guideline document that Mr. Perasmas's team is issuing to governments. This document summarizes the tenets of his 'new religion' and provides guidance for countries to transition their governments to this ideology 'quickly and effectively,' in the document's words. Dr. Honing," she said, turning to her right as the camera showed a second woman seated in the studio, "welcome to Today in Politics."

"Thank you, Doris," said the professor with a tight smile.

"Dr. Honing, tell us, please, about the changes Mr. Perasmas insists on as part of his 'new religion.'"

"Well, there are many changes, and most of them are significant. Some are brutally invasive for politicians and current governments in particular. By that, I mean Canada's as well as the US's. First, government officials and all civil servants will face a fifty-percent pay cut. The guidelines contain specific details about a new salary structure that will apply across the board, not just in government but in private industry as well.

"Another remarkable stipulation is that each government will apologize publicly for the pain and suffering they and all governments before them have caused citizens by governing in ways that benefit very few at the expense of the vast majority. These public apologies will need to be approved by a new entity called the Citizens Council Office before they can be issued.

"There is also going to be a 'war against war,' starting with retiring all ministers of defence and 10,000 of the highest paid military personnel. Firearms will be taken away from the police. Businesses approvals that require environmental evaluations will be halted until new ministries for the environment are fully operational."

The host interjected, "I understand that the new religion bans the word 'boss.' Can you tell us more about that?"

"That's right, Doris. The word 'boss' will be illegal. So it'll no longer be permissible to say, for example, 'The boss says you have to do this' or 'Do I need to remind you who's the boss around here?' Even 'Hey, boss, what can I do for you?' and things like that won't be acceptable."

"And why is this?"

"It's because the new religion is based on respect and equality for everyone. And I have to admit, although a lot of the changes are going to be very radical, they're consistent with this foundation of respect and equality across the board, starting with ordinary citizens."

"Getting back to politicians and government employees, will there be any particular measures introduced in addition to the pay cuts?"

"Yes, time-card clocks will be installed in the House of Commons and all other government offices and facilities. This is based on the principle that citizens have the right to know how their employees spend their working hours. And for transparency, all government operations will be recorded, with the Citizens Council Office having centralized control. All of this information will be available online for citizens. Mr. Perasmas calls this 'power to the people.'"

"What exactly is this Citizens Council Office, professor?"

"It's a group of nine people who are 'very intelligent, peace-loving, moral human beings with the highest level of integrity and the willingness to exclusively represent the citizens' interests.'" She read this from a copy of the guidelines that she'd brought with her to the interview. "The Citizens Council Office will have the power to replace the government, if they wish. In our country, the first Citizens Council Office being established will be led by a highly experienced judge named Timothy Gilford. The Office will keep an eye on the government to make sure it's following citizens' directives."

My cell phone rang, displaying a code that Jonathan had told us we would see whenever one of the core new religion team was calling. I lowered the TV volume and answered. It was Karen, wanting to talk about publicity for the coming days. "Great timing!" I said and began telling her about tomorrow's meeting with the PM and minister of health.

The rest of the day flew by but in a quiet, at-home way that I hadn't had in a while. I even had time for another video chat with Claire. The next day was our fifteenth wedding anniversary and we were both sad about not being together to celebrate. However, it was comforting to at least be able to keep in touch, see her face, and hear her and the kids' voices. By midnight, I couldn't keep my eyes open and hit the sack.

My escorted drive to the meeting venue the next morning was uneventful. Tasos and I were able to talk for about half an hour beforehand, in the room set up for the meeting.

"Are you looking forward to this?" I asked.

"Oh yes." He grinned mischievously. "Do you think I should make the PM go down on his knees too?"

I laughed. "I think you made your point with the president. But," I shrugged, "what're your thoughts?"

"I think you're right, my friend. I'll try to resist the temptation to humiliate him, especially if he's not arrogant."

I glanced out a window and saw Judge Gilford arriving. He was escorted up to the entrance by a burly biker. Turning to Tasos, I chuckled. "The new religion is certainly bringing together people who probably never envisioned being allies before the pandemic broke out."

When the judge entered the room, he practically ran to Tasos, grabbing one of Tasos's hands in both of his and pumping it up and down.

"I'm very glad to see you again, Mr. Perasmas. What you did with the president was very impressive. You're certainly making my job and the Citizens Council's much easier." The judge's eyes glowed.

"Thank you, your honour. I had fun doing it."

The door opened again, and several security personnel came in, some ours and some the prime minister's. Apparently, the two bigwigs were in the building and would be entering the room in a minute or so.

Security agents for the PM stood on either side of the door, inside the room. Tasos approached them and said, "Which one of you is the boss?"

The agents looked at each other, and the one on the right said, "I am, sir."

Tasos then said casually, "Do you want me to put you on your knees?"

The agent turned red. "No, sir. I do not."

"Then get this through your head: No one is the boss. Do you understand? No one. There's no place for that word and that concept in civil discourse. Not anymore."

"Yes, sir. I understand," said the agent. Although he was trained to remain expressionless, I thought I saw a flicker of fear cross his face.

At that moment, the PM and the minister of health arrived. Tasos and I shook hands with them, and the three of them sat down while I remained standing behind a tripod-mounted camera to film the meeting.

The prime minister began the discussion. "Mr. Perasmas, thank you for seeing us. It's a great honour to meet with a fellow Canadian who has saved so many lives in the last couple of weeks."

Tasos nodded his head slightly and looked intently into the prime minister's eyes but remained silent.

"Mr. Perasmas, I need your help." The PM paused, then continued, "I beg you, please save my son's life." His demeanour was very different from the president's, and I wondered how my friend would respond.

Tasos look at him for a couple of seconds, then said, "I'm

sorry to hear that your son is sick, Prime Minister. But that's pretty good leverage for me, isn't it?"

Both politicians were visibly taken aback. Then the PM said, "I appreciate someone who speaks their mind, Mr. Perasmas. Yes. It does give you leverage. And frankly, I'll do anything you ask, within reason, to save my son's life. I'll go down on my knees, if you want."

"That won't be necessary, Prime Minister. But you will need to adopt the new religion and set in motion all of the changes required to bring Canada in line with the new religion."

"Mr. Perasmas," the minister of health interrupted, "as a Canadian, when you know you can help somebody, you have a moral obligation to do so!"

Tasos's back straightened, his eyes widened and his nostrils flared. "You dare to lecture me about my moral obligation while you and your kind have ignored yours? You've got some nerve, Minister. You also have a moral obligation and a legal one to serve the citizens, prioritize their well-being, and improve their health and living conditions. They pay your salary, not mine! But you and your kind have failed. You've done nothing. Talk is worthless. So don't you sit there and lecture me, sir! As the prime minister said, I've saved many lives already. I'll continue doing that, but I'm not going to save his son's life until the Canadian government commits to a radically new way of governing."

The minister looked furious and was about to respond, but the PM put a hand on his forearm to silence him. "What you're asking is impossible, Mr. Perasmas," the prime minister said.

"Have you read the guidelines?" Tasos asked.

"Yes, and the whole Cabinet has as well. We understand that you expect us to publicly declare that the current government and all other governments before us from the beginning of civilization were useless, incompetent power abusers, and to apologize for all the pain and suffering our actions have caused to the citizens. We know you expect us to follow the citizens' mandate and get paid the same as a carpenter."

Tasos nodded.

"That's why it's impossible," the prime minister continued. "We can't agree to this."

"Well, it's only at most ten percent of the human race who will be with you on this. The ones who abuse power, steal, take advantage of working people, manipulate out of sheer greed, and love being slaves to a corrupt system. Very few won't agree that the new religion is a better way of governing. For the remaining ninety percent, the benefits will be crystal clear."

"Mr. Perasmas, you're very difficult to negotiate with," said the minister of health, scowling.

"Negotiate? You think that's what we're doing right now?" Tasos said scornfully.

"Well, what would you call it?"

"This isn't a negotiation. It's an ultimatum."

"Mr. Perasmas," said the PM in a soothing tone, clearly aware of his minister's unhelpful tactics, "you could save millions of lives. Please, whether or not you help my son, give the scientists more of your blood to develop a vaccine."

"So you and your kind can continue your corrupt, rotten policies that create homelessness, child poverty, and despair for the vast majority of the world's population? And you and your friends profit from this misery?" Tasos said. He paused, looked the PM straight in the eye, and intoned, "I will save billions of lives when the new religion is established globally. The billions of people you and your kind's policies will destroy, if I let you. I don't have time for this nonsense, Mr. Prime Minister," and Tasos began to get up from his chair.

Unlike the American president, the PM was an intelligent man who could easily see that Tasos held all the cards and would not be shaken from his conviction or his mission.

"Mr. Perasmas," said the PM, "please, don't leave." Tasos

remained standing for a few moments, then lowered himself slowly into the chair again. "Let's say that Canada and eight other countries agree to change our way of governing, to adopt the new religion. What exactly will we get from you?"

"You will each get one test tube of my blood. And I will cure your son."

"This is very generous of you, Mr. Perasmas. I see there's no other option. With your permission, I'll have this drawn up in writing, and we'll both sign the agreement." Tasos nodded his assent. "Well, we'd better start working on that," said the PM. "Thank you for seeing us. I'll be in touch with your attorney Mr. Thompson, within twenty-four hours with the draft agreement for your review."

The three of them stood up, and Tasos and the PM shook hands. The minister simply walked towards the door, clearly in a huff. Tasos shrugged and smiled at the man's rudeness.

As they and their two security personnel left, I stopped recording and stepped away from the tripod, smiling at Tasos.

Judge Gilford, who had watched the whole discussion in rapt silence, was beaming and said to Tasos, "Well, Mr. Perasmas, I can't wait to see this on the evening news! Your confidence in dealing with the PM was impressive."

"My newspaper and the CBC are waiting for the video," I said. "I'll be reviewing it shortly so we can get it to them."

Tasos smiled at him. "Nothing about the PM or his 'lofty title' impresses me or can shake my beliefs, your honour."

"But you make it look so easy," the judge replied.

"Believing in something beautiful makes everything seem easy," Tasos said. He then turned to me. "Tom, I have some other things to take care of, so I'm leaving now. But if you'll be at the newspaper's offices this afternoon, I'll meet you there. Sound OK?"

"Sounds great, Tasos. See you in a while."

I was finishing up an article to accompany the video of Tasos's meeting when Karen knocked on my door. "I took the liberty of ordering some late lunch for all of us. It'll be here in about ten minutes."

"Perfect," I said. "Tasos just texted that he's a few minutes away."

Behind her, I saw Mr. Callingham approach. His personal transformation had continued, and I now actually quite enjoyed working with him. I invited him into the office, and we sat down to go over the front page one last time. But before we could begin, Tasos came through the main doors and came striding over to my office. His personal security guard stood outside, facing the rest of the newsroom.

"Great timing, Tasos. Take a look at the front page. I think you'll like it."

Tasos and Mr. Callingham shook hands, Tasos inquiring after Jonas's health. My old "boss" smiled joyfully as he replied.

I swivelled the huge monitor on my desk around to show them the front-page layout, which I also had in print version on my desk.

It featured a half-page photograph of the prime minister and the minister of health sitting across from Tasos, the prime minister looking anxious and the minister looking like he was about to explode. Tasos, in contrast, look calm and confident. The headline above the photo read: "This Isn't A Negotiation. It's An Ultimatum."

"It's dynamite!" said Mr. Callingham. He turned to Tasos. "What do you think, Mr. Perasmas?"

"I agree. Great photo, Tom," said my friend. Smiling, he turned to Mr. Callingham. "You're very lucky to have him. I hope you know that."

"That's why he has the big office," joked Mr. Callingham. "I'll have the printers do a double run. And I can't wait to see what our online figures are once this goes live."

When lunch arrived, Tasos and I decided to eat in my office. We had business to discuss, and Karen and Mr. Callingham were hurrying to meet publication deadlines.

After a few pieces of sushi, Tasos said, "I saw Dr. Jekings this morning before the meeting, and she said all is well with my health. So I don't plan on resting, Tom. Tomorrow, I want to head to North Surrey."

"What do you have in mind, Tasos?" I asked, sipping some miso soup.

"There's a lot of poverty, misery, addiction, and crime there. These are more people the government has failed to look after. A lot of them are sick with the virus. I need to go there and help."

I sat back in my chair. "OK. It's a really dangerous area."

"I know. But Mr. Boulen's team knows it inside out, so they'll be keeping an eye on us from a discreet distance. The police will be providing aerial security. I need to do this, Tom, especially after today's meeting. Ordinary citizens need to know that change is coming, swiftly and soon."

I nodded. "All right. Let's do it. But first, let's enjoy the splash that today's 'it's not a negotiation' will make in the news." He laughed, and we tucked into our lunch.

Chapter 24

At 3:00 p.m. the next day, we met at 106th Avenue and 1356th Street in Surrey. Tasos wasn't in disguise, and this worried me. But Mr. Boulen was there with several of his team, and he reassured us.

"The people you'll be seeing today are only vaguely aware of what's going on in the wider world," Mr. Boulen said. "They've got so much misery in their own lives, they don't care about the news. A lot of them use alcohol and drugs to numb themselves." He glanced away, looking uncomfortable, then resumed. "I'm not proud of my past actions, what I've done that's contributed to this misery. My organization has made billions of dollars in the drug trade. We can't undo the damage but we can make changes. And I know that the best way to do this will be through your new religion, sir." He looked at Tasos, shame and penitence written across his tough, scarred face.

Tasos placed a hand on Mr. Boulen's shoulder and nodded. "We all have things in our past that we regret deeply," he said. "Often, we don't have the opportunity to undo the harms we've caused. But sometimes, we do. I'm grateful that you and your team are with me to support this great cause. You're vital to ensuring that the new religion spreads worldwide. In the long run, you'll end up helping far, far more people than you've hurt!"

Mr. Boulen beamed, then turned and motioned for two of his team to come over. A woman named Dominique and a man named Sebastien removed their motorcycle helmets, walked over, and shook Tasos's hand then mine.

"It's an honour to meet you, Mr. Perasmas," said the woman. "And Mr. Newman, I think you're doing an excellent job of providing information to the public. Your reporting is outstanding."

I thanked her, trying unsuccessfully to hide my surprise at how well-spoken and polished she seemed, despite her intimidating outward appearance.

She smiled. "Members of our organization don't necessarily fit the stereotype perpetuated on TV and in movies. But please don't be embarrassed. I'm used to it."

The five of us had a brief discussion about where Tasos would go and how the security detail would function. "The cops aren't involved today," said Mr. Boulen. "They stand out in this part of the city, and everybody hates them. Usually for good reason."

For the next couple of hours, we went from one scene of misery to another, travelling along streets strewn with trash. Many storefronts were boarded up. The only ones thriving were pawn shops, same-day loan businesses, and liquor stores. And there were plenty of all three.

In a squalid apartment building, we visited a family of five, four of whom were infected and clearly close to death. There was also an unemployed construction worker and his wife on the floor below. Tasos spent time with all of them and provided healing. Everyone promised to adopt the new religion.

This scenario with slight variations repeated itself over and over. We also visited a few homeless shelters and a "tent city" set up in a park, nearly every one of the tents containing sick individuals. Tasos healed everyone he met, and I recorded it all. The misery we witnessed was intense, and I had to keep reminding myself that soon, such scenes would be history.

It was near dusk and heavy, dark grey clouds were gathering as we left a church hall where a dozen of the city's poorest citizens lay critically ill. As thunder began to roll in the distance, we decided to call it a day and began walking back to my van. Suddenly from between some parked cars, three stocky men in ill-fitting suits emerged and walked towards us. Something didn't feel right. "Suits in this part of Surrey…?" I began to say to Tasos, when all three drew guns.

Tasos grabbed me and dragged me down and around behind the SUV. Bullets ricocheted off the vehicle's hood where we'd been a second before. We then heard the rev of a high-powered motorbike and the squeal of tires as Dominique approached from the end of the street, behind the men.

Meanwhile, Sebastien appeared from the other end and was returning fire on the three gunmen. In rapid succession, he felled all three with shots to their gun hands and legs.

Dominique wove expertly around the writhing men, stopped at my van, and tossed a helmet to Tasos. "Mr. Perasmas, with me!" Tasos leapt to his feet, donned the helmet, and got on the bike behind her. "Mr. Newman, Sebastien is coming for you now."

"What about the shooters?" I asked.

"Mr. Boulen will deal with them," she said over the idling motor. "We want them alive, to find out who they're working for."

As she revved the bike, Tasos gestured to me with his hand that we'd talk later on the phone. I nodded and waved as Sebastien pulled up to get me. As I too put on a helmet, I saw Mr. Boulen and two more of his team pulling the now handcuffed men to their feet. The erstwhile shooters were shrieking about the pain in their hands and legs. Although the sound of Sebastien's motorbike was too loud for me to hear the words, I saw Mr. Boulen's lips say, "Oh, yeah? Poor baby!" before we left the scene.

I didn't envy the sort of night those men were going to have. And I admit that I didn't feel a shred of pity.

By the time we arrived at my house, the adrenalin in my body had subsided but my heart was still beating faster than I would have liked. Although I had covered the news in Surrey for many years, I'd never personally witnessed a shooting let alone been the target of one. As I waved off Sebastien, who had politely declined my invitation to stay for coffee and food, I muttered to myself, "I hope this isn't something I need to get used to."

What had started off as a reasonably quiet day hadn't ended as one. I switched on the TV, grabbed a cold drink from the fridge, put some leftover lasagna in the microwave, and sat down to process the incident. Everything had happened so fast. That's guns for you. I shook my head. "Can't wait for society to be rid of the damn things."

About an hour later, the TV displayed a "breaking news" banner that said: "Shooting in Surrey: Attack on Tasos Perasmas." I was about to turn up the volume when my phone chimed, indicating an incoming request for a video chat. It was Tasos.

"Hi Tom. How are you, my friend?"

"Still a bit rattled, Tasos, but OK otherwise. More importantly, how are you?"

"Oh, I'm fine," he said. "That was a bit unnerving, but not as bad as the pirates back when I was in the merchant navy. Still, I'm glad we had Mr. Boulen and his friends there. Otherwise I don't think we'd be having this conversation."

"I wonder what information he'll extract from them about who they're working for."

"We'll find out in due course," he said. "I have to take some responsibility for it, Tom, and I'm very sorry."

"What do you mean?"

"I wasn't in disguise. That was careless of me, and it won't happen again. No more public exposure unless I'm disguised. We also won't be doing any more spontaneous visits, at least not for the foreseeable future. Planned ones only, so our security team can better manage the risks. We have a dozen lined up in the next ten days, starting tomorrow. Jonathan says we'll be at $50 billion at that point. Maybe even more."

"Amazing," I said. "So where will you be going tomorrow?"

"Well, the Greek community has asked for my help. There are some kids and some adults who need to be cured."

"May I come with you to record the healing sessions?" I asked.

"Please do. But Tom," he paused. "Wear a loose shirt and jacket, OK? Our security team thinks we should have bulletproof vests from now on whenever we're out in the community. They'll be taking every precaution to prevent our whereabouts being known ahead of time, but they'd like us to be wearing Kevlar. The vests fit under regular clothing if you're wearing something loose. Are you OK with that?"

I shrugged. "Sure. You won't find me arguing with the security experts, Tasos."

"Excellent. Then meet me tomorrow at 11:30 a.m. at a restaurant in Kitsilano called Zeus," he said.

"I know that place, Tasos. Amazing food."

He smiled. "The owners are old friends of mine. Make sure you come with an empty stomach!"

We said goodbye shortly thereafter. Getting myself a bowl of ice cream, I had a video chat with Claire and the kids, then spent a couple of hours writing about the day's events before hitting the sack.

That night my dreams were disturbing, full of dark alleys and gunfire. I woke up in a cold sweat, heart pounding. Through the bedroom window, I could see traces of rose-pink in the sky. Realizing I was unlikely to get back to sleep, I headed for the shower.

I remembered Tasos's advice about bringing an appetite to the restaurant, so kept breakfast quick and light. I then tossed on a jacket, grabbed my soft-sided briefcase and my travel mug full of coffee, and headed to the van. I wanted to stop at the newspaper to do a few things before meeting with Tasos.

As I walked into the office, the entire staff stood up and began clapping and cheering. At first, I thought it was about yesterday's shooting situation, but then I realized they were congratulating me on the article covering the prime minister's meeting with Tasos.

Mr. Callingham came out of his office and shook my hand after several of my colleagues had also done so. "Fabulous job, Tom. Will you be here for a little while?"

"About an hour. Then I'm heading out to cover a story," I said.

"If you have time, there's something I'd like to talk to you about."

As I walked into my office, Karen came in with a fresh cup of coffee and offered me pastries from the bakery a few doors down. I couldn't resist taking one.

"Thanks, Karen. I just stopped in to do a couple of things before I have to be in the city for a story."

"There's a young man here who wants to talk with you. He didn't make an appointment, just dropped in to the office hoping you'd have a few minutes."

"What does he want to talk about?"

"He's a university student with an assignment from one of his profs. I didn't want to be nosey, so that's all I know. He was keen to emphasize that he won't take up much of your time."

"Sure, please send him in."

A young man entered, tucking a surgical mask into his jacket pocket, and said, "Good morning, Mr. Newman. Thanks very much for agreeing to see me. I'm George Logan."

He was tall and slim, with blonde hair and an engaging smile. I put him at about 25. His voice was on the quiet side, but he spoke clearly and with a calm confidence untainted by arrogance.

"Please, have a seat, George, and tell me what you'd like to talk to me about." I was aware of not having much time, but I didn't want him to feel rushed.

"Well, sir, I'm a fourth-year university student doing a double major in political science and sociology. I've been reading your articles, following everything you've written and recorded about Tasos Perasmas. His meetings with the president and the prime minister were mind-blowing. I'm fascinated and excited by the new religion, and I'm working on an end-of-term paper about it—specifically, addressing criticisms of it and showing why it's the best alternative to any existing socio-political ideology. I didn't think something like this would ever happen in my lifetime, but now…it's happening! I'd like to get information about the movement from first-hand sources—you and, if possible, Mr. Perasmas himself."

I had a good feeling about this fellow. He seemed intelligent, articulate, and sincere. "Well, young man, I think Mr. Perasmas will find what you're doing very interesting."

"Really, Mr. Newman? That's fantastic."

"Please, call me Tom. I'll talk to him, George, and if he can't find the time to see you, I'll help you with details. I'll also introduce you to the Citizens Council members. They'll have a lot more information too."

George beamed. "I really appreciate this, Mr.—I mean, Tom."

"Leave your email and phone number with Karen, and I'll get back to you later today or tomorrow."

He stood up, thanking me again, and we shook hands before he left my office and went to speak with Karen.

I decided to find out what Mr. Callingham wanted to speak with me about, so I walked over to his office. The door was open and he motioned me to come in.

"Please, shut the door behind you, Tom, and make yourself comfortable."

"Thank you, Mr. Callingham." I sat down on a leather couch, and he came around from his desk to sit in a matching chair.

"Tom you've done an excellent job with your coverage of the Divine Blood. You don't need me to tell you that, but still I want to thank you for bringing our news outlet international recognition. I've been getting emails and phone calls from Europe, and I've closed a few very lucrative syndication deals. Of course, our whole financial model will be changing, adjusting to the new religion. I'm excited to think about the ways we'll be able to channel this additional revenue into social programs for our community."

It warmed my heart to see how this once angry man had gained a new lease on life, a new, positive focus for his energies. I smiled and waited for him to explain why he'd asked to speak with me.

"Tom, what do you think of recording an extended interview with Mr. Perasmas? I'm thinking an hour-long program, just you and him in conversation about the new religion, which will be broadcast globally. Do you think Mr. Perasmas would be amenable to the idea?"

I had been contemplating this notion myself for the past couple of days and had intended to ask Tasos about it after the healing sessions in Surrey. But, the mystery shooters had put that plan on hold.

"I think it's a superb idea, Mr. Callingham, and I believe Mr. Perasmas will think so too."

He smiled and said, "Then, Tom, you'll be able to retire if you want to! The money from this will be phenomenal, and..."

I held up a hand, and he stopped, looking puzzled. I

waited to see whether he would understand, and within a few moments, realization dawned on him. He looked sheepish.

"Please forgive me, Tom. I slipped back into old ways of thinking about money, profits, salaries, and so forth."

I chuckled. "It happens to me too, Mr. Callingham. It'll take all of us some practice to get out of the old ways of thinking. And that said, I would like to retire one day. But not just yet. There's still so much to do." I looked at him inquiringly and asked, "Is there anything else right now? It's just that I need to get to the city and I have a couple of things to take care of here before I leave."

"No, that's it, Tom. I look forward to hearing what Mr. Perasmas says when you ask him about the interview."

For the next quarter hour, I sat with Karen going over some details in the article about the healing session in Surrey and the surprising turn it had taken. I also told her that I would have another article tomorrow or the day after. "I'm heading out to cover the story now. I can't tell you more—for your own safety, it's better that you don't know. But I'm hoping to send you a first draft tonight."

Karen said, "Speaking of safety, one of the security team dropped off a package for you this morning." She reached down beside her desk and produced a box. "It's fairly heavy," she remarked as she passed it to me.

The box had nothing on the outside to indicate its contents, but I was quite sure it would be the Kevlar vest. I thanked her and went to get my jacket and briefcase from my office. Giving a quick wave to a few people as I left, I took the stairs two at a time and was driving towards the city within a couple of minutes.

Chapter 25

I arrived at the restaurant about five minutes early, so I opened the box as I waited in my car. It contained the vest, as I'd expected. Looking around the mostly quiet neighbourhood, I made sure no one would be looking, then quickly slipped off my shirt, donned the vest, pulled it snug around me, and put the shirt back on.

As I was doing this, a text message came through. It was from Tasos: "*Bring van 2 back door of resto pls.*"

Driving around to the alley behind Zeus, I pulled into one of four parking spaces and killed the engine. The back door of the restaurant opened, and I recognized one of the police officers in Tasos's security detail. I quickly walked from my vehicle to the door and went inside. He shut the door behind me, and my eyes had to adjust to the dimness of the interior.

"Tom, there you are. Are you wearing your vest?" Tasos's voice came to me from nearby, although I couldn't see him.

"Yes."

"Good. OK, let's go in."

From the darkened storeroom we walked quickly through the kitchen, where a few staff were busy but gave us friendly smiles and nods. As we entered the dining area, we were immediately greeted in a foreign language by half a dozen older men and women.

Tasos grinned at me and said, "It's all Greek to you, right Tom?"

"Exactly," I replied.

"They're welcoming us and thanking us for coming."

"Did you already get their permission to have this recorded, Tasos?"

He nodded, then said something to them in Greek. "Yes, but I've just asked them again, to be sure, and they confirm that they're happy to have you recording this."

One of the women stepped forward and said in English, "They're in our banquet room, Mr. Perasmas. Please, come this way."

In a large separate room, there were ten beds, each occupied. Five of the sick were in their late teens or early twenties. There were also two small children and three adults in their thirties who appeared to be the little ones' parents. Everyone looked wasted and only days from death.

Tasos said a few words in Greek, then switched to English: "Don't worry. You will all be OK by tomorrow. I promise."

At each bedside as he went about the cure, Tasos exchanged a few words with the patient. Sometimes, all the person could manage was a weak smile. He took his time, but we were still finished before noon.

As Tasos had anticipated, those who had invited him asked us to stay for lunch, and what a lunch it was. The food was magnificent, and I had the sense that for the first time in many, many months, our hosts were able to truly enjoy a meal, happy in the knowledge that their loved ones would soon be well again.

At one point, I had the opportunity to quietly ask Tasos whether we could talk afterward. He nodded. "How about we go back to the hotel where I'm staying. We can talk for as long as you like."

We cleared this with his security detail before leaving the restaurant, and they told me which route to take to the hotel. "It's important that you not follow us. Someone may know your vehicle and then make the connection with ours." The route was circuitous, taking me through Stanley Park and part of the West End, but I eventually arrived at the hotel and was ushered up to Tasos's suite.

He was reclining on a sofa, eyes closed, when I entered the room with a guard, but he sat up immediately and motioned me to a seat.

"Tasos, I can see that you're a bit tired, so I won't stay long," I began. "What do you think about us doing an extended interview for global broadcasting?"

"By 'us' do you mean just you and me, Tom?"

I nodded. "Yes. I'm thinking an hour, no commercials. It would be me asking you questions about the new religion. People want to know what it is, what it will involve, what it will lead to. This would be 'New Religion 101' in an hour. A special broadcast for the citizens from the biggest champion of the citizens." I paused. "What do you think, my friend?"

Tasos looked at me seriously, then a huge smile broke across his face. "I think it's a fantastic idea, Tom. Yes! Let's do this. And the sooner the better. When were you thinking of?"

I shrugged. "How soon can you be ready?"

He got up and fetched a small notebook from a side table. Flipping it open, he said, "Well, tomorrow's healing session is scheduled for 2:00 p.m., so how about tomorrow morning? I can spend the remainder of today resting. I don't feel particularly tired, but I have to keep Dr. Jekings happy." His eyes glinted mischievously.

"Sounds great," I said. "I'll arrange for cameras, lighting, and the rest. And I'll talk with the security team to put them in the loop."

I got out my phone to text Superintendent Cooper and Mr. Boulen, then saw that the superintendent had texted me a few minutes earlier: "*need 2 meet asap pls call me.*"

"As it happens, the superintendent wants to meet with me,

Tasos," I said.

"Well, how about I call you at 6:00 p.m., and you can update me?"

"Sure. Oh, before I go, one more thing." I told Tasos about my visit from George Logan, and the student's request to learn more about the new religion, preferably first-hand. "I'm going to ask our security team to run thorough checks on him, of course," I said. "But if everything checks out and there's no red flags, how would you feel about him watching the interview then asking you a few questions afterwards?"

Tasos nodded. "Tom, I trust your judgement, as you know. If this George Logan is legit, he sounds like another potential messenger of the new religion. We need honest people from all walks of life, including academia, to achieve this enormous transformation."

We said goodbye and I was soon back in my vehicle, leaving the hotel parkade. I called the superintendent.

"Mr. Newman," he said, "thank you for calling me back so quickly. Can you meet me now?" He gave me the address for a coffee shop in Kerrisdale, which I was able to reach in about twenty minutes.

He was sitting at a table when I arrived, but got up and said, "Let's go outside rather than talk in here. I'll meet you in the park across the street."

I quickly purchased a large dark-roast coffee and went to join him. We shook hands.

"Superintendent, I was going to text you, but you beat me to it. Seems we both have things to talk about, although it sounds like yours are more urgent than mine."

His face was serious as he nodded. We began to walk briskly along a path away from the street.

"I'll get right to the point," he said. "We have a big problem. The commissioner of the RCMP has issued a warrant for Mr. Perasmas's arrest."

I choked on my coffee and had to stop walking.

"Here, let's sit down on that bench over there," he said.

Seated, I said to him, "How is this possible? Is it because of the interview with the PM?"

He shook his head. "I don't know. I haven't gotten to the bottom of it yet. I'm just one of 187 superintendents across the country, so it's taking me some time to find out. I have to be careful who I talk to. I do know that the minister of health, the minister of justice, and the commissioner belonged to the same fraternity in university, and they're all Freemasons, so…"

"Wow." I exhaled slowly. "Do you think they bypassed the prime minister?"

"I think they did, and he's going to be furious. But they might be taking a calculated gamble. The two ministers are arrogant pricks, and if they figure they can get the rest of the Cabinet on their side, they might even try to oust the PM. We'll have to see how that political side of things plays out in the coming days. But right now, our immediate problem is keeping Mr. Perasmas from being arrested."

"What do you suggest?"

"Ideally, he needs to disappear for a week or two, until we see how this unfolds in the political arena."

I rubbed my face with both hands and exhaled slowly. "I understand, but I think we both know that's not going to happen. He has an urgent mission, and he's not going to go into hiding."

"I was afraid you'd say that, and I know you're right. I'm not quite sure what to do at this point. I'm meeting with the entire security team in two hours." He sighed. "What was it you wanted to speak with me about, Mr. Newman?"

"Well, it might be something you don't want us to consider at this point. But we plan to do an hour-long interview tomorrow, just me interviewing Mr. Perasmas about the new religion." I told him what Tasos and I had discussed, and that he was ready to do it as soon as I could organize the camera and lighting crews. "But I'm guessing you don't want this kind of exposure right now," I concluded.

To my surprise, the superintendent's face displayed keen interest and even some relief. "Actually, I think this is perfect," he said.

"Really?"

"Yes. You said it would be broadcast globally, right?"

"That's correct. I suggest we coordinate with the BBC, like we did for the meeting with the president. They already have all the syndication relationships in place, the satellites, the whole nine yards. And they're the most reliable, trustworthy broadcasting corporation in the world," I said.

"Then I think we should go ahead with this as soon as possible. Are you OK with conducting the interview in the suite where he's staying?" he asked and I nodded. "Good. That keeps things simple. Now, in terms of your camera and lighting crew, please don't be offended, but we can't take any risks about a security leak. Nobody can find out where Mr. Perasmas is staying. So instead of using your colleagues, I'd like to use some of our security team. A few of Mr. Boulen's organization are skilled camera operators and lighting technicians."

I was surprised. "Really? They don't strike me as film types."

He looked at me pointedly with one eyebrow raised. "They're involved in a branch of the film industry that isn't particularly…mainstream, if you get my meaning."

Realization dawned in me after a few moments. "You mean—?"

"Yes, the adult movie industry. Nothing illegal or unsavoury, though."

I shrugged. "As long as they can do a professional job of it, their prior experience is irrelevant as far as I'm concerned."

"Then let me bring them into the plan at the meeting this evening."

"Great. But Superintendent, why do you think this is a good idea, given there's a warrant out for Tasos's arrest?"

"Because once the interview airs, the citizens of Canada and the rest of the world will see what the new religion is about. They'll understand how it will bring down corrupt governments worldwide but without bloodshed—unless those governments dare to make war on their own citizens. Then, there's no way the commissioner will arrest Mr. Perasmas. There will be such a hue and cry about the warrant that the commissioner will be forced to cancel it. The PM will then be able to rein in his rogue ministers. Maybe he'll even fire them; that would be the smartest move. In any case, the interview will force that trio's hand. They'll be totally blindsided."

As the beauty of this simple plan became clear to me, I started to grin. "You know, it's like Tasos told me. This is all part of a larger design, and things are unfolding as they should."

Chapter 26

The next morning, I joined Tasos for a hearty breakfast in his suite. We were both looking forward to the interview, and as the camera and lighting crew arrived, the atmosphere in the room was lighthearted and congenial. "No outside observer would guess that this room contains Canada's most wanted man," I said to him.

"Most wanted, but by different people for very different reasons!" he joked. I marvelled at his composure and put it down to the strength of his belief—in himself and in the cause he was devoted to making a reality for the entire world.

My smartphone pinged. It was a text message from the superintendent, informing me that one of the security team was about two minutes away bringing George Logan. During my conversation with the superintendent the previous day, I'd let him know about George. It hadn't taken him long to get back to me with an "all clear." "Clean as a whistle. He's been arrested twice: once at an Occupy Wall Street protest and the second time more recently at a Fridays for Future gathering. Both times, a few police got carried away and started slapping handcuffs on people they said were threatening violence. Videos taken by onlookers showed it was actually the officers who'd been making the threats of violence, so he was released without charge in each situation, and the officers were disciplined." He shook his head. "Bloody embarrassment, some of the police officers I've had to deal with over the years. Frankly, it'll be a relief to me that they're no longer carrying guns!"

True to the superintendent's text, George soon appeared accompanied by a guard. I shook his hand. Tasos was already seated in one of the interview chairs, gazing out a window. I said to George, "We need to get the interview under way. I'll introduce you to Tasos afterward. You'll be in a better position information-wise to ask him questions then."

George nodded vigorously, and I invited him to take a seat on one of the couches, out of the interview chairs' sightlines. One of the camera crew brought him a glass of water. "If you feel like you're going to cough, drink some water. If you still feel like you're going to cough—or if you think you're going to sneeze—then get up as quietly as possible and leave the room. We can edit out background noise, but it's easier if the noise isn't there in the first place."

Shortly before 9:30 a.m., Oliver the crew supervisor said, "Mr. Newman, Mr. Perasmas, we're ready when you are."

We sat down in two comfortable armchairs angled at ninety degrees to one another, and one of the crew fitted us with lapel mics. The lighting technician made a few adjustments, then gave a thumbs up to the three camera operators.

"OK," said Oliver when I gave him a nod, "roll it."

I looked into one camera and began. "A year ago, no one could have predicted the scale of death, or the physical and psychological suffering of humankind that is occurring worldwide right now, due to the apocalypse virus. Until six weeks ago, it seemed this pandemic spelled the end of our species. But inside this terrifying darkness of biblical proportions, a bright light appeared. I'm Tom Newman, senior journalist for the Surrey Post, and today I have the honour of being here with the man who is that light: Mr. Tasos Perasmas. For the next hour, we'll be talking about the new religion, bringing clarity and understanding about it to citizens around the world. Thank you for agreeing to this interview, Mr. Perasmas." I turned to him.

"Thank you, Tom, for giving me this opportunity. And please, Tasos is fine."

"OK. Well, Tasos, there are so many things you've done in such a short time, but I think I'll start with a simple question that a lot of people are asking: Who are you? Many people call you the 'Divine Blood' or the 'Light Worker,' saying your ability to miraculously cure people of the apocalypse virus means you're here with a divine purpose. Are you a divine being?"

"Well," smiled Tasos, "I can save people's lives, but I'm not sure about the divine being thing. The scientists are saying that my blood cells are like a combination of kamikaze fighters and the mythical Hydra, which had an infinite capacity to multiply and rejuvenate themselves. So, maybe there is a more down-to-earth explanation."

"With your divine blood, you've already saved hundreds of lives for free, and you're charging the rich to save their lives. As a result, you've quickly become one of the wealthiest people on the planet. You've also spoken with the President of the United States and with the Prime Minister of Canada. About two billion viewers saw you dominate and humiliate the president, making him beg you to save his son's life. Virtually overnight, you've become a very powerful man, and this has some people inspired and other people scared. You say you're bringing the 'new religion.' Tell us about this new religion."

"With pleasure, Tom. It all begins with respect and equality," said Tasos. For the next several minutes, Tasos sketched the basics of the new religion, from its foundations of respect, equality, and power to the people, through to the three basic principles of abolishing guns and the word 'boss,' and making protection of the environment a sacred responsibility for everyone. He spoke about the Citizens Council Office and the establishment of governments that citizens can actually trust.

He also went into the details about how earning structures would be radically redefined, and corporate profits reallocated to support social programs.

"All of the change, Tom, starts by addressing the fundamental cause of the bad, unfair things that currently bring suffering to humankind. As an old saying goes, the fish stinks from the head first. The governments currently in charge are corrupt, and the responsibility for the massive scale of human suffering globally is a result of their immorality and misdeeds. It's their fault that so many citizens are suffering, and living in perpetually high states of stress and fear for their futures and their children's futures. Governments across the political spectrum have lost the trust of citizens. They fail at the most basic level of ensuring citizens feel safe. In fact, they and the wealthiest one percent of the population ensure that ordinary people feel unsafe, insecure, and constantly at the mercy of governments, stock markets, and the almighty profit motive. Ever since Hiroshima and Nagasaki, ordinary citizens have lived in fear of nuclear annihilation. Now, with our complete dependence on digital technology, some pissed-off terrorist could send us back to the Stone Age, paralyzing our basic infrastructure, and turning us against each other like savages just to get food and clean water.

The AV pandemic that has wiped out more than a billion people is yet another instance of government failure on a massive scale. So yes, this looks like a biblical End of Days. But in reality, it's simply that humankind has reached a turning point in how we are going to function as a society. And around the corner is not total annihilation but a new dawn, not just for our species but for the whole planet." Tasos smiled.

"Can you tell us more about this turning point, Tasos?" I asked.

"I'd love to," he replied. "From the beginning of time, when humans began organizing themselves into communities, towns, cities, and countries, the leaders of these communities, towns, cities, and countries have shaped our societies by imposing laws, rules, and regulations on citizens. Now, after a few thousand years of these laws, rules, and regulations being updated and twisted to look after the interests of fewer and fewer of the citizens, we've reached a point where citizens have had enough. Enough of the authoritarian governments that create homelessness, wars, and lack of healthcare coverage. Enough of corporations' complete disrespect for the environment. Fortunately, the amazing communication technology available to us today has allowed for the exposure of the corruption that lies at the heart of our governments and our economic systems. We're finding out about expense scandals, about physical, sexual, mental, and emotional abuse by those with power, about 'public servants' paid obscenely high salaries while children go to school inadequately clothed and undernourished. The evidence is there. It's clear who has the money and who calls the shots.

"War, terrorism, famine, and other crises are in the news every day. We've become numb to the scale of suffering all around us. And all the while, those in power are swimming in their millions and billions of dollars. Our political and religious leaders live like kings, lacking nothing. For citizens, only one thing is sure apart from their ongoing suffering; drastic change is absolutely necessary. Social inequality must end. The devastation of our environment must end. The flagrant disregard for life—human and nonhuman—must end. A new way of thinking is the only thing that will save us and the Earth. It will be an approach where science and spirituality meet for the good of all humanity. Then we will live on a planet without war and without human-made environmental disasters, where citizens live in peace rather than fear and don't need to worry about how they will look after themselves and their families." He paused and reached for a glass of water, taking a long sip.

"So really, you're proposing a deep and lasting equality, justice, and happiness for everyone?" I asked.

"Exactly, Tom. The new religion is a 'happiness-creation belief.' There will be a tiny percentage who will be very unhappy with the new religion, but those are the power abusers, the trust abusers, the unethical, corrupted, authoritarian, selfish ones, those who until now have been the cancer of our societies. These will be publicly shamed, the way we shame drunk drivers and sex offenders," Tasos explained.

"Can you give us some examples of how you'll achieve social equality?"

"There are so many things that we can and will do, but the first priority for the government, the new citizens' government, will be to eliminate child poverty and homelessness. We'll need strict time frames, and this will be one of the areas the Citizens Council Office in each country will oversee. Goals without targets and deadlines are doomed to fail, and failure is not an option for the new religion. Not a single person will be homeless. Not a single child will go to school hungry ever again. The governments have failed, and the citizens will discipline them for their incompetence. Previous so-called housing strategies haven't been enough. They never were. Everyone has the right to a safe, clean, adequate home, and it's the job of governments to provide this. By providing shelter and food, and reinforcing every single individual's human dignity, all of us can become useful and productive members of society. In some cases, we'll confiscate properties for developments that will benefit citizens. The rich will be forced to recognize that capitalism and authoritarianism have failed. Societies the world over that have bred corruption, abuse of power, mistreatment of citizens, inequality, racism, discrimination, division, and so many other deformations of human dignity, are doomed. From now on, the new religion will be putting the power into the citizens' hands."

"Tasos, these are very drastic changes that have to take place," I said.

"Yes, I know and I realize that governments will have to work hard. And I say it's high time they did, so citizens finally see the government working for citizens' benefit," Tasos replied with a smile.

"Can we talk a bit about the plan to get rid of guns, even from the police and the military?"

"Of course, Tom. Well, the devastation caused by wars and other violence needs no explanation, does it? Mothers, fathers, brothers, sisters, friends, have voids in their hearts from losing loved ones to war, to terrorism, to acts of planned or random violence. In any war, far more innocent civilians end up suffering and dying than military personnel. In the past decade, we've been witnessing the largest movement of refugees globally since the Second World War. And let's not forget the drug wars, where innocent people get killed by stray bullets as they walk along the sidewalk or sit peacefully in their living rooms.

"Guns kill people, and you're several more times likely to die from gun violence if your skin isn't white. The United States is drowning in gun violence. How many more lives have to be lost at the hands of lunatics that have access to guns and want to go out in a blaze of carnage? The psychological and emotional pain of a person who has lost a loved one from gun violence never goes away. And it isn't just random lunatics. A small but deadly percentage of police walk around every day, exercising lethal force against citizens, most of the time with impunity.

"And how about our military leaders and diplomats who fail to promote peace, holding phony conventions and summits that have peace on the agenda? Meanwhile, their own countries are manufacturing the guns, bombs, jets, and surface-to-air missiles used in the very wars they pretend to be opposing. So all these 'peace talks' are pure, monumental hypocrisy.

The same people in government that pretend to be pro peace turn around and declare wars, commit atrocities like bombing civilians and hospitals, killing innocent kids by the dozens, so the so-called peace-loving governments can establish control over other nations' citizens—in the name of democracy and freedom. If a smaller, weaker country doesn't agree to be 'liberated' by one of these more powerful countries, they face military invasion or political destabilization from forces within that are financed and armed by the powerful nations.

"So in order to stop genocides, famine, homelessness, refugees, and so much more psychological and physical human suffering, there is only one action the citizens can take. We need to declare war on war, and this starts by banning guns and other high-powered weapons of any kind." Tasos said with passion. At my prompting, he then went into some detail about removing the top-earning military officials so the funds could be used for constructive purposes such as social programs, and then gradually phasing out armies altogether.

"What about all the army personnel who will lose their jobs?" I asked. "How will they support their families?"

"Those in non-combat occupations—doctors, cooks, mechanics, electricians, and so on—will be assisted with finding employment outside of the armed forces. Those who have been trained to fight and to kill will also be helped to reintegrate into civilian life. They'll require more assistance, but when it comes to funding, the vast amounts of money that will be shifted away from waging wars and maintaining huge standing armies, over to caring rather than destroying will, I'm confident, be more than sufficient to rehabilitate and retrain everyone. We're talking trillions and trillions of dollars every year, Tom, and that's just the US military. The sums are phenomenal."

"So no guns and no armies at all?" I asked.

"Some people say it's premature to talk this way. I say that these people are either blind, or fools, or working for the guns and weapons manufacturers."

"What if another country attacks us and we don't have an army to defend and protect ourselves?" I asked.

He nodded. "Look, I'm not naïve. It's going to take about fifty years to fully achieve this outcome, and we will dismantle the armies gradually. During that phasing-out period, we can recruit veterans who are still capable, in cases of extreme emergency. So we're not going to be in more danger than we are right now," Tasos replied.

"Earlier, you mentioned refugees. How do you believe the current global refugee crisis should be resolved, and who should pay for that?"

"The countries that produce weapons and other military equipment, which are responsible for this misery, will cover the costs," Tasos replied.

After a few more minutes discussing how the plight of war refugees would be addressed, I raised the topic of migrants displaced due to economic hardship and climate change. This led Tasos to spend a significant amount of time on the no-pollution principle. He explained in detail why this was crucial, and how the current harmful regulatory practices would be halted and replaced with systems that were genuinely dedicated to protecting the planet rather than corporate profits.

Tasos summed up by saying, "It's well known that Mother Earth can provide us with geothermal energy that, if properly harvested, will last thousands of years. Plus, we have wind, water, and solar energy. Citizens know this and aren't willing to wait any longer. We're not going to allow the destruction of our planet to go beyond the point of no return. With the new religion, the citizens will put a stop to this outrageous abuse of our precious Earth. We won't just halt the destruction; we'll rejuvenate the world."

"What about oil and natural gas extraction, Tasos?"

"Again, we have the technology to use non-polluting sources for power generation. We just have to work on expanding these other sources. And this will create just as many jobs as the ones that will be eliminated by getting rid of oil and natural gas use," he replied.

"Tasos, what if other countries don't want to cooperate?" I asked.

"Well, the countries that follow the new religion are only going to do trade and business with each other. Any country that doesn't follow it, well..." he shrugged. "Frankly, they're going to die out, Tom. I refuse to provide help to anyone who continues to believe that the old, corrupt, profit-driven ways should continue. It's that simple."

"Let's talk a bit about the profit motive, Tasos. What is the new religion's perspective on profit?"

He smiled and replied, "Profit and all the ugly things that represent and stem from this motive will be gone. There are far more beautiful things to be motivated by, like social equality, respect, and the right of everyone to live without fear about an uncertain tomorrow for themselves and their families. The only acceptable profit will be profit in knowledge."

"So what actions will be taken to deal with existing profits, some of which are humongous, generated by corporations or individuals?"

"The government will find ways to return the profit reaped by any individual or company to the rightful owners: the citizens. One method will be by companies with massive profits reducing the price of the products they sell. And the result will be deflation," he explained.

"Oh Tasos, the rich aren't going to like you very much," I said, smiling.

He shrugged and smiled as well. "Any kind of social change makes some people unhappy and disappointed. If the wealthy want to get out and protest, that will be their right. And I wish them lots of luck, because they're going to need it!"

"Tasos, we've ranged across so many topics during this hour, and there are many more that we could cover."

"Well," he said, "I'll be happy to do more interviews, Tom."

"And I'm sure our viewers will be thrilled to hear that. For now, I want to ask about one more very important matter. How will the new religion handle the opioid crisis, an epidemic that has been sweeping through societies for much longer than the apocalypse virus?"

"Ah, that's such an important question, Tom. I'm glad you've asked it. This is about freedom. Freedom to express ourselves without harming others, freedom to get outside of our own heads sometimes. Humans have been using mind-altering substances since prehistoric times. The new religion is big on promoting personal and individual expression and self-actualization. With all the helpful citizens' programs that will be put in place, those who use harmful substances will be able to get help with no criticism or judgement. Addiction will no longer be stigmatized. And those who just want to have some fun safely will be able to do so legally. Addiction is another symptom of the disease and misery that the profit motive has created in our societies. When people are no longer living in constant pain, fear, anxiety, and helplessness, they'll feel less and less driven to use substances that numb them. Addiction is a complex problem, and I'm not going to pretend that it will be magically fixed overnight; but doing away with the corrupt social and economic systems that have poisoned this country and other countries will set in motion a chain reaction that will help many, many addicts emerge from their private hells into a world of healing, health, and happiness."

"One last thing," I said. "It's been widely publicized that you're already a multi-billionaire. What do you plan to do with that money?"

"Tom, this money doesn't belong to me. I've taken it from

the ultra-rich so I can return it to the rightful owners, the citizens. All of this money will be used for their benefit, and their benefit alone. In the new religion, it's not cool to be rich."

"Tasos Perasmas, I want to thank you for your time. You've enlightened me and the millions of citizens watching this interview about this beautiful way of thinking called the new religion."

"You're very welcome," Tasos replied. Then turning to the main camera, he said, "Power to the people begins right here, right now."

Chapter 27

I leaned over to shake Tasos's hand after the interview had ended, and the filming crew as well as everyone else in the room broke into applause.

"Thank you, Tasos," I said. "How do you feel about the interview?"

"I look forward to it being broadcast, Tom," he replied. "When is the air date?"

"As soon as possible," I said. "Tomorrow evening at 6:30 p.m., right after the main news is what I'm aiming for. It'll be broadcast at different times in the various time zones, of course. And there will be repeats in the coming days. Plus, Jonathan will have a streaming option on the new religion website; that way, people can watch it anytime they want if they have Internet access."

Out of the corner of my eye I saw George patiently waiting for a moment with Tasos. "Tasos, do you have the energy to meet George Logan, the UBC student?"

"Of course!" he said, reaching for the pitcher of water and glass that still sat on the table between the interview chairs.

I motioned for George to come over. "George, I'd like to introduce you to Tasos Perasmas. Tasos, this is George Logan. I'm going to talk with the filming crew while you two chat."

As I wrapped things up with the crew, I could see the two of them talking animatedly. After about fifteen minutes, they stood up and walked over to where I was standing. George extended his hand to shake mine. "Mr. Newman, thank you so much for inviting me. I can't tell you how grateful I am for this privilege. And I'm really looking forward to writing up my paper and presenting it to my supervisor and seminar group."

"Let us know how it goes, George," I said, and Tasos nodded his agreement. Security escorted George out of the suite, and I turned to look inquiringly at Tasos.

"Tom, I'm going to take it easy for the rest of today and tomorrow," he said. "I'll have meetings with the security and legal teams, but those will be done by video. I need some time to rest and think about next steps. You and I can talk later."

I nodded. "Of course, and I'm glad to hear you'll be taking a bit of a break. I'll let you know once I have the broadcasting details for the interview."

Heading home by another different route, I stopped at the grocery store to pick up a few items for dinner. I'd already mentally outlined a new article and was preparing for a night at the computer. Once home, I spoke with Mr. Callingham about the interview which he was thrilled to be airing. And I also had a video chat with Claire and the kids before settling down to start writing. When I was satisfied with what I'd accomplished, I watched my favourite late-night talk show then went to bed, glad that I didn't have to set the alarm.

While I was having a late breakfast the next morning, I got a text confirming the 6:30 p.m. airtime for the interview, which I sent to Tasos. I then realized that I couldn't remember when I'd last gotten any proper exercise. Tasos had free weights, a rowing machine, and other equipment at his place, and he'd said I should use it anytime while he was staying away in the hotel. So I got changed into shorts and a t-shirt and spent a couple of hours working up a good sweat.

By the time I had showered and dressed, it was almost mid-afternoon. I switched on the BBC World News and made myself a smoothie. An announcer was informing audiences of the upcoming interview broadcast. "Some are already calling this the epoch of Tasos Perasmas," he said, "so radically is he set to change the face of human society around the globe. He doesn't want money or glory. He simply wants to make our world a better place for everyone. Many call him the Divine Blood for the numerous lives that his remarkable blood has already saved. The greatest minds in immunology, virology, cytology, genetics, and biochemistry are at this moment working around the clock, trying to decode why his blood has this apparently miraculous quality and then use this information to save our species from the apocalypse virus.

"In just a few hours, we'll be airing a one-hour, BBC-exclusive interview of Mr. Perasmas by his close friend, Canadian journalist Tom Newman. Titled simply 'The New Religion,' this program will take us into the heart of the radical reorganization of politics, economics, and climate-change strategies that some countries are already adopting. Join us, if you can. After its initial broadcast, we'll be repeating the program over the coming days. You'll also be able to stream it from the new religion website." The URL for the site appeared at the bottom of the TV screen.

I busied myself until about a quarter past six, then put something in the oven for dinner and tuned into the BBC again. Advance viewing figures suggested that more than two billion people would be watching the interview. As the broadcast began, I sat back and marvelled at Tasos's charismatic presence. The camera operators and the film editor had done a superb job. I had already previewed it on my computer when the crew had sent it to see whether I had any feedback on their work. But there was something magical about seeing it on TV, knowing that a third of the world's population was watching it too. Sometimes, I still couldn't quite believe that I was living in such extraordinary times.

Once the program had ended, I got myself dinner and checked email. There were a dozen job offers from major news outlets, each praising my work with Tasos and indicating very large salaries. I smiled wryly. Although I was flattered, it was interesting to see that these people clearly still didn't grasp the essence of the new religion—rejection of the almighty dollar as a measure for success and the eschewal of socio-economic inequity. But of course, our entire culture and ways of thinking were built on capitalist-based assumptions, the worship of profit above all else. It would take time to change not only the system's structures but, even more importantly, people's thinking habits and the moral underpinnings of their behaviours.

There was an incoming video-chat request on my computer from Tasos and I immediately clicked "Accept." His beaming face appeared on my screen. "Hey, Tom. Congratulations, my friend. You and the film crew did an excellent job. I couldn't have asked for better."

Never mind the job offers, I thought. This was the one person's feedback that really mattered to me.

I thanked him and he went on, "Have you seen that demonstrations are being planned for tomorrow in major cities around the world?"

This was news to me, and I glanced at my TV, which I'd had on mute with closed-captions since the interview ended. I read, "Thought leaders on social media are calling for peaceful demonstrations around the globe tomorrow, October 15, in support of Tasos Perasmas and his New Religion. Half a billion people are expected to turn out in major cities around the world."

"Wow, Tasos. I mean, I figured there'd be a response to the interview, but this is huge!"

He nodded. "Yes, my friend, it is indeed huge. Do you want to come to my suite tomorrow to watch coverage of the demonstrations and talk about what might happen in the coming days?"

"I'd love to," I said.

"OK, whenever you like," he replied. "Text me when you're ready to leave your place, and I'll let the security team here know to expect you."

We chatted for a bit longer about various things, then said good night. I felt relaxed and surprisingly tired, given the long sleep I'd had the night before. Then I remembered the earlier hard workout and smiled. I'm getting out of shape, I thought. Hopefully, my life would get back into a routine one day soon, or I'd find some middle-age flab showing up in unwanted places.

I had just done a final perimeter check of Tasos's place and mine before locking up for the night, when my phone rang. George Logan's number was displayed, so I answered. "Hi George, how's it going?"

"Hi Mr. Newman! I hope I'm not calling too late."

"Not at all, George. What can I do for you?"

"Well, after the interview recording, I went home and spent the whole night writing. At my seminar today, I asked whether I could present my paper a week early. My prof and everyone else was fine with that, so I did." He paused. "It went really, really well, Mr. Newman! My supervisor was blown away by the fact that I'd met Mr. Perasmas. He asked me to send him a copy of my paper right away, which I did. He called me this evening and said that he'd been on the phone with the president of our university."

"Really?" I said. "That's neat. She's a very prominent political scientist, if I remember correctly."

"That's right," said George. "My supervisor had sent a copy of my paper to her, and she was really enthused. She's actually cancelled all classes at the university tomorrow so that students can attend the new religion demonstrations being organized in and around Vancouver."

"Wow, cool," I responded. "Tasos will be pleased."

"There's something I think he'll be even more pleased about, sir," George said, and I could hear the smile in his voice.

"Oh? What's that?"

"The president is going to nominate Mr. Perasmas for an honorary degree in sociology and political science. It has to go to the university senate for approval, but she's positive it'll be approved."

"Well, that's great news, George. Thank you for letting me know. I'm going to be seeing Tasos tomorrow, so I can tell him then."

"Thanks, Mr. Newman! The senate meets tomorrow evening. As soon as I hear anything, I'll call you, if that's OK."

"It's definitely OK, George."

"All right! Bye for now, Mr. Newman!"

After I hung up, I thought about texting the news to Tasos but decided to wait until tomorrow. I wanted to see the look on his face.

Chapter 28

The next day, I woke early. Not wanting to risk waking Tasos, I decided to have a coffee, then do another, shorter, workout before showering and heading to the hotel. As I merged onto the freeway, I was surprised at the volume of traffic, then realized that it was of course because of the demonstrations due to get under way in a few hours.

I listened to a local talk radio station that was giving information on demonstration locations, traffic advisories, and additional public transit services being provided to facilitate people's journeys to and from the events. It felt like a major storm was in the offing. The prospect of these large demonstrations was exciting, and the thought of them going on around the world gave me goosebumps. But would they be peaceful? Or would violence break out? How would the police in the various countries react? And would any subversive elements of the public or, more likely, the disgruntled, threatened one-percent elite have organized groups to initiate or incite violence? Thugs could be hired, and since the new religion's plans to remove guns from general circulation were not yet complete, a number of very bad scenarios were possible.

As I joined Tasos in his suite, he smiled, and motioned me to a couch. He asked whether I'd had breakfast and in response, my stomach growled. We both laughed, as I realized I'd forgotten to eat before leaving the house.

He ordered breakfast from room service, then we settled back to watch things unfold on the big screen.

I told Tasos George's news about the honourary degree. He smiled broadly, his eyes twinkling, and said, "Well, I don't want to assume that the university senate will agree with the proposal. But it would be a great honour if they do."

The Canadian Broadcasting Company and the various local stations were all covering the demonstrations across the country. The CBC was providing updates on gatherings outside of Canada as well. In each case, people were present in the thousands, some carrying placards or banners. Participants at various times were chanting, or giving speeches, or stopping to be interviewed by members of the media. Even anarchists had shown up, and the camera at one point showed placards reading "Anarchists Love Tasos!" and "No Anarchy with the New Religion!"

A reporter interviewing one of these placard holders asked, "Why do anarchists support Tasos Perasmas and the new religion?"

"We're anarchists because we don't want governments and politicians to tell us what to do or not do, and what to say or not say," said the young woman. "With the new religion, citizens will be telling governments and politicians what to do or not do, and what to say or not say."

By noon, the estimate of half a billion people participating globally had been exceeded. In most countries, the demonstrations were absolutely peaceful. Many participants carried signs extolling peace and celebrating the banning of guns. However, in the States, the results were mixed. Staunch defenders of the First Amendment were out in force in some cities, supported by the National Rifle Association. I saw Tasos frown at this. "I hope the president is going to do something about this," he said ominously, "otherwise I may need to have another stern conversation with him on live television."

As if on cue, the CBC announcer said, "We've just received word that the President of the United States, in an unprecedented move, this morning phoned the head of the NRA to request his cooperation. The NRA has just issued an official statement, condemning any violence engaged in by its members at these demonstrations, and announcing that it will be entering into discussions with the United States government on how to implement the peaceful phasing out of firearms throughout the country."

Tasos let out a low whistle. "Well, that may be the best news I'll hear all day," he said. He looked at me, grinning. "It's happening, my friend. It's all happening!"

Sadly, the coverage soon shifted to scenes of police brutality in countries with repressive regimes. Tear gas and rubber bullets were used on the crowds. In some places, live rounds were being used as well. There was screaming, blood, and citizens being beaten with batons or savagely thrown to the ground and handcuffed. I saw tears slide down Tasos's cheek.

"It won't be easy in some countries," I said quietly.

He sighed. "There's still a long road ahead, Tom. And I don't know how I'm going to deal with the suffering of citizens in countries whose governments refuse to embrace the new religion. There will be great misery and many, many deaths."

I spent all day at the hotel watching the coverage and talking with Tasos about next steps. We also made tentative plans for reuniting with our families. At one point in the late afternoon, a video call came in on Tasos's phone. It was Mr. Robinson, and his news gladdened us both.

"The governments of Canada, America, Japan, and Norway have all officially signed agreements accepting the new religion, sir," he said. "And we expect Brazil and Australia will come on board very soon, too."

A couple of hours later, around 8:00 p.m., Tasos and I were sharing a large pizza when George texted me: "*may i vid-call u now pls?*" I replied with a thumbs-up emoji, and a few seconds later, his animated face filled my phone's screen.

"Hello Mr. Newman. Oh, hello Mr. Perasmas!" he exclaimed as Tasos leaned over to wave in front of the phone camera.

"Hang on, George, I'm going to switch to my laptop so the three of us can talk more easily."

Once I'd done this, I said, "OK, go ahead."

"The university senate voted unanimously in favour of granting Mr. Perasmas an honorary degree. They also want to have a special ceremony rather than make it part of the graduation ceremony for other university students. The president asked me to give you her phone number so she can personally congratulate you and find out how best to make the arrangements with you and your security team."

"Sure," said Tasos. "You can text the number to Tom."

"When do they want to hold the ceremony?" I asked.

"Fourteen days from now," said George. "The new sports centre at the university has a seating capacity of only 5,000, so they plan to erect huge, outdoor viewing screens and marquees outside the centre for the overflow."

We talked with George for a few more minutes, then thanked him for his good news and wished him a good night.

"I think we should invite him to become part of Team Tasos," I said.

Tasos laughed loudly. "Team Tasos—I like the sound of that, Tom! And I agree, George would be a valuable addition to our team."

As I drove home that night, the streets were alive with people. What a contrast from all the months of relative emptiness with a few face-masked people scurrying to destinations, the city and suburbs subdued under the weight of the pandemic. Now, the air vibrated with celebration and optimism. I smiled but felt a pang of loneliness as I anticipated my house, which held only echoes of Claire and the kids.

Sighing as I closed and locked the front door, I heard my phone ping. It was a message from Tasos: "*u home yet? call me pls, good news.*" Putting on the kettle to make some tea, I poured milk into a mug, tossed in a tea bag, and called Tasos.

He was beaming. "Hello, Tom! I won't keep you long."

"No problem, Tasos. What's the good news?"

"I didn't want to wait until tomorrow to tell you. I just got off the phone a few minutes ago with Superintendent Cooper. All nine countries I stipulated should agree to the new religion have confirmed! Germany, the Netherlands, Sweden, Iceland, Norway, Japan, Australia, America, and Canada are all now on board. They've signed the official documents, and each has already established a Citizens Council Office to oversee the transition process. The new religion is becoming a reality, my friend."

"That's fantastic, Tasos!"

"This means the day after tomorrow, I'll be giving each country two vials of my blood, as agreed in the negotiations. The blood will be drawn, packaged, and sent off from Vancouver International Airport to their destinations as quickly as possible."

"Isn't the airport a risky location?"

"Actually, no. As a busy international airport, YVR already has a comprehensive security system in place. Getting me there will be done very quietly and covertly with no fanfare, no public announcement. Once we're ready to draw the blood, we'll begin broadcasting, so people in all of the countries can see that it really is my blood. Crowds will likely gather once the broadcast goes live, but Superintendent Cooper and Mr. Boulen are taking care of security. We'll use the same film crew as at the interview—Mr. Boulen's taking care of that. I'll email you the details so you can be there as well, of course. Can you get in touch with the BBC to coordinate the broadcast?"

"Absolutely," I said. "I'm sure there won't be any problems."

"Great, thank you. And Tom," he paused, "I know you're missing your family. I'm missing Themis and having a regular family life too. With everything going so well now, we'll be able to bring them home very soon."

Chapter 29

On the morning of the blood-collection day, I arrived at Tasos's hotel suite early to go over security details with the superintendent. Mr. Boulen and his team were already at the airport getting the film crew set up and ensuring that on-site security would be tight but discreet. The broadcast was set for noon, so we planned to arrive at the secure airport location by 11:15 a.m.

Tasos wore a crisp white dress shirt, open at the neck, that contrasted with his olive skin. Charcoal-grey casual pants, comfortable shoes, and a stylish but unassuming matching jacket completed the simple outfit. The drive to the airport took less than twenty minutes, and we entered an employee-only zone that brought us around to a part of the airport shielded from public view. We got out of the vehicle and were whisked through a heavy double door into an elevator. We rode up to a conference room, where the lighting and film crew had just finished setting up. A reclining chair like they use in blood donor clinics was set up at ninety degrees to one wall, with a high table on each side of the chair. On one was a jug of orange juice, a tall glass, and a plate of cookies. On the other was the paraphernalia for drawing blood.

Tasos had asked me to be the presenter on this historic day, so I rehearsed a few times with the camera and lighting crews, to make sure everything would go smoothly. At the stroke of

12:00 p.m., we began the broadcast and I announced to the world what was about to take place.

Dr. Jekings was in charge of the procedure. She began by inserting a needle into the prominent vein on the inside of Tasos's right elbow. With his strong heartbeat and healthy blood pressure, it took very little time to fill the tubes. There were eighteen in total, as Tasos had decided to give each country two rather than just one. Each pair of tubes was put into a specially labelled, insulated stainless-steel carrying case. When the cases were closed, they were lined up in a neat row for the camera and we ended the broadcast. The whole thing had taken only half an hour, but I knew the impact would be tremendous.

We remained in the room for another forty-five minutes, at Dr. Jekings's insistence. Tasos drank juice and ate a couple of cookies, as did everyone else in the room. Tasos and I stood looking out a window at the various runways, watching planes take off and land.

Superintendent Cooper approached us and Tasos turned and smiled. "Have you been able to arrange it?" he asked. I didn't know what they were talking about.

The superintendent nodded and said to me, "Tom, Mr. Perasmas will be stopping at the art gallery downtown and making a short speech on the gallery steps. I wasn't sure whether we'd be able to get the necessary security in place in time, but we have. We're ready to go. People are already gathering there, hoping that Mr. Perasmas might talk to them."

The steps and outdoor concourse areas of the Vancouver Art Gallery had for many decades been a place where the people congregated for rallies, protests, and political gatherings. So it made sense that they'd be going there today, and I knew our security team would have plenty of experience with how best to secure that area.

"Ready when you are," I said.

The police had cordoned off a direct route from the airport to the art gallery, so we got there quickly. Apart from the route blocked off for our vehicles, the surrounding streets were thronged with people. As Tasos got out and walked from the car to the concourse then up the gallery steps, the crowd broke into wild cheering. Chants of "Tasos, Tasos, Tasos, Tasos," echoed off the surrounding skyscrapers.

At Tasos's request, I walked with him all the way to the microphone. As the two of us looked out at the throng and listened to the swell of voices, Tasos smiled at me. "This is real love, my friend. This is what will propel the new religion and transform our world."

Tasos lifted his right arm and waved to the crowd for a long time. Then he raised both arms in a gesture entreating them to become quiet. A hush fell as everyone waited for him to speak.

"Hello everyone. Thank you for coming." His rich voice flowing out through the speakers had a mellifluous quality that had a tranquilizing effect on the crowd. Even the few babies who had been fussing were quiet. "I did what I promised to do. The vials of blood for all nine countries are on the way to their destinations. Here in Canada, they'll be going to the Public Health Agency's main research centre in Ottawa."

Cheering broke out and more chanting of his name.

Tasos let it go on for a while, then motioned again for quiet. "From now on, our governments will do what the citizens want. I know that citizens want to live in a peaceful world, where wars are a thing of the past. Citizens know and understand the importance of protecting our environment for future generations and for all of the species on this planet. Most of all, citizens want to reshape our society based on fairness and equity. From now on, we'll teach our kids about living in a world without armies. We'll teach them that saving and restoring the environment is of paramount importance. We'll teach them that no one is anyone's boss, and profit isn't the key to success or happiness. The new religion is where spirituality meets science for the betterment of humanity. Together, we are going to make this a reality around the globe. Thank you." He then waved at the ecstatic crowd for a long time, smiling, and looking very, very content.

When he was done, security escorted us back to the waiting vehicle. Although Tasos's hotel was nearby, we couldn't risk giving away its location. The security detail took us to Vancouver Police headquarters, where we transferred to a different vehicle in the secure underground parking area. We were back in his hotel suite by mid-afternoon. By then both of us were ravenous and room service brought up a large lunch.

As we were waiting, sipping coffee that I'd made in the small kitchen area, Tasos said, "Tom, I've had several meetings with the research scientists at the local centre, who've been studying my blood since I provided them with the first sample weeks ago. I've also been doing a lot of reading on my own to learn about genetics, hematology, virology, and other areas, trying to understand the secret to my blood. And I've come up with the answer, which I'm going to reveal tomorrow evening at a special gathering of scientists, doctors, and the media. It'll be at the World Trade and Convention Centre here downtown at 5:00 p.m. If you could bring the BBC into the loop for international broadcasting and issue a press release to the Canadian media in the morning, I'd greatly appreciate it. I'll take care of contacting the scientists and doctors."

I nodded. "No problem."

"And Tom," he had a glint in his eye now, "I'm afraid that I'm going to keep you in suspense by not telling you what I've discovered. It's not that I don't trust you…I just want you to feel the same kind of excitement and thrill as everyone else at the same time. You've been working so hard for weeks and weeks, never getting a chance to be a regular citizen—one of the people who'll be benefitting from the new religion. Will you let me have this small, childish pleasure?" He really did look like a big kid, delighted at the prospect of giving me a huge surprise the next day.

"Of course. If it'll make you happy, then it'll certainly make me happy."

Chapter 30

I arrived at the Convention Centre shortly after 2:00 p.m. the next day to review the arrangements and make sure everything would go smoothly for Tasos's "great reveal." By 3:00 p.m., the camera and lighting crews were all set up. Anticipating that attendees would start arriving in an hour or less, I took advantage of the short break to walk in the sunshine along the promenade that encircles most of the Convention Centre. The Northshore mountains still had snow on their peaks, and the sun's rays reflected brilliantly off the pristine slopes. I felt a surge of optimism for the future.

Looking back at the city from my vantage point on the promenade, I could see the streets were filling with people hoping to catch a glimpse of Tasos on his way to the Convention Centre. In the wee hours of the morning, I had issued a media release about the special announcement. The information had made its way onto the early morning news and was being repeated regularly on various channels and radio stations. Everyone knew that Tasos would today explain how and why he was the Divine Blood, and how to defeat the pandemic other than by using drops of his blood. Even from this distance, the excitement of the crowd was palpable.

Glancing at my watch, I decided to get back to the room where the announcement would be made. As I walked through the door, I saw Tasos and Mr. Callahan, the head of Tasos's personal security, standing next to a long table set up on a low platform at the far end of the room. A podium was positioned at the table's midpoint, and five chairs were arranged on each side of the podium. Rows of additional chairs had been arranged in the rest of the room, which could accommodate about 160 people.

"Hey Tom, how are you, my friend?" Tasos asked as he shook my hand.

"Excellent, Tasos, and yourself? Are you ready to deliver your big revelation?" I replied, smiling.

"I certainly am. Thank you for taking care of the media side of things once again."

I looked around the room, which was beginning to buzz with attendees, and recognized the minister of health, and Rachel Johnson and Christopher Cornish, two scientists from the hospital's pandemic research group. Superintendent Cooper was there as well, of course, overseeing security.

At five minutes to five, the superintendent stepped to the podium and said into the microphone, "Thank you all for coming. Could you please take a seat so we can begin this very special event and broadcast?" The camera crew knew to begin filming at this point. I had pre-recorded the introduction to the broadcast shortly after arriving at the Convention Centre. Knowing all was in hand, I decided to relax and enjoy the moment.

Tasos was seated directly to the right of the podium from the audience's perspective, and I sat next to him. Various Canadian scientists had been assigned places at the long table, marked by name cards.

Canada's minister of health seemed to have undergone quite a transformation since the hostile meeting between him, the prime minister, and Tasos. His eyes were glowing as he stood up to speak.

"Ladies and gentlemen, thank you all for being here. Because you being here means you want to help humanity. I would like to thank Mr. Perasmas for giving so much of his divine blood to help humanity, and for his willingness to help humanity further today by revealing helpful information to our scientists. He has promised that with this information, they will make crucial advances in the fight against the devastating AV pandemic, which has brought so much pain and suffering around the globe." Turning to Tasos, arms outstretched in welcome, he said, "Honoured guests, I present Mr. Tasos Perasmas."

The room erupted in a standing ovation, and some began chanting, "Tasos! Tasos! Tasos! Tasos!"

Tasos stood up and smiled, then placed his right hand on his chest in a show of gratitude. After a few moments, he raised his hands to request quiet and everyone resumed their seats. I looked out at the crowd and saw a sea of beaming faces.

"Thank you for coming," Tasos began. "Humanity needs your brilliant minds. You and only you can take us to a safer future. This evening, I'm going to share with you my beliefs and knowledge so you can accelerate humanity's recovery from the pandemic. Not only this, but we'll also be able to ensure that the human race never faces this situation again." Tasos took a sip of water and continued.

"First, I want to explain how and why I have this, so-called divine blood," Tasos said in a deep, strong, clear voice. The room had gone completely quiet. "To put it succinctly: I am a more evolved human being."

The room began to buzz, and I could see that many in the audience weren't quite sure how to interpret this. Tasos waited for almost a minute, observing the room, then raised a hand to request quiet again.

"Let me elaborate a bit. The first tip that I am going to give you is that there are many more people who have the divine blood. Because the divine blood is nothing more than an activated gene, an epigenetic modification. I have taken the liberty of naming it the gene of defence, or G, O, D."

This time, the response was even more pronounced, and several people in the audience as well as at the table began speaking, some of them trying to get Tasos's attention.

Tasos pointed at someone in the first row, who stood up and said, "I'm Dr. Harvey from Heidelberg University in Germany. You said an activated gene. Can you explain how it's activated and what kind of defence you're talking about?"

"Yes, I can do that, Dr. Harvey," Tasos said with a smile. "The gene is activated by the brain. In my case, the GOD inside of me was inherited in an already activated state, which is why I said I'm a more evolved human being. For the gene to be activated in others who have it, certain conditions must be fulfilled. The brain that will activate the GOD must believe in beautiful things, like peace, and the importance of not using violence to achieve peace. It also needs to have great respect for the environment and to believe in the fundamental equality of all human beings. A person who strongly believes these things has the greatest chance of activating their GOD. Basically, it's gene activation on demand." Tasos's voice was quiet but passionate.

"Ha, ha, ha!" An older gentleman in the audience who had a bit of the crazy scientist look about him had begun to guffaw.

Tasos smiled gently and said, "You're finding something funny, sir?"

"Yes," the man said with a clearly derisive tone. "I'm Dr. Verinsky, Professor of Biology and Head of the Epigenetics Research Facility at McGill University. With all due respect," he practically spat out those words, "gene activation on demand is BS. For two dozen years, the best genetics researchers in the world haven't established that such an outlandish thing is possible."

"Thank you, Dr. Verinsky. I have the greatest respect for your opinion, and I would ask you to please let me complete my explanation," Tasos said. "This on-demand expression can only take place under the very specific cognitive conditions I have described. The human body is like a doctor who refuses to treat a patient because the patient is harming himself—for example, a smoker who is ill but doesn't stop smoking. Like that smoker, humanity has believed that we need to amass weapons and wage war against each other. We've believed that we can use and abuse the planet's resources for our personal needs and pleasure, and the almighty profit motive. All these beliefs are self-destructive, as many scientists and other great minds have been pointing out for decades. The human race is heading for extinction just as surely as a man diagnosed with advanced lung cancer who won't quit smoking. This is why the human bodies containing the GOD have refused to activate it—because humanity is on a suicide mission that will destroy our species and the planet as well. If you start looking for others with an activated GOD, you won't find it in people with ugly beliefs, only in people who have embraced the principles of the new religion: no army, no pollution, no perpetuation of social inequality and injustice. The new religion is a happiness-creation belief, and it activates the GOD. The new religion is where spirituality meets science for the betterment of humanity."

Dr. Verinsky sat back with crossed arms, looking unconvinced. But that didn't seem to bother Tasos, who continued unperturbed. "I'd like to return to answering Dr. Harvey's second question, which was about what kind of defence the GOD can provide. Two brilliant scientists are sitting at this table, Dr. Johnson and Dr. Cornish," he motioned to them. "They have been working full-time trying to develop a vaccine or cure for AV. They're the ones who have determined that my blood is like a combination of a kamikaze fighter and the mythical Hydra." Turning to the two scientists, he said, "Dr. Johnson, Dr. Cornish, am I describing it accurately?"

Dr. Johnson stood up and said, "Yes, Mr. Perasmas, that is

what your blood is doing. The cells attack the virus in this case, or any other intruder, and they die in the attack. But when the cells die, they explode and multiply, like the Hydra, who when its head was cut off would sprout many new heads rather than dying. So a body containing the activated GOD has an unlimited capacity to eliminate any invader."

"Thank you, Dr. Johnson," said Tasos. He turned back to the epigeneticist. "Dr. Verinsky, my scientific and academic knowledge is not a fraction of yours, but when I came to recognize the so-called 'divine' quality of my blood, I began to study intensively to try to understand what was going on, and why me. I took into consideration the histories of my family members—their beliefs, personalities, ways of life—and I examined my own life too. Of course, this involved educating myself sufficiently to understand how the human body's systems work, and how something such as the activation of the GOD could occur. I understand your skepticism of anyone claiming he can change his body simply with the power of thought—like stopping cancer cells from developing or progressing. What I am suggesting, though, is that we can use the power of the brain to initiate the magic of neuroplasticity. That's how we will change human beings from who they are now, into beautiful moral creatures. For years, scientists have harnessed patients' mental activity to help them heal from various physical ailments. There is significant evidence of the powerful healing effect that specific brain activity can have on the body using visualization, or guided imagery, or biofeedback. The brain creates mental images and as a result can initiate physiological changes."

The rapt attention of the room was focused on Tasos as he described the beautiful simplicity of what he had discovered. "Dr. Verinsky, this isn't some sort of magic," he said. "I know that the neuroscientists at this table and in this room will confirm that neuroplasticity can work real-life wonders. I am telling you and everyone else here that positive messages on a massive scale can retrain our brains and, in turn, activate this part of our genetic code. What I'm proposing is a natural, organic way to turn on the GOD in each person who possesses it. And I believe that most humans do have it lying dormant in their DNA."

Tasos spread his hands and said, "I invited brilliant people to come here today so that they can take my ideas, expand on them, and research them. I think that you'll find the mechanism I am proposing makes sense within the science we have already established; about how negative experiences and thought patterns and stress can have profound adverse effects on our bodies. Psychoneuroimmunology, which is the study of how psychological processes interact with the nervous and immune system, has shown this to be true time after time, in study after study. If this is the case for negative ideas, then why not for positive ones? Belief in and practice of the new religion will stimulate the release of helpful neurotransmitters, ones that will counteract the stress hormones and other toxic substances that build up in our bodies when we're constantly subjected to mental, emotional, and environmental stresses. This is what I mean by the new religion being a happiness-creation belief, and one that will cause a cascade of physical changes that activate the GOD. In people who don't yet possess the gene, epigenetic modification will begin to occur. It will take two or three generations to complete the change throughout our species, at which point everyone will inherit the gene of defence."

A gentleman in the third row raised his hand. "Yes sir," Tasos said to him.

"I'm Dr. Monouar, Professor of Neuroscience at Kalas University, in Greece. Mr. Perasmas, are you saying that once the GOD is activated, human beings will no longer become ill?"

"Dr. Monouar, I believe that will be the end result, yes.

Citizens will no longer need antibiotics or retroviral therapy or chemotherapy or radiation treatment. None of that. The activated GOD signals the perfection of the human body's immune system. It's also my belief that as our bodies evolve in this new way, our senses will become enhanced, and our pineal gland will be activated to such an extent that we will finally experience what mystics for thousands of years have described as the vision of the third eye."

Dr. Verinsky at this point got up and began walking toward the door. I thought his behaviour was inexcusable, but Tasos seemed slightly amused. He called out, "Dr. Verinsky, I'm sorry to see you go. I'm offering you something here that is even better than my divine blood: the knowledge of a way to ethically transform the human race at the genetic level and guarantee the preservation of humanity and the planet for good. My name means 'reincarnation of the passage,' and surely that isn't coincidental. It's a sign of the gift, the opportunity I was destined to bring to humanity." Dr. Verinsky paused but now waved his hands dismissively and turned again to go. "Before you leave," said Tasos, "answer one question: Is what I have described at least theoretically possible? You're a man of science, and I know that you'll answer me truthfully even if you're highly skeptical."

Dr. Verinsky frowned, then mumbled something.

"I'm sorry, I can't hear you, Dr. Verinsky," said Tasos. "Could you please speak a little louder?"

"Yes, it is possible," Dr. Verinsky said loud enough to be heard by everyone in the room.

"Thank you, doctor. I appreciate your honesty. And again, I'm sorry that you feel the need to leave." Dr. Verinsky hurried from the room as Tasos continued, "Could everyone in the room please, by a show of hands, indicate who is a scientist or a physician?"

About half of the room raised their hands.

"Now," he said, "could everyone in the room who believes what I said is possible please raise your hand."

About three-quarters of the room responded positively, and some people even got to their feet in their enthusiasm, including everyone sitting at the head table.

I looked at Tasos and saw his eyes fill with tears. His lips trembled and he swallowed a couple of times to control his emotions before saying, "Thank you all, thank you from the bottom of my heart. Your acceptance is the greatest reward for me. I am very happy that the greatest minds on the planet will work on studying the GOD and how we can help bring about this evolution of the human species."

Most of the room began to applaud, and I saw that even those who had seemed skeptical were swept up by the enthusiasm of the renowned scientists at the table and their colleagues in the audience, all of whom demonstrated their overwhelming support for Tasos's ideas.

The session ended very soon after this, although for another hour or more people approached Tasos to shake his hand, thank him, and ask him questions. I could see that behind all of the smiles, he was becoming tired, so I was grateful when Dr. Jekings intervened. Quietly putting her hand on Tasos's forearm, she said to the surrounding crowd, "Mr. Perasmas could use a break now. As his personal physician, I'm afraid I'll have to insist that we call it a night."

Before I left, Tasos reminded me that the following day, the Canadian government and the various other governments around the world that had accepted the new religion would be making formal, televised apologies to their citizens, present and past, who had suffered wrongdoings and injustices. "Tom, if you're up for it, why don't you come to the hotel and watch these with me?" He leaned in and said quietly, "I think that within the next few days, it'll be safe to bring Claire and the kids back, and I'll be able to return to my house with Themis.

So this may be our last chance to have a guy's night with pizza and beer." He winked at me mischievously.

I knew that he was as weary as I was of being without our families, but I went along with the pretense. "Absolutely! I'll bring the cold ones and you can arrange the pizza, my friend." We embraced briefly, then I said goodnight and headed home.

Chapter 31

I was biting into a second piece of pizza when the CBC broadcast began at 6:00 p.m. Tasos was sitting in one of the hotel suite's recliner chairs, sipping a beer and smiling in anticipation at the TV. I had arrived only twenty minutes earlier, famished after a busy day at home. I'd spent some of the morning writing, then the remaining hours cleaning the house from top to bottom, in anticipation of Claire and the kids' return. There were flowers in the kitchen, and I'd put fresh sheets and comforters on the beds. I'd even vacuumed the upholstery in the living room and office. The kitchen shone as if any minute, Martha Stewart would come waltzing in to whip up something special for dinner. After my exertions, the pizza and beer seemed especially delicious and refreshing.

"I sure am looking forward to this, Tom," Tasos said with a huge grin as we settled into our seats. "Did you have a chance to look at the requirements I specified for each country's head of state when delivering their apology?"

I nodded. "Yes. It needs to be passionately delivered in simple language that everyone can understand, and must be said with genuine humility and contrition."

Tasos began to chuckle at the image of habitually arrogant politicians humbling themselves on national and international television.

At that point, the broadcast began. After a brief preamble

by the respected anchorman who presented the national news each weeknight, the Canadian parliament appeared on screen and the camera zoomed in on the prime minister, who commenced his speech.

"My fellow citizens, this may be the first time in our nation's history that all the individuals in this house concur. We agree that all of us have treated you, the citizens, very badly. I am here before you to apologize for that. I am here to apologize on behalf of the house of parliament and on behalf of all past Canadian governments and politicians. We have done a great wrong. We made laws, rules, and regulations not for the citizens' well-being but for our political and personal benefit, for power and for money. I apologize for that. The fact that we have homeless people, and there are children in this country who go to school hungry, and there are families living in dire poverty—we are responsible for those wrongs. On behalf of myself, the entire parliament, and past governments and politicians, I apologize to you."

I looked at Tasos and saw that tears of happiness were running from the corners of his eyes.

The prime minister continued, "My fellow citizens, I am here in front of you to promise that from now on, we are going to truly serve you. We will be reclassifying our profession, because we are no longer going to be called politicians. Our political ideology is irrelevant to our job, which is to follow your mandate, and that is what we are going to do. My government will consider it an honour to continue governing during the transition period to the new religion. My fellow citizens, our government's mandate is to do what the citizens want. And the citizens want to live in a country with no army or any other means of destruction, and no authoritarian organizations. The citizens want to live in a country where protecting the environment is the law and a top priority, alongside respect and fairness for everyone. This is exactly what we are going to work on and achieve, what we are dedicating ourselves to from now on."

Tasos was smiling, very satisfied with the prime minister's speech so far. "I love it," he said then focused again on the TV.

The prime minister looked directly into the camera and said, "From this point forward, citizens' well-being and environmental protection will be the top priorities of all decisions, laws, rules, and regulations. I apologize for taking so long to see what is right. Thank you all for joining me on the exciting road ahead for our country and for humanity." The prime minister bowed slightly and sat down.

The broadcast then showed in succession the public apologies of the other world leaders who had signed agreements.

Tasos sighed and visibly relaxed. "Tom, this is what I was trying to accomplish. I'm very happy. My son will live in a better environment than I have. And I know that I have personally contributed to this result. This is the happiest I've ever been."

"Tasos, you did much more than just contribute. You flipped the world upside down, all by yourself. It still amazes me, all that has happened in the past year."

Tasos smiled broadly and said, "I think it's time for you to open the envelope, Tom."

He had messaged me that morning, asking me to bring the envelope that he had given me such a long time ago, just after he had saved the lives of my family. I had kept it in a locked box, which I now placed on the table, suddenly feeling the solemnity of the occasion.

Unlocking the box, I withdrew the envelope and looked at it, overcome with a flood of strong emotions. I had brought a letter opener with me and used it to carefully slice along the length of the envelope. Withdrawing a single sheet of paper, I looked at Tasos. "Go on, Tom, read it out."

So I began reading:

A Perfect World

My world is beautiful; my world is shining. There is no army in any country in my world. What a beautiful world I am living in, knowing that there is no war.

There is no pollution of any kind allowed in my world. What a beautiful world I am living in, knowing that the Earth is respected.

There is no "boss" word in any language in my world. What a beautiful world I am living in, knowing I will go to work where there is no master-servant dynamic.

What a beautiful world I am living in, knowing that I live in a perfect world.

The hair stood up on the back of my neck as I realized that even then, he had seen what his mission would be, what he would achieve.

"You knew that you were going to change the world, didn't you?" I asked.

"Yes, my friend, I knew from the moment that Themis, my beautiful, dying son, said to me on July 27, 'Dad, I'm hungry.' The day he recovered from the virus. Remember me showing you that he was back playing in the tree house again?"

I nodded. "I'll never forget it."

"That day, Tom, I realized my purpose in life. I knew what I had to do. I understood why I hadn't become infected, even when I was trying to get sick. I understood it was because of my beliefs. I realized the opportunity and I realized that I was the best person to live this experience."

"So when you gave me the envelope and said that you needed me to help you do something. That 'something' was to flip the world upside down, right?"

"Yes."

"Tasos, you've changed the world, you, one man with no education, English as a second language, and no expertise in political science or sociology or neuroscience. The only thing you had was your divine blood. You've shown humanity the way to achieve a perfect world, a utopia, a world that is going to progress 500 years in just fifty years or less."

"Something like that," Tasos said quietly.

Two days later, we drove to John and Sherry's farmhouse to bring our families home at long last. It was an emotional reunion, with many tears and a lot of laughter. The journey home passed as quickly as the previous two days had dragged.

For nearly a week, we basked in the luxury of each other's company. There was still plenty to be done, of course. Tasos and I attended various meetings, and I continued writing and taking care of matters at the newspaper office. But the tremendous pressure of the preceding many months had been lifted.

The day of the honorary degree ceremony arrived, and we travelled there together, leaving mid-morning so we could enjoy the beauty of the university campus beforehand.

As we entered the university endowment lands, not far ahead I could see that thousands of people were already gathered along the road, some standing and some walking, presumably toward the venue for the ceremony. I slowed down to make sure we could pass through safely, and several people began chanting, "Tasos! Tasos! Tasos!" This continued all the way to the sports centre, where security directed us to a reserved parking spot, then escorted us inside.

An area within the gymnasium had been curtained off, where we stood, receiving brief instructions from the ceremony organizer. The venue was packed. I glanced over at Tasos, wondering how he was feeling.

As if reading my mind, he grinned at me. "So, Tom, the big

moment has just about arrived. I'm a bit nervous. Does that seem silly to you?"

I shook my head. "Not at all. But I hope you'll be able to enjoy the experience nonetheless."

"Oh, I think so," he said.

The ceremony started and the university's president Dr. Song took the stage. She was a tall, slim, Southeast Asian woman in her late fifties with silver hair.

"Ladies and gentlemen, thank you for being here at this unique ceremony to honour a person who has changed the world. His brilliant philosophy, the new religion, has opened our eyes. We now know how to create a utopia. The social standards that his philosophy dictates will guide us to that utopia. Please join me in welcoming, with great honour, Mr. Tasos Perasmas, the Divine Blood."

The five thousand people in the room went wild and started chanting, "Tasos! Tasos! Tasos! Tasos!"

Tasos walked to Dr. Song and shook her hand, then faced the ecstatic crowd and waved to everyone, his beaming face reflecting the joy in theirs. After a minute, the president thanked them for their warm welcome and asked them to be seated. Then she smiled at Tasos and said, "Mr. Perasmas, I have the great pleasure of presenting you with an honorary doctorate in sociology and political science. From the bottom of my heart, I thank you for enlightening us." Dr. Song handed Tasos a beautiful parchment-paper certificate decorated with elaborate calligraphy and a purple velvet ribbon.

Tasos bowed, then stepped up to the podium and said into the microphone, "Thank you, Dr. Song. I am tremendously honoured to receive this degree. The university's recognition of my philosophy delights me. This is a moment I will always remember. Thank you so much. And thank you all."

The rest of the day was spent enjoying the festivities. We got home quite late, feeling completely satisfied with the day's events.

For a month, we enjoyed the family life that we had missed so much. During that time, we all decided to move to a new neighbourhood. Tasos promised to build another tree house, even better than the old one. Our society continues to flourish as change after change transforms every aspect of life. Korea, Argentina, and China have initiated the new religion as a way of governing. Sadly, Russia and Brazil have decided to maintain their authoritarian regimes...and the pandemic continues to rage there. For countries embracing the new religion, the future looks very bright, and we haven't given up hope of eventually bringing the entire globe into this new age of enlightenment. But that will be another story.

Made in the USA
Monee, IL
14 June 2020

32506834R10144